Didn't I Say to Make My Abilities Average in the Next Life?!
Lily's Miracle

VOLUME 1

Veil

Lily

Didn't I Say to Make My Abilities Average in the Next Life?!
Lily's Miracle

VOLUME 1

BY

Kousuke Akai

ILLUSTRATED BY

Itsuki Akata

Airship

Seven Seas Entertainment

Watashi, noryoku wa heikinnchi dette ittayone! Lilly no kiseki
God bless me
© FUNA/Itsuki Akata/Kousuke Akai 2019
Originally published in Japan in 2019 by
EARTH STAR Entertainment, Tokyo.
English translation rights arranged with
EARTH STAR Entertainment, Tokyo,
through TOHAN CORPORATION, Tokyo.

Seven Seas press and purchase enquiries can be sent to
Marketing Manager Lianne Sentar at press@gomanga.com.
Information regarding the distribution and purchase of
digital editions is available from Digital Manager CK Russell
at digital@gomanga.com.

Follow Seven Seas Entertainment online at
sevenseasentertainment.com.

TRANSLATION: Diana Taylor
ADAPTATION: Maggie Cooper
COVER DESIGN: Nicky Lim
INTERIOR LAYOUT & DESIGN: Clay Gardner
COPY EDITOR: Jade Gardner
PROOFREADER: B. Lillian Martin
LIGHT NOVEL EDITOR: Nibedita Sens
PRINT MANAGER: Rhiannon Rasmussen-Silverstein
PRODUCTION MANAGER: Lissa Pattillo
MANAGING EDITOR: Julie Davis
ASSOCIATE PUBLISHER: Adam Arnold
PUBLISHER: Jason DeAngelis

ISBN: 978-1-64827-335-3
Printed in Canada
First Printing: November 2021
10 9 8 7 6 5 4 3 2 1

Dedicated to all the heroes,
both in this world and all others.

CONTENTS

Lily's Miracle

Lily

The eldest daughter of Margrave Lockwood. Born deaf, her existence was hidden from the world.

Lafine

A maid at the Lockwood manor who looks after Lily.

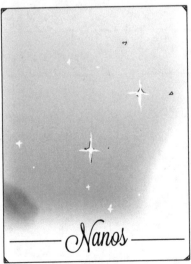

Nanos

The nanomachines, which receive and actualize the thoughts of all living things.

Veil

A young C-rank hunter. Looks after the children of the slums.

C-Rank Party "The Crimson Vow"

A girl who was granted "average" abilities in this fantasy world.

A strong-willed female hunter. Specializes in combat magic.

A swordswoman. Leader of the hunting party The Crimson Vow.

A hunter and healing magic user. A timid girl, but...

Previously

When Adele von Ascham, the eldest daughter of Viscount Ascham, was ten years old, she was struck with a terrible headache and, just like that, remembered everything.

She remembered how, in her previous life, she was an eighteen-year-old Japanese girl named Kurihara Misato who died while trying to save a young girl, and that she met God...

Misato had exceptional abilities, and the expectations of those around her were high. As a result, she could never live her life the way she wanted. So when she met God, she made an impassioned plea:

"In my next life, please make my abilities average!"

Yet somehow, it all went awry. a

In her new life, she can talk to nanomachines, and although her magical powers are technically average, it is the average between a human's and an elder dragon's...6,800 times that of a sorcerer!

At the first academy she attended, she made friends and rescued a little boy as well as a princess. She registered at the Hunters' Prep School under the name of Mile and made a grand debut with the Crimson Vow—the party she formed with her classmates. At this point, she's been sought after by royals and elven scholars, meddled in wars, and even fought elder dragons?!

Then one day, the Crimson Vow were running amok all across the land when they came to the borderland fief of a certain margrave...

CHAPTER 1 |
A Chance Meeting

L ILY, the eldest daughter of Margrave Neiham Lockwood, was born deaf. With only nine short years of life under her belt, she could never have guessed what was to become of her, her beloved family, and the mansion that they lived in.

On the evening that it all began, the first thing she became aware of was Lafine, her loyal attendant, rushing into the room and taking her by the hand, dragging Lily into a cramped, dark armoire.

"Wha?"

"——!"

Lafine pressed a hand over Lily's mouth, a sharp look upon her face as she placed her pointer finger to her own lips, shaking her head from side to side. She did not speak, but had she spoken, Lily would not have heard it.

Nevertheless, Lily could easily understand that this was a signal that meant, "Don't make a sound." She was very intelligent, after all, partly because she'd spent most of her life reading. The day it was discovered that she had not been blessed with one of the most treasured of senses, she'd been hidden away from the world, left locked in her room so no one would know of her. As a result, she passed nearly all her waking hours with her nose in a book.

"Mm..."

Though she did not know why it was so important that she stay silent, Lily simply nodded. Lafine leaned the back of her head against the wall of the armoire and breathed a gentle sigh.

Her arms around her knees, Lily looked up at Lafine from the base of the wardrobe. Lily's father, Neiham, had brought Lafine into the Lockwood household one day, intending her to serve as a maid—but a peculiar kind of maid, who never did any washing or cleaning. Lafine had light brown hair, warm ruby eyes, and a perpetually weary expression. She always seemed placid, even as she was shunned by the other staff, which had led to her becoming the attendant of their deaf little interloper.

Just as these thoughts crossed Lily's mind, Lafine looked down at her, and their eyes met. Lily smiled. Yet Lafine swiftly averted her gaze, scratching her head and scowling.

She felt no affection for anyone.

Loyal attendant or no, she was always like this. Rarely did she bother to communicate. The only bond Lafine and Lily shared was a written one—an exchange of necessary words, penned at the necessary times. Nothing more, and nothing less. However, as much as she acted as though Lily was a bother, she always fulfilled her requests, no matter what they were.

Lily needed her, yes—but more importantly, she didn't dislike her. Lafine may not have been particularly chatty, but she was the only person who paid even the slightest attention to the girl.

Still, Lily had no idea why they were hiding in the armoire. She would understand it better if she were the only one who had been shut inside. It would be like the time bullies had locked her inside a storeroom, or comparable to the way she'd been confined to the second floor of the mansion, as though she were a foul smell her family needed to conceal from the rest of the world. And yet, Lafine was right there beside her. Whenever she had been shut away before, she had always been alone.

Lily pondered.

Lafine, did you do something bad, too? Is that why you've been locked in here with me? But you got in here yourself. Did you bring me in here with you because you're lonely? Or are you afraid of the dark?

Lily giggled.

Goodness, Lafine, you're hopeless! Here you are, even older than me. Don't worry, though, I'm right here with you. It's cramped in here, but I don't mind it. It's nice and warm with both of us, and there's some kind of fruity scent in the air.

Lily gave a quick thumbs-up and a forceful nod, her eyes sparkling.

"...?"

Lafine was biting her bottom lip. Her forehead was creased, and her eyes were weary.

Hm! What an interesting expression...

Minutes ticked by, but Lily was never able to decipher either the meaning or motive behind Lafine's actions. At some point, she fell asleep. When she opened her eyes again, Lafine had vanished from the armoire.

Timidly, she pushed the door open.

"Uh?"

Her room looked strange. There were muddy streaks on the carpet, like it had been trampled upon. Her carefully arranged bookshelf had been toppled, and her beloved books were scattered everywhere. Still, her bed was untouched, and everything else appeared as it normally did. Her parents had never given her much besides those books, after all.

"Uh... Huh?"

The door to her room was ajar. The lock on the door opened only from the outside, per her parents' decree, and it was unusual to see it unlocked.

No, that wasn't it. Something had broken the lock, and the metal shards were lying on the carpet.

The hallway was in worse shape than her room. It had practically been destroyed. Her father's decorative armor had been violently knocked over, and several paintings were missing from her mother's collection. But that was not all. Even the mansion's walls were damaged.

Seeing all this, the girl began to feel the queasiness of worry for the first time. Finally, she understood. It was robbers. Robbers had infiltrated their mansion, which was why Lafine had hidden the both of them away.

"Uuuhhuh——!"

Lily screamed wordlessly, but there was no reply. Normally, Lafine would come running, albeit begrudgingly.

She walked down the long hall. One by one, she opened the doors on both floors of the house.

And yet, she found no one. Her father's study, her parents' chambers, and her siblings' rooms had all been similarly ransacked. There was not a single soul in the servants' quarters nor in the kitchen where the chefs were normally found.

A cold night wind blew in through the shattered glass windows and the crumbling outer walls. The only thing that moved was the hem of Lily's dress, which now seemed out of place in the ruined mansion, swaying with the breeze.

Nothing else stirred. Nothing at all.

She was all alone in the vast Lockwood mansion. Lily Lockwood, the little deaf girl, had been left behind.

That was exactly ten days ago.

Lily remained in the abandoned mansion. She managed to subsist on the steadily spoiling food in the storehouse, awaiting the return of her family or servants.

And yet, no one came—not even Lafine, who had saved her life that night. Lily had not seen any sign of her since she had woken up in the armoire.

A few more days passed, by which point Lily had eaten

through all the edible stores that remained, and her small body was beginning to grow weak. If she ventured out into town, someone might offer her help. However, in the eight years since her condition had been discovered, she had spent her whole life locked in her room. Her only knowledge of the outside world came from her books.

And so, she waited. She knew of nothing else she could do. She opened all the windows and thrust open the half-destroyed front door. She pulled the blankets from the bed she knew so well and slept in the entrance hall.

She did this in the hope that someone would someday come back to her—in the hope that she could be there, to welcome them with a smile.

Soon, even waking became a struggle. It was not until the very end that she came to feel, deep within her bones, that she was wasting away. Yes, the end—however, not *her* end. For as it turned out, Lily Lockwood had the good fortune to make this distinction.

As Lily stared outside, her eyes half-lidded with fatigue in a way she recognized from her one-time maid, her consciousness fading, four girls appeared beyond the open front door.

"..."

She had never seen these girls before. Obviously, there was no way she could have known that they were the Crimson Vow, a promising group of rookie hunters from the capital branch of the Hunters' Guild in the Kingdom of Tils, traveling to make a name for themselves.

All Lily knew was what she could see.

The first of the girls was tall. She had blonde hair and a handsome face, and her hand sat on the hilt of the sword that hung from her hip.

"Don't let your guards down. The robbers that were targeting the margrave might still be around here somewhere."

"What're you talking about? Why would they stick around? The kind of pea-brained idiots who run in bandit circles always beat it the moment they've gotten what they came for. It's pointless to go shuffling around."

A short but imposing red-haired girl waved the tall girl's concerns away, tromping ahead with confidence.

"I-I guess so, but if we don't keep our eyes peeled—"

"Oh?"

The redhead locked eyes with Lily.

"There's a kid here. She looks pretty thin. Wonder where she came from."

"She has the same violet eyes as the margrave. Think she's his daughter?"

As though this were their cue, the remaining two girls stepped in through the front door. There was a girl with brown hair and a gentle air about her, and another who was small and cute—probably the youngest amongst them. For some reason, Lily thought, there was something strangely captivating about this foursome.

The brunette turned to the younger girl beside her and asked, "The margrave's son and daughter were only supposed to be five and three years old, weren't they?"

"Yes. At least, that's what they told us at the guild when we accepted the investigation job. This girl looks like she's probably eight or nine."

The redheaded girl's eyes narrowed.

"So, who's this kid, then?" she asked, pointing toward Lily.

The four hunters tilted their heads simultaneously.

"It's probably best if we ask the girl herself..."

The smallest of the girls called out to Lily. "Hello there, young lady. It's super dangerous for you to be here right now. Where did you come from? And who might you be?"

But rather than answer, Lily just tilted her head—since, of course, she had not heard a single word of the girls' conversation.

Next, the tall girl spoke up. "She's probably not feeling well enough to speak. Hey, kid. Are you hungry?"

Lily's cheeks were sunken, her whole body propped listlessly against the wall like a broken doll. She could do no more than stare up at these four strangers with curiosity. Seeing that they were taking turns speaking to her, she pointed to her own ears. Then, she pointed to her mouth and made a sound.

"Uh..."

With that, the girls understood—the weakened, emaciated girl could not hear them.

"Oh!"

"She—"

"Looks like she's deaf."

The tall girl whispered to the gentle-looking one, "Hey, Pauline. Can you heal her with your magic?"

"I can try."

The girl named Pauline crouched down in front of Lily, put her hands on both sides of her head, over Lily's ears, and closed her eyes.

What a big chest she's got, Lily thought to herself. It was right in her face.

"Heal the injuries, regenerate the nerves, repair blood vessels. *Mega Heal!*" Pauline announced, but even once the spell had been completed, nothing had changed. In truth, this was to be expected—Lily had not lost her sense of hearing to illness or injury; she had been born this way.

"Mile, do you think *you* could do it?" asked the tall girl.

The smallest girl, the one called Mile, shook her head.

"Hmm, if even Pauline's Mega Heal had no effect, it's unlikely this is from injury or sickness. Which means it'll be hard to handle with regular magic."

"I see..."

For some moments, silence overtook the hall. Seeing that they had stopped talking, Lily, unable to tell what was going on, smiled broadly.

The tallest hunter lowered her eyes.

"Hey, Reina—"

"Mavis, we can't," Reina, the redhead, spoke curtly. "We've still got work to do, and we're going to have to pass through some dangerous places. We can't bring her with us. Plus, what happens to her after we get back home? She's not some kind of house pet."

"Guh... I-I mean, I know that..."

Mile, the smallest one, opened her mouth.

"How about this, then? We can leave her with a few weeks' worth of preserved food and potable water, and as soon as we're done with our job, we hurry back to the capital and tell the guild about her. Then, the guild can contact the local orphanage, and they can look after her."

"Oh, yeah. Good thinking, Mile."

"You really do always manage to come through at times like this. How are you such an airhead the rest of the time?"

"I'm not an airhead! That's so *rude*!"

Clearly a bit disgruntled, Mile began pulling dried meat, cooked vegetables, and loaves of bread out of thin air.

"Hup! Heave ho! Here we go!"

To the pile, she added a great big cask.

Ka-thud...

"?!"

Lily's jaw dropped at the preposterous scene unfolding in front of her. She knew from her reading that there were people in this world who had access to the convenience that was storage magic, but hearing about something was far different from seeing it with your own two eyes. It was amazing just to watch as so many different things were produced from *nothing*, right in front of her.

Whoa! Whoa!

Her cheeks pinked with excitement, and she clapped her hands.

"Oh, she seems to be enjoying this," Mavis observed.

"Well, I mean, what can any of us do but laugh in the face of that unnatural magic Mile's got?"

"Reinaaa, you don't have to say it like *that*!" Mile whined.

"Whatever. Just hurry and finish up."

"Okay... Hup!"

A ball of water popped into existence above the cask. A second later, the water splashed perfectly inside.

"There we go. That should be enough to keep her from starving for now."

"It should. It's unfortunate that we couldn't heal her illness, but hopefully she can hang in there until someone from the guild can come to get her."

"For sure."

Mavis picked up some of the bread and dried meat, offering it to Lily, who was still sitting with her back to the wall.

"Here, eat up."

"Mavis, you dummy. She needs water first." Reina stepped in, offering the girl a cup full of water.

"N-no fair, Reina! You're just trying to win her over first because she's cute."

"I-I am *not*!"

Lily looked back and forth between their faces, then weakly bowed her head, taking and emptying the cup before accepting the meat and bread. She took a small nibble, grinned, and bowed her head again. The four girls wordlessly nodded. Mile smiled in satisfaction.

Good. They understood my thanks.

After that, the four girls watched over Lily for a time, before they finally turned to leave. As they walked away, the smallest girl, who was trailing at the back, stopped, and turned back to Lily. She closed one eye, placed her pointer finger in front of her lips, and softly whispered, "Your hearing can't be healed with magic. At least with *normal* magic. But wait just a little bit, okay?"

"...?"

What had the girl said? Lily watched, perplexed, as Mile walked away, and then took another nibble of her meat and bread.

It had been roughly half a day since the girls had departed. Lily drew some water from the cask that had been left behind and quenched her thirst.

She hated the nighttime. Without her beloved family and their kind servants, the mansion was like a great beast, the jaws of its immense, pitch-black maw opened wide. Then again, she supposed that she had been biding her time inside of that very mouth, which was rather amusing. As she imagined it, she began to giggle.

Lily was a cheerful girl by nature, and now, she felt a flood of optimism. She stood, drew another cup of water from the cask, and drank. Now that she had food in her, her tired body was suddenly able to move again. She truly had to thank those girls.

"Phew..."

Once more, she considered her situation. The mansion had most likely been attacked by bandits. Their lands bordered the Albarn Empire, and though her father, Margrave Neiham Lockwood, had a substantial personal guard stationed outside the estate, it seemed something awful had happened to them. After all, if any of those guards were still safe and sound, they would have come to her rescue long ago.

Indeed, it was clear that something terrible had happened to both her family and their personal guard, as well as their servants. If she waited here forever, she would probably begin to waste away once more.

She clutched her hands to her chest.

Yes. Okay. Tomorrow morning, I'll have to set out.

Just as the thought crossed Lily's mind, a small figure walked in through the open front door. Her heart leapt at the irrational thought that this might be her brother or sister.

"Uh...wh—?"

Lily's eyes opened wide as she looked up at the figure in front of her. It was one of the girls from earlier that day, the smallest one of the bunch with the adorable face.

It was Mile—though, of course, Lily did not know her name.

"Ha! I thought I would slip out after everyone had fallen asleep, but that took a lot longer than I thought. They started getting suspicious, and in the end, I had to use a bit of magic to force them to drift off."

"...?"

Lily tilted her head. All she knew was that Mile was standing there, her lips moving. She could surmise that she was saying something, but she had no idea what.

"Oh, right. You can't hear me, can you? Just a second!"

Mile suddenly produced paper, a quill, and an ink pot out of thin air. Using a pillar as a writing board, she swiftly wrote across the page.

"Hopefully you can read."

She then handed the paper to Lily.

"I'm going to heal your ears so that you can hear," was written on it.

"?!"

Lily held her hands out in a grabbing motion. Mile handed her the quill and paper.

"But the mages all said that my ears can't be healed with magic," Lily wrote.

"Don't worry. I have a special kind of magic. Before I heal you, though, you have to promise me one thing. You can never tell anyone about what is about to happen here. Not anyone. You can't even let anyone know that you were healed. If anyone asks you, please tell them that your ears just healed on their own."

Lily tilted her head.

"Um. Here. Just pretend that this is all a dream. We're both in your dream right now, actually. This isn't reality."

This girl is pretty weird, thought Lily. *It's actually a little spooky...*

"Anyway! You won't tell anyone you were healed! Forget I ever existed! Got it?!"

There was no way this girl could heal her. Her parents had brought dozens of famous healing mages in to examine her. However, the result had always been the same. Nothing had changed.

However... Yes, *however.*

This girl was maybe three or four years older than her. Looking at her now, with her rapid and desperately changing expressions, her mouth flapping, Lily smiled comfortably and nodded. Clearly, the girl's intentions were good. Lily might as well let her try, so that this girl could feel she had made her best effort.

Lily moved the quill across the page.

"Yes. I promise."

"Then, let's begin the treatment. Please relax."

Putting down the pen, Mile looked not at Lily but off into the distance. Lily reflexively followed her gaze upward into the air but saw nothing but the dark ceiling above her.

"Nanos, you here?"

Huh?

Lily had no idea who or what Mile was talking to. She appeared to be staring at nothing at all.

I MEAN, WE'RE EVERYWHERE...

"I don't think there's something wrong with her ears but maybe with her brain? Her temporal lobe or something?"

YES, THAT IS ABSOLUTELY CORRECT.

Mile's pointer finger shot up.

"In that case, could we just alter her temporal lobe to be the same as a normal person's?"

WE COULD DO THAT. THAT IS, WE *CAN* DO THAT, BUT...

"What is it?"

WE SHOULDN'T. WE OBVIOUSLY SHOULDN'T.

Mile's expression twisted as she spoke.

"Why not?"

ALTERING THE BRAIN VIA SURGICAL METHODS IS A TECHNIQUE THAT DOES NOT YET EXIST IN THIS WORLD. PLEASE REFRAIN FROM BRINGING TOO MANY MEDDLESOME EARTH ARTS INTO THIS REALITY.

"Come on, Nanos! That doesn't matter. There's a cute little girl in trouble! Look! Look how squishy her little cheeks are! Look at her!"

Mile pinched Lily's cheeks, pushing and pulling and squishing them all around.

"Humweh, pwah, mwuh..."

"And just listen to her! It's too cute—it's just too *cute*, I *can't stand it*!"

As the assault on her face continued, Lily's gaze roved around the hall. But sure enough, there was no one in sight. However, the girl before her was definitely talking. Not only that, she appeared quite animated.

Are there spirits here or something? she wondered.

YOU KNOW, THE ODDS ARE FAIRLY GREAT THAT THAT FIELD OF STUDY WILL PROGRESS BEYOND OUR RESTRICTIONS WITHIN THE NEXT FEW HUNDRED YEARS...

"Shut up, shut up, *shut uuuup!!!* It doesn't matter if they haven't gotten there yet! If it seems like it's going to get there eventually then I or one of my descendants will probably manage it sooner or later!"

YOU'RE BEING ABSURD. BUT...

"I don't need your lectures! I'm not listening anymore! Just stop quibbling and do it! This is over! This conversation is over!"

Mile clasped her hands over her ears. *That will probably keep her from hearing,* Lily thought to herself.

AH, WAIT. PLEASE DON'T CANCEL OUT THE VIBRA-TIONS OF YOUR TYMPANIC MEMBRANES WITH MAGIC. WHAT ARE WE SUPPOSED TO DO IF EVEN *YOU* CAN'T HEAR US? COME ON. BESIDES, YOU KNOW IT'S POINTLESS ANYWAY. EVEN IF YOU CANCEL OUT THE VIBRATIONS, WE CAN JUST SPEAK DIRECTLY INTO YOUR TEMPORAL LOBE... CAN YOU HEAR US? LADY MILE...?

Mile removed her hands from her ears, eyes opening wide. She clamped her mouth shut and returned a thought pulse.

Shut up! Don't speak directly to my brain like that! It's creepy!

CREEPY? THAT'S NOT VERY NICE. WE ONLY HAD TO ADDRESS YOU THIS WAY BECAUSE YOU WERE US-ING THAT VIBRATION CANCELING MAGIC TO TRY TO IGNORE US. OKAY, FINE. WE GET IT, WE GET IT. WE'LL DO IT. WE MAY AS WELL. BUT WE HOPE YOU'LL TAKE RESPONSIBILITY FOR ANY CONSEQUENCES THAT MAY ARISE AS A RESULT OF THIS. NOW, LET'S HAVE THIS GIRL GO TO SLEEP.

*Why didn't you just say so from the beginning? Thanks, Nanos.
I can always count on you.*

WELL, OF COURSE. AND NEXT TIME YOU USE THAT
CANCELING MAGIC, MAKE SURE YOU DO IT PROPERLY. IF
YOU DON'T, YOU MIGHT END UP LOSING THE ABILITY TO
HEAR ANYONE ELSE AROUND YOU.

I knew that! Thank you, Nanos.

Knowing that she had won, Mile grinned devilishly.

However, she had no idea exactly what was about to oc-
cur. Even the nanomachines she had been conversing with did
not know the full extent of what it was they were bringing
about.

"...!"

Lily gasped, her eyes opening impossibly wide.

Ba-dump...

Her heart fluttered at a brand-new sensation, something
she was feeling for the first time in her life. In that moment, Lily
Lockwood *heard*. She heard an impossible voice and a high, girl-
ish one—not via the vibration of her eardrums but via thought
pulses. Directly into her temporal lobe.

Then, Lily knew: There were spirits in this world known as
Nanos. (Though, in truth, they were not spirits but nanomachines, the minuscule scientific beings that were the true source
of the power that the people of this world referred to as "magic."
But Lily, who knew only what was written in her books, firmly
believed that these were spirits.)

NOW THEN, LET'S BEGIN.

Not in the least bit aware of Lily's dawning awareness, the nanomachines began their treatment.

"If you would, Nanos. Now, as for you," Mile turned to Lily again. "Time to take a nap... Hang in there. Hang in there and keep on living. There are so many wonderful sounds in this world waiting for you..."

Before Lily could ask Mile about the spirits' voices, she was overtaken by a powerful spell and sunk into a deep slumber.

When she awoke to the sounds of birds chirping, Lily was so struck by the beauty of their song that she wept. Her heart swelled as the gentle, wonderful resonance filled her head.

At last, she knew how many joyous sounds flowed throughout this world—the wind, the rustling of the leaves in the trees, the birds and insects, the calls of animals, and even the sounds of her own humming.

Her world was expanding.

At the age of nine, Lily Lockwood, born without one of her senses, finally *heard*.

Or, so she thought in that moment.

CHAPTER 2 |

Her First Adventure

HER EYES WERE CLOSED, but she had been awake the whole time. She was listening to the sounds of the night—the wind that shook the windows, the cries of the birds and insects, the sound of her own breathing.

She couldn't get enough of it. It was just as the girl had told her. The world was full of wonderful sounds.

"Uh-uhh..."

That was *her* voice. Her own still-wordless voice.

Up until this point, she had always understood words by picturing the written letters in her head, but everyone else distinguished these words by their sounds...

It's really amazing! I hope I can speak one day. I'll have to start studying words.

She thought of her beloved family. What had their voices

been like? Lafine must have had a clear, beautiful voice. That was what Lily imagined.

If only she could hear them... Deep down, she knew that she would probably never get the chance.

Lily opened her eyes and gazed through the open front door at the moon that hung low in the sky. Just then, what seemed like countless raucous sounds, all of which she had never heard before, came rushing in from outside. Lily turned to watch as ten-odd men came in through the front door.

"...!"

For a moment, she had been overjoyed at the possibility that her family or a few servants had returned, but now she tilted her head at the stranger at the head of the bunch, a burly man she had never seen before.

Who's this?

The man snatched her up by the scruff of the neck.

"Wah! Wahh!"

"What's with this brat?"

"Uh, eek!"

Lily's limbs flailed wildly, but her nine-year-old body was powerless to resist as she was hoisted up close to the man's bearded face.

"Ow?"

His beard grew from ear to ear, from his sideburns all the way to his chin, and the perimeter of his mouth bristled with hair as well.

He's like a big scruffy bear. It's kinda cute, actually. Lily thought. *I wanna touch it.*

"Hey! Don't pull my beard! Ouch! Kid, who are you?"

"Aah, uh?"

She had no idea what he was saying. Because she had yet to learn the sounds of words, the man's question was nothing more than a series of noises to her. If the conversation were somehow beamed straight to her temporal lobe via magic, she would have been able to understand it. The spoken word, however, was still beyond her.

"Boss."

"Yeah?"

A smaller man came up beside him, wearing an odd smile.

"This place really was trashed. Seems like those rumors about the Lockwoods being attacked and vanishing to the winds were true."

"No valuables left at all?"

The small man shrugged.

"Not sure. The rest of the guys split up and are combing the mansion now, but if those attackers came here to strip the place, then I doubt there'll be anything left."

"Now, hold up," the burly man puffed out his chest and proudly declared, "If anyone is gonna be diggin' up any treasures around here, it's gonna be us! The wimpy robber gang, the 'Ashen Alleycats!'"

"Heh heh, y'got that right. Heh heh heh."

"Bwa ha ha ha! C'mon, let's go get our loot on!"

As the man dropped Lily, a thought occurred to her, and she smiled to herself. *Wow! That big man and that little man were talking to each other. I'm so jealous. They were smiling as well, and it seems like they were having a lot of fun. I want to have a conversation, too...*

Let's do it!

Lily opened her mouth, smiling wide.

"Uwh-auh. Awoh. Ah! Ha ha!"

"Uh? What's with her? She laughin' at us? It's...kinda creepy. She's really bustin' a gut."

"Maybe it's because your face is so funny-lookin', Boss?"

"Ha ha ha. I see. My face, eh? ...I'm gonna smack you into next week, idiot."

The small man pointed to Lily. "But actually. Who the heck is this kid?"

"Who knows? Figure she's probably one of the Lockwoods? She was here, anyway."

The small man put a hand to his chin and tilted his head.

"Thought the Lockwoods only had one son and one daughter. I've seen both of 'em before, and they're both littler'n her. Think the boy's only 'bout five years old."

Recall: The Lockwood family had not only locked Lily away—they had concealed her entire existence from the world. The burly man shoved Lily toward his associate.

"So then, who's this?"

"I'm sayin' I have no idea. That's why I was just askin'. I mean, she's probably just some kid from the slums who wandered in here, right?"

"Huh. Think this kid's one of us? Awful young start for lootin'... But I can tell she's got a lotta potential! Let's take 'er with us!"

The boss yanked Lily back again, staring fixedly at her.

The small man raised an eyebrow. "What? You really got an eye for this li'l squirt? I mean, she's got a pretty face. But she's *way* too young t—"

Before he could finish the sentence, the boss protested, veins bulging on his forehead, "You dumbass! Ladies don't hit their peak until they're in their late thirties at least!"

"I mean, I think that's all a matter of opinion."

Oh, this seems like so much fun. I have no idea what they're talking about, but I am so ready to have my first conversation! I hope I can learn some words soon.

Lily was so excited she could burst. Dropped summarily onto the floor, she looked up at the boss.

"Boss, that brat might run on us."

"I mean, she can run if she wants to. We ain't bandits or slavers. Fightin' or killin' her would be stupid."

"There ya go again with that goofy set of morals, Boss!"

The burly man looked a bit ashamed.

"Anyway, what're we gonna do with somethin' that conspicuous if some hunters show up? They'd take a guy like you down on sight."

Despite the small man's concerns, however, Lily made no attempt to run. She could not wait to see what this amusing duo might do next.

A few minutes later...

The Ashen Alleycats tottered down the dark road, shoulders slumped—with little Lily bouncing briskly behind them. Not only was she *not* running away, she was following them. Quite closely. Of her own accord.

Danger was not a word that existed in Lily Lockwood's vocabulary.

Walking just behind the boss, she tugged his clothing lightly with her fingertips.

"Uh? What? Oh, yeah, well, you see, there wasn't much of anythin' of value left in there. I mean, it wasn't a total wash, but this was pretty much a wasted effort. We might even have to break up the Alleycats soon. There aren't that many wasted places to loot, anyway," the boss kindly explained, but Lily, unable to understand, only tilted her head.

At length, the group made it out of town and climbed into a boat that sat moored on a sandy beach. Then, they rowed out onto the waves.

"Whoa! Whoa!"

It was her first time seeing the sea. And her first time in a boat. It was like soaring through the darkness, the girl thought, the boundary between night sky and sea nearly indistinguishable. Her heart pounded. She stood at the bow and stared down into the dark, roiling water.

"Whoa now, little lady! Don't fall in."

"Huh?"

She leaned forward and stretched her hand out, then scooped up some of the water and licked it. For a moment, her face crinkled, but then a smile broke across her face.

"Waha!"

It's so salty! Is this all salt water? It's just like the ocean I read about in my books. They say that despite all this salt, there's way more fish here than in the rivers. Ah! This is just too exciting. The outside world is so much fun.

Finally, the boat rounded a triangular rock face, which jutted several hundred meters out into the sea. On the other side of it was a cave, carved out by the lapping waves, which the little boat proceeded to enter. It wasn't dark inside, thanks to all the torches that lined the cave's interior.

"This is the Ashen Alleycats' top-secret base," the boss explained. "Not that there's much of anything in it. C'mon, we gotta walk from here. Let's get you out of this boat."

He gripped Lily by the sides and hoisted her up. She sunk ankle-deep into the salt water.

"Waha! Wah!"

It's cold! But it feels so nice!

"Hey now, quit splashin'. You keep kickin' up water like that and you're gonna muddy up that pretty dress you got from the Lockwood place."

Of course, the boss had no way of knowing that the dress had been Lily's to begin with.

"Wuh?"

Once she had made her way out of the water and onto the floor of the cave proper, Lily began frolicking around again.

Everything was so new to her. A home inside an ocean cave was just like something out of her pirate books. She could hear the crackling flames of the torches, the soft and rhythmic lapping of the waves. And, most importantly, the sounds of many voices. They echoed throughout the cave, shifting into a strange melody. It was as though the people were repeating themselves with a second's delay.

Deep within the cave, there was a doorway, which opened up to a wider area. Unlike the outer part of the cave, this space had been carved cleanly into a rectangular room.

A living room?

In the walls of the living room were a number of other doors, which Lily imagined led off to bedrooms or something similar. The men all headed off in separate directions. Only the boss and the smaller man remained, sitting down at a large table.

"Looks like we came up empty again, eh, Harris? We got all that food that was sitting in front of the Lockwood house for some reason, but there's a lotta us. We're gonna bottom out in the next few days."

"Well, then we just get all the guys together again for a big fishin' meet-up. Or, we could sell that girl off to slavers..."

"Hmm..."

The boss's gaze fixed on Lily. The moment their eyes met, she smiled. She turned to the bearded man and gave a little wave.

"Nope. We can't do that. We're not criminals. We're just a buncha petty looters. Plus, we wouldn't get much for her, since she can't talk."

"I noticed that. Why *can't* she talk? Seems like she can hear, and I'm pretty sure she weren't raised by monsters or beasts. They might not be able to write much, but even kids from the slums are pretty good at talkin' nowadays."

The boss put his hand to his chin.

"Writing... Writing, eh?"

"Oh, right, yer surprisingly good at writing, aren'tcha, Boss?"

"What's so surprising about that? I'm gonna kick you into next week... Anyway, let's try it."

The boss brought over a paper and quill. Suddenly, Lily's eyes began to sparkle. He gestured for her to join them at the table, and he sat down across from her. Then, he ran the quill across the page.

"Can you read, little lady?"

Lily took the quill from him and wrote across the same page, *"I'm great at reading and writing!"*

The boss and the smaller man looked to one another.

"Well now, that's a shock. Whaddya think of that, Harris?"

"Well," Harris said. "It's obvious she's no wild child raised by beasts. Can't be some waif from the slums, either. Her writing's good. The letters are nice. Better'n yours, even."

"Shut up. Sorry my writing's *so messy.*"

"And so's yer face."

"Right, yeah, and so's my face, huh? I seriously am gonna kick your ass."

The boss snatched the pen away from Lily.

"What's your name?"

"It's Lily."

"Hmm. Lily, huh? Yo, Harris, there any kids named Lily in the Lockwood family?"

Harris shook his head. "Not as far as I know. Could be one of the servants' kids?"

"Could be."

The boss seemed to ponder something, then leaned across the table and tapped the middle of Lily's chest with one chunky pointer finger, loudly and clearly enunciating, *"Li-ly."*

"...?"

Lily tilted her head.

"That's yer name. *Li-ly.* C'mon, you say it now. *Li-ly.*"

Lily's lips parted faintly.

"Lihleey?"

The boss nodded firmly.

"That's right. You're Lily. And I'm the boss."

"Ain't that the part where you'd tell her yer name?"

The boss ignored Harris's interjection and pointed to himself, repeating, *"Bo-ss."*

"Bawhss," Lily repeated, nodding.

"That's right. I'm the boss. And you're Lily."

"Boss. Lily... Lily."

A strange warmth began to spread throughout her chest. For the first time ever, she had heard herself called and she had spoken her *own name* with her own two lips. *Lily.* The name that her beloved family had given her.

What was this feeling?! She was happy! She was ever so happy!

Lily pointed to herself.

"Lily!"

"Yeah. Lily. So, w—"

The boss thought for a moment and then began writing with the quill again.

"Lily, we, the Ashen Alleycats, have abducted you."

"Uh?" Lily furrowed her brow.

"I'm bringing you into the gang, and we're going to raise you up into a right proper looter, just like us! You've got a bright future ahead of you, kid!"

"There you go again with those mixed-up morals, Boss."

"Shut up."

Lily took the pen back.

"No way."

"Why not?! How else is a brat like you supposed to live on her own?"

"Well, looting is bad. Bad things are no good. That's what my books said."

Both the boss and Harris's faces twisted at this earnest answer.

"Seems Miss Lily here's got no idea just what kinda position she's gotten herself into here, Boss. Why don't you show 'er what it means to face down a wicked leader?"

"Sure."

The boss swung out his legs and thrust them up onto the table with a thud. Lily's eyes went wide at the sudden loud noise.

"Heh heh, look, now she's shakin'."

Lily, however, took up the quill again.

"Why are you putting your feet on the table? Isn't that bad, too?"

The boss snatched the pen back.

"That's just how we do things around here. You get it now? Why don't you j—"

Before he could finish writing, Lily also hoisted her legs up—and plopped them atop the table. Her skirt was hiked up, baring her legs all the way to the thigh. Lily looked a little bashful as their legs faced one another's.

As the boss stared at her, mouth agape, Lily gestured for him to hand the quill pen her way.

"Sorry, Boss. I didn't know this was how we were supposed to do things here. Thank you for showing me. This seems bad for your posture, though."

Lily chuckled as she passed the paper back.

The boss and Harris read her response, looked at one another, and then shook their heads simultaneously, faces serious. Then, the boss brought his own legs down and abruptly grabbed Lily's. He pulled them off the table, carefully tugging her dislodged skirt back into place as well.

"It was a joke. You should be more modest."

Lily looked confused.

Harris smacked his palm to his face and muttered, "You've gotta be kiddin' me..."

"Anyway, you're sleeping here tonight. The other guys have already taken all the other rooms."

"Okay. Thanks, Boss."

"You sure?" asked Harris. "Shouldn't we lock her away?"

"I don't think she's gonna be rowin' off on her own."

"Guess you're right."

So, Lily ate with the Ashen Alleycats and went to sleep. Snuggled up in her blanket, she wondered what might happen next. *It seems I've followed some bandits home. They don't seem like bad people, but I certainly can't live here with them this way. How could I face my parents and siblings if I grew into a criminal? I'd be dragging our title through the mud.*

But I have no idea how to row that boat. How am I supposed to get out of here? If only I had someone to talk this over with...

Suddenly, she thought of the girls who had rescued her from starvation. They had produced all that food and water out of nowhere and shared it with her without reservation. Judging from the swords and staves they carried, they were probably hunters.

She heaved a sigh. *If only those girls were here,* she thought wistfully. But then, she remembered. *Hadn't there been someone else, too?* She had not seen them, but she remembered them just the same—the spirits who had fixed her hearing.

Wait, she thought, *don't tell me. Yes, of course!* There were those mysterious voices that had seemed to echo inside her head.

And so, Lily Lockwood began to "speak," focusing her energy around each word.

Hey, uhm, Spirits? Might you be around here somewhere?

It was nothing less than a miracle. Just a day ago, this would have been utterly impossible. Lily had been born without hearing, and thus, she did not speak.

Yet as a result of her unhearing ears and silent tongue, Lily had spent her life honing her thought-pulse reception, which was far stronger than that of the average person in this world. And as a result, she had been able to hear the nanomachine when it had "spoken" to her and Mile.

Spirits, are you here?

Even if she were able to transmit thought pulses, clearly there was no one around to hear them. She was perfectly aware that her "spirits" (which were in fact the nanomachines) existed, but perhaps there weren't any in this cave.

I guess those Nanos aren't here...

?!

What Lily did not know was that the all-purpose entities known as the nanomachines only spoke when directly addressed—which was why, in this moment, they were able to reply.

Hm? Um, were you perhaps speaking to me? Am I supposed to be this "spirit"?

Oh, you are here! Yeah! That's right, I was talking to you, Mr. Nano!

After an interminably long silence, the nanomachine replied with the shortest possible word in its expansive vocabulary.

Huh?

The nanomachine was bewildered. However, Lily continued to speak.

Oh, yes. Thanks for my ears, Mr. Nano.

Well, no, that was Mi— The nanomachine stopped and corrected itself. We could not take the credit for that. We were only able to act because the mage who was present insisted on our aid.

Lily's heart leapt. She was having a conversation, somehow or the other. She could not recognize words by their sound, but via thought pulses, communication was simple. *If only everyone in the world could communicate in this way,* she thought.

WELL, YOU SEE, AS FAR AS A MEANS OF CONVEY- ING ONE'S INTENTIONS TO ANOTHER PARTY, DOING SO DIRECTLY VIA THOUGHT PULSE IS A FAR MORE PRIMI- TIVE METHOD THAN SPEECH, SO IT IS PROBABLY FOR THE BEST THAT THIS IS NOT THE STANDARD MODE OF COMMUNICATION. HOW LONG HAVE YOU BEEN ABLE TO HEAR US, MISS LILY? AND HOW IS IT THAT YOU KNOW THE TERM "THOUGHT PULSES" IN THE FIRST PLACE?

Since the night you fixed my ears! When that mage lady covered her ears, you were talking to her by thought pulses, right? I heard the conversation you two were having then.

OH, GOODNESS! IT'S ONE THING TO EXPECT SUCH A SLIPUP FROM MI...*THAT LADY.* BUT FOR ME TO DO SO... IT WAS RECKLESS TO ASSUME THAT YOU COULD NOT HEAR US.

The spirit seemed troubled. Perhaps, Lily wondered, calling out to it had been wrong?

I fell asleep before I could tell you, and when I woke up, that mage lady was gone, so I couldn't ask anyone about it. I can't believe you've been so close this whole time and I never realized it!

Of course, Lily still had no idea that the nanomachines existed throughout the entire world, serving as the source of all magic. Naturally, the nanomachine that she was currently speaking to was not one of the individuals that had been involved in healing her ears, but all nanomachine units shared information with one another. Yet it was quite unreasonable to expect Lily—or anyone without Mile's very particular background—to understand any of this. It was closer to science than to magic, after all.

WELL, the nanomachine seemed to sigh, resigned. WHAT'S DONE IS DONE. SO, WHY IS IT THAT YOU CALLED FOR ME?

Lily clapped her hands together and smiled.

There's something I want to know.

LILY LOCKWOOD, AS YOU ARE ABLE TO HEAR AND SUMMON ME, YOU HAVE OBTAINED A LEVEL-3 ACCESS AUTHORIZATION. HOWEVER, THE QUESTIONS I AM ABLE TO ANSWER MAY BE LIMITED.

Lily tilted her head.

I'm not sure what you mean.

OF COURSE NOT. ANYWAY, IT'S NOT SOMETHING I WOULD BE ABLE TO EXPLAIN TO YOU SIMPLY, SO JUST ASK AWAY. IF I CANNOT ANSWER YOUR QUESTION, I WILL TELL YOU SO.

Ah, thank you, Mr. Nano! It would seem that this was a benevolent spirit. *Um, so, are the Ashen Alleycats bad people?*

ACCORDING TO THE STANDARDS ESTABLISHED BY HUMANS, THEY WOULD BE MINOR SCOUNDRELS. IN THE KINGDOM OF TILS AND THE ALBARN EMPIRE, AND IN FACT MOST PLACES, LOOTING ABANDONED BUILDINGS IS CONSIDERED A CRIME. THEY WOULDN'T BE KILLED

FOR THIS, BUT THEY MIGHT AT LEAST BE SENTENCED TO
SEVERAL YEARS OF INVOLUNTARY LABOR IN THE MINES.

Lily's expression faltered.

That sounds terrible.

WELL, THAT IS SIMPLY HOW THEY HAVE CHOSEN TO
LIVE. WHAT IF YOU WERE TO STOP THEM?

Me?

THERE IS A FAIR AMOUNT OF VALUE IN THE FACT
THAT YOU HAVE BEEN ABDUCTED AND DETAINED.

She did not understand. All the kidnapping talk aside, she
had followed them willingly, and though she was ostensibly being detained, she had not been bound or locked away anywhere.
She had far more freedom here than back at the Lockwood
manor—not that she would be taking advantage of it, since she
wasn't about to go sailing out across the waves all on her own.
But if there was some way that she could stop the Alleycats from
wrongdoing...

*What should I do? Try and persuade them? All I can do is write
to them!*

FELLOWS LIKE THESE ARE FIRM BELIEVERS IN
STRENGTH ABOVE ALL ELSE. SO, YOU JUST HAVE TO
SMACK THEM DOWN AND TELL THEM TO LEAD A MORE
RIGHTEOUS LIFE. THAT SHOULD BE ENOUGH TO PER-
SUADE THEM.

Smack them down? Lily supposed that was something she
might have been able to do if she were like the mages and hunters
who appeared in her books. But...

I can't use a sword or magic.

MISS LILY, HAVE YOU EVER GOTTEN CLOSE TO A FLAME? EVER SUBMERGED YOURSELF IN COLD WATER? EVER BEEN BLOWN ABOUT BY A WIND SO FIERCE YOU THOUGHT YOU MIGHT SOON TAKE FLIGHT?

She had tried touching the flame in a lamp before. Naturally, it had burned her. As a noble, baths were a luxury afforded to her, so of course she had tried dunking herself. And, as far as the wind, she had tried to close the windows of her room before during a storm and been blown back. Still, she could not possibly imagine what use these experiences might be to her.

I have.

GIVEN YOUR LEVEL-3 AUTHORIZATION, YOU SHOULD ALREADY BE ABLE TO USE MAGIC. IN FACT, YOU MAY HAVE ACCESS TO EVEN MORE POWERFUL MAGIC THAN THOSE WHO TYPICALLY ARE REFERRED TO AS MAGES.

Lily shook her head.

Even if that's true, I can't say any magical incantations. I don't really know the connections between language and sounds, so I can only talk via these thought pulses.

THE INCANTATIONS ARE NOTHING MORE THAN A FORMALITY, MEANT TO STRENGTHEN THE INTENT BEHIND YOUR MAGIC. PLEASE DON'T TELL ANYONE ABOUT THIS, OF COURSE. BUT THE SPELLS THE MAGES OF THIS WORLD USE ARE MADE UP OF VERY POWERFUL WORDS, AREN'T THEY?

That was certainly the case in Lily's books. There were mages who spoke of flames as hellfire, invoking fearsome images of purgatories that one could not even prove existed in their incantations.

THOSE WORDS ARE MERELY A BIT OF SELF-SUGGESTION—A WAY OF REMINDING ONESELF JUST HOW HOT A FIRE MUST BE. THEN, ONE USES ONE'S THOUGHTS TO SPREAD THAT SOLIDIFIED IMAGE OF A FLAME FROM DEEP WITHIN OUT INTO THE WORLD AROUND. FINALLY, WE NANOMA—ER, NANOS—RECEIVE THOSE IMPULSES AND INVOKE IT AS MAGIC.

Lily folded her arms and gave a slow nod.

Yep. I have no idea what you're talking about.

OF COURSE NOT. UNDERSTANDING AN EXPLANATION LIKE THAT WOULD BE IMPOSSIBLE UNLESS YOU WERE BORN INTO RATHER UNUSUAL CIRCUMSTANCES—LIKE THAT MAGE WHO HEALED YOUR EARS. WE CAN ONLY CONFER A LEVEL-3 AUTHORIZATION UPON YOU, WHEREAS THAT MAGE IS A LEVEL-5. SHE'S AN EXCEEDINGLY HIGH-LEVEL MAGE, BEYOND MOST HUMANOIDS.

Lily still had no idea what the spirit was talking about, but she got the feeling it was implying that that little mage was an incredibly powerful person.

I want to try some magic.

IN THAT CASE, TRY IMAGINING IT. CRYSTALLIZE THE IMAGE OF FIRE AND WIND WITHIN YOURSELF.

Done.

NOT JUST THE COLOR AND FORM OF IT BUT THE HEAT AND OTHER PROPERTIES?

Yep!

THEN, TAKE THAT IMAGE, FORM IT INTO A THOUGHT, AND TRY RELEASING IT INTO THE WORLD AROUND YOU. IT'S THE SAME METHOD BY WHICH YOU'RE SPEAKING TO ME.

Okay.

Lily closed her eyes and tipped her chin slightly upward.

She imagined flames above her. The bigger, the better. It was magic, after all. And, beneath that, the image of a gale, even stronger than the squall that had threatened to break her windows. Carefully, intentionally—as though she were morphing the words from her storybooks into a reality.

ARE YOU FINISHED?

Let's go!!!

She released her stored-up impulses all at once, and immediately, an immense pillar of flame darkened her vision. Well, not *only* her vision. Fanned by the squall beneath it, the flames grew even more intense, and in an instant, the pillar extended, smashing through the ceiling of the cave like a volcano erupting, sending rocks flying into the ocean around and bathing the night sky in a crimson light. The whole place was overtaken by the roar, the vibrations, and the stench of smoldering.

Lily's lips flapped wordlessly.

"Wah...?"

....

The whole top of the triangular jetty of rocks that marked the edge of the cave had been fully blown away. The remaining rock was still glowing a hot red, like the mouth of a volcano after an eruption. Indeed, it was no longer rock but lava.

Miss Lily Lockwood. The nanomachine squeaked out her name.

Yes?

How to put this... Perhaps we ought to start your lessons by teaching you about limits.

"Mwehh..."

Lily sunk down on the spot, horrified. She had no idea how she was going to apologize to the Ashen Alleycats for blowing up their entire base. She put her head in her hands just as the last of the molten rocks, which had flown into the air like shooting stars, finally crashed down into the sea. As they did, there was an explosion of steam, and the deep red that glowed at the edges of her vision faded into white.

It was like peering into the end of the world.

The ocean breeze billowed from out of the newly opened crater, and a fog rose from the sea around the Alleycats' hideout. Harris and the boss kicked open the warped wooden doors of their rooms, practically tumbling out. The rest of the Alleycats followed shortly after.

"Wh-wh-wh-wh-what the hell was that?!"

"Boss, what was...?!"

They looked at Lily, crumpled on the floor, and the scene around her, then fell to their knees.

"Whoaaa...?!"

"What is going *on*?!"

Their shock was to be expected, of course. The roof of their base had just been blown off. Furthermore, large portions had been melted away, as though by an intense flame.

"Wh-wha... Wha...uh? L-L-L-L-Lily...?"

"Did an underwater volcano erupt?! Or are the Albarnians launching an attack on Tils or something?!"

"Calm...c-calm down, Harris."

"I'm calmer than you, Boss! Here, drink something!"

The boss chugged the water that Harris offered him and placed the cup down on the charred table. He looked down at Lily and then took up the quill that was still strewn on the table, writing not upon the now-charred paper but the surface of the table itself.

"What happened out here?"

Lily wobbled to her feet and sat down in a chair. The boss pushed the quill into her hands.

"I tried using magic. And I kind of messed it up."

The boss's face twisted.

"Kind of?! This is what it looks like when you *kind of* mess up?!"

Harris surveyed the area mournfully. The walls were charred, everything from the ceiling upward blown fully out of existence.

In fact, it was not only the ceiling but the whole enormous rock formation above it. It should have been fully solid in composition, and yet, not a single fragment remained.

Harris and the boss looked to one another, their faces pale.

The boss returned to the table, carefully circumventing Lily, and moved the quill pen.

"You did this?"

"Yeah, I did. I destroyed your base. I'm sorry."

The quill tumbled from the boss's trembling hands. His eyes filled with fear.

"B-B-B-Boss. Boss! Come—c'mere a second!" Harris grabbed the boss by the shoulder and forcibly wheeled him around, dragging him into a room where Lily could not see them.

"This is bad," Harris started. "You didn't say she was a mage..."

And a fairly skilled one, at that. To cause something as immense as that pseudo-eruption, she would have to be an A-rank hunter or higher, or something like a court magician, would she not?

"This is the first *I'm* hearing of this, too, dumbass! How was I s'posed to know she's some kind of magical monster?!"

"*Sh-shhhh!* Don't let Lady Lily hear!"

The pair looked back at once to Lily, who was grinning up at them, her head cocked slightly.

"Oh, right. She still don't understand words... But let's remember, we don't have any fighters here! If we get on the little lady's bad side..."

"I mean, she already blew up the base. Doesn't that mean she's already pretty mad at us?"

The hairs on the backs of both of their necks stood on end as the pair shuddered.

"It's because you told 'er that we'd kidnapped her, Boss! What're we gonna do?!"

"D-don't put this all on *me*! Lily was the one who decided to come with us!"

"Then *why* were ya tryin' to take credit for kidnapping her?! Just puttin' it that way totally changes things!"

The boss averted his gaze sorrowfully and spat, "I just wanted to sound like a proper villain for once."

"*Boooooosss!!!*"

"Uh...?" Lily's voice could be heard from the center of the room.

Harris hurriedly muttered, "Anyway, Boss, whatever it is she wants, you gotta give it to 'er. Then she can just go on home. I'm done with this."

"Y-yeah." The boss rushed back to the table, where Lily was moving the quill.

"*No fighting. Got it?*"

"*Yes, ma'am.*"

"*And also, no more doing bad things. That includes stealing.*"

"Huh?"

The boss turned his gaze to Lily.

"*If the Ashen Alleycats want to keep working together, you should make a living fishing or making something. If you don't...*"

You'll be captured and enslaved. And then, you'll all be separated. Lily, having lost her family, understood better than anyone how lonely this could be. However, she was certain that all of these men would know this, even without her spelling it out for them. She had faith that there was a goodness somewhere deep down in the hearts of these kindly fellows. Having faith was a virtue, after all.

Yet these formerly stalwart men still seemed remarkably unsettled.

"Boss," Harris said, "she is definitely threatenin' us."

"Y-yeah, I know. If we say we're gonna keep on stealin', then she's gonna..."

They looked up at the now-missing ceiling. That had been a demonstration. For even a sturdy rock face to end up in such a state... It went without saying that, should a normal, non-magical person be struck head-on by such an explosive spell, they would be blasted to smithereens. Not that Lily would ever do such a thing.

The boss's Adam's apple bobbed as he gulped.

"Harris. I'm sorry. But I guess this is the end of our thievin' days."

"Think it was high time anyway. Never been too lucrative a business fer us... Y'all good with that?"

Harris and the boss looked out at all the other men. Not one of them possessed the courage to raise an objection.

"D-definitely better than bein' slaughtered by the little lady..."

"Guess from now on we make a livin' on fishin' boats or somethin.'"

"We all do love fishin.'"

"Sounds good to me." One man chimed in. "If we do this right, the missus might even come back."

It was partly because these men lacked confidence in their own strength that they had not become bandits or pirates, instead leading this half-hearted life of looting. Yet even the fact that the Ashen Alleycats had not fallen into outright thuggery proved they were mostly a decent lot. And, of course, this was due in large part to the rather vapid man they called their boss.

"I guess this is our chance to start over."

"Guess so. Let's go out after some fish or somethin' tomorrow."

And thus was born the fishing industry in Tils...

The boss stepped forward and took up the quill pen.

"Understood. Lily, we'll honor your request. So, please leave my men alone. If you would."

He turned his bearded face to Lily and passed her the quill.

"I'm not going to do anything to them."

The boss lifted his head, expression calm.

"Okay. It's decided. We'll let Lady Lily go. Harris, get a boat ready."

"On it."

After some time, Lily was placed into a little boat and returned to the sandy beaches of the shoreline.

The boss and Harris bowed their heads to her one final time, returned to their rowboat, and set back out onto the seas with a wave.

Lily looked up into the starry sky. All she heard was the sound of the waves. Left all alone upon the beach, tears shone in Lily's eyes.

But whyyy?!

She clutched her head.

Mr. Nano, are you here?!

This should not have happened. Lily had assumed that she would be helping the Alleycats out in their new career, but here she was, banished.

I AM HERE. WE EXIST EVERYWHERE IN THIS WORLD.

Why did they leave me alone?

IT WAS BOUND TO HAPPEN. ANY NORMAL HUMAN WHO LAID EYES UPON SUCH A POWERFUL DISPLAY OF MAGIC WOULD WISH TO DISTANCE THEMSELVES FROM THE CASTER, NO MATTER WHO THEY WERE.

This was dreadful. Here she was, alone again.

YOU DID WELL THOUGH, DIDN'T YOU? IT SEEMED LIKE THEY HAD A CHANGE OF HEART. NOW, THERE SHOULDN'T BE ANY CHANCE OF THE BOSS OR HARRIS ENDING UP ENSLAVED IN THE MINES.

Lily looked up to the night sky and thought a while, then swiftly changed her mind.

Hm... I guess that's good, then.

She was worried about the men, but she also needed to start thinking about what she was going to do now. If she did not come up with a plan, she would start to waste away again within the next few days. And so, she set off along the beach, considering her future, when suddenly, she heard a voice addressing her across the sand.

"Goodness, what a shock! So this is where you went. You're doing better than I expected."

Lily looked up reflexively at the sound of the quiet yet lilting voice. There, on the edge of the beach, stood Lafine, not in her usual prim and proper uniform but dressed rather roughly.

"Huh?"

The maid's tired eyes narrowed suspiciously at Lily.

"Did you just...react to my voice?"

Though Lily could hear the melody of her words, she still could not understand them. Lily blinked twice and then tilted her head. Lafine let out a sigh, scratching her light brown hair.

"What a bother. Can you not understand anything without a paper and pen around?"

"Uh..."

Lily gestured, pointing underfoot. Lafine's gaze followed, pointing downward, as Lily knelt down upon the sand and began writing with her fingertip.

"Lafine!! Where is everyone?"

Wearily, Lafine carved a reply with her foot.

"I don't know. By the time I got out of the armoire, everyone was already gone. Judging by the state of the manor, it wasn't good. I'm sure you can imagine what happened as well as I can."

Lily looked up to her and nodded sadly.

They had been attacked in the night by brigands, her whole family gone to who knows where. She had to help them. She might be the only one left who had the freedom to do so.

"What are you doing here?"

"There was a red light by the sea just a little while ago, so I came here to see what it was. Pretty sure we'll be seeing a lot of

*rubberneckers soon. Have you been here this whole time? Did you
see what it was? An underwater volcano?"*

Lily looked around to see that a number of townsfolk had
begun to gather on the beach.

"It was magic. I did it."

Looking utterly exhausted, Lafine scribbled back, *"There's no
way a brat like you could use magic. You can't even hear—how could
you cast a spell in the first place?"*

*"But I can hear. Um, see I can't really explain it, but a mage
healed me, and now I can hear. Though I still can't really put voices
and words together, or talk."*

"What?"

Lily cleared her throat and tried to make a sound. At first, all
she could get out were noises. "Ahh, ahh." Then, she tapped her
pointer finger to her own chest. "Lily."

Lafine furrowed her brow fiercely and placed her right hand
to her chest.

"Lafine."

"Lahfeen. Laahfeeeenuh."

"That's amazing... You really *can* hear."

Lily tilted her head.

"Ah, you can only say your own name. I see."

Lily bent down to the sand again. *"Let me show you some magic!"*

She closed her eyes and imagined a flame—or rather, she
started to, but then Lafine clapped her hands together loudly
right in front of Lily's face. She sunk down to the sand and began
to write furiously.

"Wait just a moment! I still don't think I believe you, but if any of this is somehow true, you can't go throwing around magic like that in a place like this."

A number of onlookers had gathered following the explosion at the Ashen Alleycats' cave, and even without them, this was a border town, where people were always on guard, in no small part thanks to their proximity to the Albarn Empire.

"Oh, I see. What should I do, then?"

Lafine just shrugged.

Lily thought back to the spells the youngest of that group of four girls had used. Of course, she could never go pulling all those random items out of thin air, but perhaps she could manage the spell that had filled the cask with water.

Okay...

Could she do the spell, just like that girl had? If Lily recalled, she had produced a ball of water in the air and lowered it down into the cask. She could do that. She could definitely do that.

Water! Water! Mr. Nano, give me water!!!

She closed her eyes and clenched her fists.

"Mmmmm!!!"

Suddenly, the light of the moon dimmed, as though obstructed by clouds. Lafine looked casually up to the sky, and her eyes popped wide open.

"Wha...what are you...?!"

Her words broke Lily's concentration.

"Uh?"

And at that moment, a tidal wave of water poured down atop the pair's heads in a torrent that was nothing short of a flash flood.

"Gyaaaah! Blargh!"

"Gaaah! Bwaaah?!"

The pair were toppled by the force of the water, which washed them along the beach all the way to the edge of the waves. They quickly pulled themselves up out of the shallows, both of them coated in sand.

I am in such trouble now, Lily thought.

"Lily, *you little...!*"

"Wha..."

Lily sprung to her feet, hurrying to write an apology in the sand, but Lafine grabbed her by the collar, leaving her feet swinging wildly.

I'm sorry! I'm really sorry!

With a power that seemed unlikely given her slender arms, Lafine picked Lily up under the arms and took off running like a bat out of hell. Lily looked timidly up at her, wondering what was going on.

"...?"

"Bwa ha ha ha! Heh heh! You're amazing!"

Lily had no idea what Lafine was saying, but for whatever reason...she didn't seem angry with her.

As they ran, Lafine continued, "A lovely little girl with a promising future as a mage, who can now hear! Ah ha ha ha! I've got myself a real prize!"

Cackling and clutching Lily tight, Lafine ran on, dodging the gazes of the onlookers, and the pair ran off into the night.

An array of sounds filled Lily's ears.

The voices of men and women, high or low, with rhythms and intonation depending on age and personality. Lily noticed how the voices of children had playful, excited tones, while adult cadences were as still as a prairie. The boss had a voice that seemed to resonate throughout her whole body, but this seemed unique—even those of most other adult men were not quite so impressive.

There were so many different kinds of voices.

And so many other noises, too, like the sound of wooden wagon wheels moving down the streets, with their strange, incessant *ka-chunk-ka-chunk, ka-chunk-ka-chunk.* Now and then, a cart might run over a rock, and the carriage would sway as the rhythm was broken.

There was the clang of horseshoes that rang out each time the powerful draught horses took a step. Sometimes, the sound was drowned out by that of the wheels, but if she strained her ears, Lily could let the comforting, regular noise of hooves fill her consciousness.

The footfalls of the hunters escorting the carriages were rather soft. So soft she could scarcely hear them. Their rhythm was erratic, but that was probably because they were circling the wagon, keeping an eye out up ahead.

Closer by, there was the sound of Lafine's breath as she slept. As she...spoke? She seemed to be mumbling something in her sleep.

Lily's eyes were closed, but she could see the entire world. Hearing was such a wondrous thing.

She opened her eyes. Traveling in such a small wagon was in no way comfortable, but nevertheless, getting to hear all these sounds made her heart dance.

And at this very moment, I'm here in the outside world!

Seated across from her, their fellow passengers, a family of four, were in the midst of a lively conversation. Like a visitor to a foreign land, Lily still could not parse the meaning of their words and had no idea what they were talking about. Still, it was a novelty to just listen to the sounds of their voices. Previously, they had tried speaking to her as well, but they seemed to have gathered something of her situation based on the way Lily had only tilted her head and smiled in reply, and had ceased trying to communicate.

Beside Lily, Lafine slept, her mouth hanging open in a most unseemly fashion. When Lily tried to wipe the trail of drool from the corner of her mouth with a handkerchief, Lafine had mumbled something again and pushed her hand away, looking disturbed.

"Mmnn!"

Goodness, Lafine!

Lily tucked her handkerchief back into her breast pocket as the children sitting across the way tittered at her. They were a girl and a boy, smaller than Lily—perhaps an older sister of six and a brother two years younger.

Suddenly, Lily thought of her own brother and sister, who had been missing since the night that the Lockwood manor was attacked. Of course, the pair had lived in a different part of the house from her and were too young to have even conversed with her via writing. Still, she had watched them from afar. Watched, and thought how darling they were.

She hoped that they were all right.

That said, where *was* this carriage heading? She had boarded it with Lafine dragging her along, but it was clear that they had long since passed through the border town that was home to the Lockwood manor. If they were not heading back into town, then where could they be going?

Shaking Lafine did not wake her, and even if she were to try asking the family sitting opposite, her meaning would never get across without a paper and pen on hand.

How troublesome.

Wait, don't tell me, has Lafine abducted me? Oh dear. I seem to have an odd knack for this. First the Ashen Alleycats and then my own servant. I don't think it would be an exaggeration to say that I'm a prodigy at being abducted. Of course, even if we went back to the town around our manor, it's not as though anyone would be at the mansion. I waited there a very long time, and no one came back. They might not ever come back. So I suppose being kidnapped is better than having no future at all. Yes, far better. Probably. This is at least more fun than sitting around in my room.

Lily sighed happily. She truly was having fun. It was almost as though she had become the protagonist of one of her storybooks. From here on out, she would be facing a world of unknowns. She had no idea what might be out there waiting for her—but that was fine.

For some time, she sat in her carriage seat, letting her imagination run wild and listening to the sounds around her. Finally, she began to grow sleepy and leaned back. However, perhaps because of the rocking of the carriage, she could not get comfortable. Lafine was probably able to sleep because she was in the corner seat, so she had the carriage wall to lean against. In which case...

Quietly, gently, Lily rested her head against Lafine's arm.

"..."

Good, she's still asleep. I guess her being so sloppy does have its uses. She makes a great pillow.

Lily closed her eyes and swiftly fell into a slumber. The carriage continued swaying all through the evening—en route to the capital of the Kingdom of Tils.

As the sun sank and darkness spread around them, the carriage paused in a field on the side of the highway. Apparently, this was where they would be making camp for the night. The three hunters who had accompanied the carriage as guards were surveying the area to make sure there were no monsters or bandits around.

Lily peeled back the curtain and stepped down from the wagon. When she looked up to the sky, she let out a sigh of amazement.

The stars were a beautiful sight. Perhaps because they were away from the lights of town, there were so very many more stars overhead than she was accustomed to seeing. It was like looking into a chest full of jewels.

"All clear. No threats as far as we can see."

"Thank you. I guess we'll rest here tonight, then. I'll have to ask you all to keep watch," said the driver. The hunters, all young men, nodded.

"You got it. The Flaming Wolves have got your back."

The hunters turned back to the passengers.

"Let's introduce ourselves again. I'm Brett, leader of the Flaming Wolves. This is Chuck, my fellow swordsman. Daryl's a lancer. We're all C-rank hunters. We've got a plan in place for protecting you all, so if anything happens, just do as we say."

Lafine opened her mouth, half-yawning. "A sword, a sword, and a spear. Pretty imbalanced party. Hope we'll be all right."

The hunters looked troubled by this rude interjection. Daryl started to open his mouth, annoyed, but Brett, the leader, stopped him with a grimace. "You don't need more than three hunters to guard a carriage this small," he said. "Hiring any more would just raise the burden of cost on you passengers. Right?"

The driver nodded dimly. "Y-yeah. With the current fare, three is the most we can hire. That's why I requested the Flaming Wolves."

Lafine, however, was ruthless.

"Nah, that's not what I was talking about. I meant that all three of them are vanguard-types. You don't have any archers or mages? Did you not consider this when you were forming your party?"

"Uh..."

Lafine snorted, rolling her eyes at the now-silent Brett.

"Well, whatever. That's none of my business."

Chuck took Brett's place and shouted, "It's not like he just didn't think about that! Until a little while ago, there were five of us! We had a female archer and a mage, but a party full of nothing but handsome studs took them away from us!"

"I see," Lafine bluntly replied. "Sounds like you got lucky."

"What?! What are you talking about?!" Chuck raged.

Lafine remained cool. "I mean, it sounds like now you don't have to trust some idiot women who don't know how to keep the business separate from their pleasure to guard your rear. Am I wrong? Or don't tell me you all were playing at hunter just to pick up chicks, too? Bet you're regretting that now, if so."

All three hunters were lost for words as Lafine gazed at them with sleepy eyes. They looked at one another, and then Brett stepped up again to rebut.

"Well. Obviously not. We Flaming Wolves are s-serious hunters, after all."

The situation was falling apart.

After that, a minimal bonfire was lit, and everyone ate whatever meals they had brought with them—primarily hard crackers and salted meat. Lily chomped on some jerky. It was a pain to chew, but she did not dislike the flavor. It was far inferior to the luxurious dishes cooked up in the Lockwood kitchens, but there was just something fun about eating out here, in the wild plains, beneath the stars, with all sorts of people around.

"What're you smiling about?"

"Uh?"

Lafine, by contrast, looked utterly unenthused and somewhat irascible. There had clearly been tension brewing between her and the hunters not long ago, but now, any bad feelings had seemed to resolve themselves without incident. Now, the irascible Lafine was using a rock for a chair, her elbows propped on her knees as she stared out into the distance with half-lidded eyes. She glanced down at Lily, who sat directly on the ground next to her, tugging at Lafine's sleeve.

"I don't have any paper or pen." Lafine gestured, holding an invisible pen with her right hand, and then spread both hands out wide.

"Mm..."

Able to grasp her meaning from Lafine's gestures, Lily nodded once. It was hard to write in the dirt out here in the grasslands.

It was best that she resign herself to a lack of communication for now.

"If this were a merchant caravan, they'd probably have paper and pens for doing their calculations, but no dice with a cheap carriage share like this." Lafine sighed. "You've got no idea what I'm saying, so no use telling you this, but something's odd here," she went on. "The Flaming Wolves said they didn't see any monsters or bandits around, but they haven't moved an inch away from this campsite. For them to not need to even move to tell us that means that there's absolutely *nothing* around at all."

Lily nodded along with the sound of Lafine's voice.

"But isn't that all the more odd? We're in a field. Shouldn't there at least be *animals* around? And if there were animals, the Flaming Wolves would have had to go out and make sure that they weren't monsters. We have plenty of time right now, and it wouldn't take much effort to do so."

"Uh..." Lily wrinkled her forehead, listening.

Suddenly, Lafine smacked the girl lightly on the top of the head.

"Huh?"

This was an incredibly rude thing for a servant to do to a noble who employed them, but Lily did not seem to mind.

"Don't act like you understand me when you have no idea what I'm saying. That drives me nuts."

"Uh..."

Truth be told, though, Lily *did* understand what Lafine was saying. It had occurred to her when she was watching the family across from them in the carriage earlier that if she got Mr. Nano to translate for her, a conveyance of meaning would be possible via speech. However, this mysterious spirit did not seem to wish for its existence to become widely known. In other words, though it was happy to translate other people's words for Lily and convey them to her via thought pulses, it was less keen on using magic to vibrate those people's eardrums so that they could hear Lily's thoughts. Thus, Lafine was left to monologue.

"The fact that there are no animals or monsters means there's a fair chance that something else around here poses a threat to even them. At first I was wondering if the Flaming Wolves might be in league with some bandits, but they don't actually seem bright enough to pull something like that off, to be honest."

Ah, thought Lily. So Lafine had purposely provoked them earlier to get a better sense of the men.

"Still, that doesn't mean that there's *nothing* here in these grasslands." Lafine placed a hand over her mouth, mumbling something. "Well, hopefully I'm just being paranoid. Just in case, it's probably best that we not sleep tonight. How annoying..."

Lafine is amazing, Lily thought to herself. *She can guess all that about the Flaming Wolves from just a short exchange. It seems amazing that she's just a servant that my father, Margrave Neiham Lockwood, brought to the manor. I wonder what she used to do before this... Could she actually have been some kind of hunter?*

Yet Lily's newfound appreciation for Lafine was fleeting. Once they had finished eating, the woman fell asleep before anyone else, snoring loudly. Lily tried prodding her cheek, but she only twitched her brows, showing no signs of waking. She poked more forcefully, but again, Lafine only swatted her hand away.

"Mmmmnn!" Lily groaned, but Lafine gave no reply.

Well, fine! I'll have to be the responsible one!

Blessedly, there were so many sounds for Lily to hear that she could never grow bored, even lying back in the darkness. She could hear a sound, open her eyes, and look for the source of it. It was a fun game to play on her own. Only bugs turned out to be particularly difficult to locate via their noises. She had never thought that such tiny little creatures would make such resonant sounds.

Finally, the crackling of the bonfire began to die out, as did the voices of the other people. The wind was quiet tonight. Soon, the only noises that remained were the yawns or sighs of the Flaming Wolves as they took their turns on watch, along with the shuffling sounds of their pacing through the grass, the gentle snores of the passengers, and the incessant cries of insects.

The first thing to catch Lily's attention after that was the sound of horseshoes. The draft horses had suddenly stood up.

Lily's eyes shot open. Because she had them shut for so long, the dim light of the moon was enough to see by. She could not see far, but she could see well enough.

Crunch, crunch.

In her dull vision, she could make out Brett of the Flaming Wolves, yawning as he paced. Was nothing happening...? No, the horses were definitely agitated. And also...

She focused all her attention on what she could hear. Aside from the footsteps of the current Flaming Wolf on watch, she heard a great number of clipped sounds rushing toward them along the ground.

Crunch, crunch. That was Brett, of the Flaming Wolves.

Shf, shf, shf, shf. That was the racing sound.

Even as she listened, someone was snatching Lily up by the collar and hoisting her up into the air.

Wa-waaaah!!!

The form that had grabbed Lily turned away from the approaching steps and took off running.

"...!!"

A whisper reached her ears: "Keep it down!"

It was Lafine. Lily had no idea whether she had woken up a moment before, or if she had been awake the whole time, but regardless, she was much different from her usual slow-moving, disinterested self. She raced away from the wagon, stalking through the field like a wild animal. Her footsteps were almost entirely soundless.

With Lily still in her arms, Lafine dove behind some rocks a short distance from the camp. Then, she pushed one hand down on the top of Lily's head and looked toward one corner of the wagon, her eyes sharp.

"Bandits...?!"

It was at that moment that Brett could finally be heard calling for the other two Wolves to wake. However, it was already too late. Lafine was unable to do anything but whisper as ten-odd figures materialized from the shadows, surrounding the wagon, Flaming Wolves and all. The driver and passengers, now finally awake as well, all paled in terror.

"Augh. It's all over now. There's twelve—no, thirteen—of 'em."

There was no point in trying to either fight or run just after waking. Even Brett, who had been the only one with his sword drawn, placed his weapon at his feet and put his hands up in the air—a surrender.

The whole group knelt on the ground, the three Flaming Wolves included. No hunter was stupid enough to honor their job over their life. They worked only for the sake of living, after all.

"I feel bad for the driver and that family. They've only got those cheap, worthless hunters to protect them. If they take his horse away, he'll lose his livelihood. And as for that family—we might be about to see the woman and kids get snatched away."

Lily, of course, could say nothing.

"Keep your head down, Lily. If we're spotted, we won't be safe. You might be a bit better off considering you're still a little squirt, but I'm pretty much a Ten. We need to wait for our opportunity and try to slip away, get some dista—uh, huh?! What are—?!"

Lily had squirmed her way out of Lafine's arms and brushed the dirt from her skirt. Now, she began walking back toward the campsite.

"W-w-wait a—!!"

Lafine was shouting something from behind Lily, but she was already too focused on her conversation with Mr. Nano to hear.

INDEED. THERE IS LITTLE CHANCE OF ANY WOMEN WHO ARE CAPTURED HAVING A COMFORTABLE LIFE HENCEFORTH. YOU, MISS LILY LOCKWOOD, ARE NO EXCEPTION TO THAT.

I see... I'm going to try asking the bandits to just go home, then.

One of the bandits spotted Lily as she walked calmly toward them.

"Hey, there's another kid over there!"

"Why's she walkin' this way? Was she off takin' a leak or somethin'?"

Another bandit furrowed his brow.

"Hey, is that little lady *waving* at us?"

Yet another bandit pointed to the kneeling family.

"Idiot, who the hell'd be waving at a piece of crap like you?"

The bandit twisted up his face and pouted.

"*You're* the idiot. Obviously a kid like that ain't travelin' alone. So she's probably with this family...right, old man?" the bandit asked the father of the family. Then, with his foot, he struck the kneeling man in the gut. The man looked down, face distorting in anguish.

"Gu...ah..."

The woman and children scrambled to help the man as he collapsed on the ground, unable to reply. Seeing this, Lily's face tightened in anger.

MISS LILY, IT IS POINTLESS TO TRY TO PERSUADE THEM. IN ORDER TO EVEN TALK TO SUCH PEOPLE, YOU HAVE TO PROVIDE THEM WITH A DISPLAY OF STRENGTH. THAT SAID, BECAUSE YOU CANNOT SPEAK, YOU WILL HAVE NO WAY OF COMMUNICATING WITH THEM AFTERWARD, EITHER.

Well, I think Lafine can take care of that part for me.

Lafine was still hiding behind the rocks, peeking out toward the scene. Apparently, she no longer intended to run.

PLEASE BE CAREFUL IN LIMITING YOUR POWER. IF YOU CAUSE TOO MUCH OF A SCENE, IT MAY RESULT IN

PROBLEMS LATER, the nanomachine warned, but Lily was already in the process of letting out a full-force thought pulse— something far, far more powerful than what she had unleashed upon the Alleycats' cave.

Don't worry! I'm just going to fire it into the air!

PERHAPS WE OUGHT TO HAVE TAUGHT YOU HOW TO USE MAGIC *AFTER* TEACHING YOU A BIT MORE ABOUT COMMON SENSE.

Three of the bandits were already running toward Lily, surrounding her. They reached out to grab her without hesitation. After all, for all they knew, she was a child of a mere nine years who didn't even have so much as a crude knife. However...

Lily pointed her right index finger toward the sky.

Everyone followed her gesture, looking up. Then, the darkness was shattered. For a few seconds, the whole field around them was bathed in an orange light so bright it was as though day had broken, the heat intense enough to scald one's skin. Everyone there except Lily—including the bandits with their weapons drawn, the three unarmed and kneeling Flaming Wolves, the resigned captive family of four, and Lafine, peeking out from her hiding place behind the rocks—looked up to the sky.

The draught horses whinnied in fear, falling to the ground as their knees buckled.

In the sky floated a great spherical object, looking like nothing less than the sun itself. This sphere, a pale orange wholly reminiscent of magma, roiled, unleashing a wave of heat upon the grasslands with each burst of its surface.

One of the bandits, trembling in fear, stammered, "A f-fireball...?"

No, it was not a fireball. It was something else.

So then, what *was* it? Truth be told, even Lily herself, the one responsible for bringing this thing into existence with her magic, had no idea. The only beings in this world who might perhaps be able to accurately name the composition of this phenomenon were the nanomachines and that young mage girl that Lily had met on the fateful night when her ears had been healed.

It was largely hydrogen, with a scant bit of helium, plus less than a percentage point of other materials that we'll ignore.

It was, in fact, most akin to the actual sun.

Lily, it should go without saying, had never touched the sun and certainly had no idea what it was made of, much less would she have any notion of a star in the astronomical sense. So then, *how* had she come to craft such a thing?

Thus far, Lily had spent most of her days in the world of storybooks. Among those books was contained the fantastical notion of "science," a force that could make inscrutable, mysterious phenomena into a reality...primarily in the works of a certain Miami Satodele.

Her earliest works were profuse with narrative gimmicks so entertaining that other authors could scarcely hope to compare. Anything that might be beyond the understanding of the people of this world, she denoted as stemming from the fantastical enterprise known as "science." And this fantastical enterprise was absolutely part of the appeal of her works.

Lily certainly did not know the details of disassembling water molecules in order to produce pure hydrogen. Quantum mechanics was beyond her, and she had no idea how large the sun truly was. Furthermore, she would not know that helium was a gas that the atmosphere contained trace amounts of. However, thanks to Miami Satodele, she had grasped the notion of the sun's true form, and so she could imagine it. That was enough to send the nanomachines into action—indeed, were that *not* enough, most mages in this world would be unable to use magic at all, since all magic was a product of human imagination.

Which was why, currently floating in the sky, was...

"Wh-whoooaaa?! What the hell is *that*?!"

"M-magic...right?"

Lily twirled the finger she had pointed toward the sky, and the miniature sun began to revolve along with it. She had to show them her power. She had to let them know that the sun-like thing floating in the air was under her control.

"Uh-wuh-huhh?!"

Still spinning the sun above her, Lily took a step toward the bandits—all with a calm, beatific smile, the sort one might see on the face of one of those allies of justice, those so-called heroes who appeared in the tales of Miami Satodele.

She took one step and then another.

"Hey, this looks kinda bad. I can feel the heat off that thing all the way over here."

"What d'you think would happen if that thing hit us...?"

"Should we...run?"

"Keep it together!!" shouted the man who seemed to be the leader of the bandits, putting a sword to the neck of the patriarch of the family of four.

"Eek! H-help!"

The bandit seized the man by the hair as he tried to escape from his place on the ground, pushing the blade harder against him.

"Whoa there, not another step, little lady. Don't you care what happens to yer daddy here? I've got no idea how powerful that spell of yers is, but if you toss that thing at us, yer gonna hit the hostages, too," threatened the leader with a vulgar laugh.

"...!"

Lily stopped in her tracks.

"Sh-she stopped. Ha ha, looks like she's stopped!"

"H-heh heh, little idiot."

"Well, naturally," the leader spoke up. "It's her dad. Use yer heads, dummies. Even we'd have to surrender if someone took our kinfolk hostage."

Of course, this man was not Lily's father. This man was a complete and utter stranger. That said... Though it may have been common sense in this world to value one's own safety over that of a stranger, Lily simply could not abandon the people sitting right in front of her. The heroes of her storybooks always did the right thing. In that moment, Lily was not a citizen of this world but of the world in those tales.

As already noted, Miami Satodele was the author of the bulk of those books. She was furthermore the very mage who had healed Lily's ears. Plus, she had been reincarnated from another world into this one. And so her novels were founded on common sense principles that belonged not to this world but another one entirely.

The safety of others was just as important as one's own.

Lily had no idea about any of this, of course, but that only meant that Miami Satodele's tales had all the more effect on her as she grew.

Thus, Lily Lockwood was an ally of justice.

"That's right, don't you move! Boys, go tie up that little mage. Can't have her usin' any magic. Gag her, too, so she can't cast any spells."

"On it!"

Four bandits surrounded the woman and children of the family, along with the driver. Four more bandits held their weapons around the Flaming Wolves. A third set of four approached Lily from all directions, watching her carefully. The moment there was no one left behind the leader...

A woman materialized from the darkness without a sound, flew toward the bandit leader, and put her hand around his throat, pressing the tip of a knife softly against the nape of his neck.

"...?!"

The blade pierced his skin, slicing through flesh, until it pressed against his carotid artery.

"No one move a muscle. If you so much as blink, this man is dead."

The listless voice seemed to echo across the quiet field.

Confusion overtook the scene. The father of the family froze, with a blade still at his neck as the rest of his family looked on, weeping, bandits surrounding them. The bandits approaching Lily and the Flaming Wolves, who were still kneeling with their hands in the air, all stood stock-still at the sound of the woman's voice.

This time, even Lily herself was surprised.

"...?"

Lily's eyes opened wide. Her jaw dropped. The woman standing behind the leader with a knife at his throat was Lafine. She had the man pinned with her legs around his waist, her left hand gripped around his thick neck, and a blade in her right hand.

The leader could not lift even a finger. Or rather, should he dare to, she could end him with a flick of her wrist.

Lafine spoke in a bored, casual voice, commanding the speechless hostages as though she could barely be bothered to do so. "You there, man. Don't just sit there staring. Take your family and the driver and get out of here. *You're in the way.*"

"Uh, uh, o-okay!"

The man scrambled past the frozen bandits, scooping up his two children and running by Lily with his wife in tow. The driver tottered after them a moment later.

Uncertain what to do, the bandits remained still, petrified.

"What're you lookin' at? All of you, drop your weapons. Flaming Wolves, get it the hell together, pick up *your* weapons and go stand by that girl."

"Huh?"

"Don't you *huh* me! Are you all not hunters?! Do your jobs!"

"Y-yeah, y-you're right... Chuck! Daryl!" Brett shouted, grabbing for his sword, as Chuck and Daryl followed suit. They retreated to Lily's position, surrounding her as though to fend off the bandits. Seeing this, the corners of Lafine's mouth turned up wickedly.

"All righty now, bandits. Time for us to have a fun little bit of negotiation."

"N-negotiation?" the boss squeaked in reply.

"Do I need to spell it out for you? Let me set the scene. After I kill you and get out of here, that girl over there is going to blast the rest of your little squad with that crazy-looking spell of hers. No hostages left to get in the way, after all."

The bandits trembled in fear. There were, in fact, no hostages left anywhere around them.

Lafine continued, "So, the long and short of it is, do you all wanna leave this boss of yours behind and run away? Or would *all* of you like to die here?"

"Wha—?! You bitch! You can't be seriou—"

Lafine moved the knife in her hand subtly. The boss, petrified, swallowed his words as a drop of crimson fell from his neck.

"I wasn't talking to *you*. No point in negotiating with you, after all. The only choices I have to offer *you* are to perish, here and now, or to be captured and live out the rest of your days in the mines."

In short, the choice Lafine was offering was this: The bandits could leave their leader to take the fall and make their retreat, in which case, Lafine would let them go. Or, if that left a bad taste in their mouths, they could all remain here together and be fodder for that magic spell.

"Say, Wolfboys," Lafine called.

"Y-yes, ma'am!"

"If we were to capture all these bandits here, there'd be no way to get all of them to the capital, given that there's just the three of you, right?"

Brett nodded.

"I-It'd be impossible. The three of us can't keep an eye on this many crooks. Too much of a risk of a revolt along the road. We'd be in trouble if we got taken hostage again. We've got children with us, too."

"Well then, guess we gotta leave the small fry behind. Safer bet just to hand over the leader to the authorities and get a reward from the guild, right?"

"Yeah, that's right."

Lafine closed one eye and grinned.

"Welp, let's say the glory's all yours then, Wolves. Just gimme half the reward. The two of us aren't hunters, so if we tried to collect on him, it'd just make things confusing."

All three of the Wolves nodded enthusiastically. They were the ones who had been defeated at the outset. Lafine would be well within her rights to demand the full sum of any reward. Getting both the credit and half of the reward was a pleasant surprise, as far as they were concerned.

"Th-that, well, yes. Um, well, honestly we're more than happy just to make it through this in good health and be able to get our weapons back."

"Then it's settled. Time for a nice bonus." Lafine turned to the bandits. "Look, just get outta here. What're you doing? Do you all actually wanna die here? Oh, wait. Before you go, drop all your weapons. We'll sell 'em all off later."

The bandits looked to one another, then up at the sun floating above Lily's head, and put down their weapons, one after another.

The leader shouted frantically, "H-hey, you bastards! You can't seriously be thinkin' of leavin' me here! Who the hell d'you think's been lookin' out fer you guys this whole time?!"

"Shut up. Don't scream in my ear."

"Ow! P-please, stop this! I'm beggin' ya!"

Lafine moved the knife ever so slightly, scaring the leader back into silence. The twelve other bandits took this opportunity to slip off into the dark grasslands. After watching them go, the Flaming Wolves bound the bandit leader with rope and lashed him to the carriage. Thus, the incident of the midnight ambush was concluded.

Or was it? Lily thought to herself. She had made this sun-like magic just to see if she could, but what should she do with it now? It was still burbling all over its surface, sending out a wave of heat each time one of the bubbles burst.

"Lily? You can put that thing out now."

But how? Lily wondered. She got the sharp impression that if she were to let her guard down even a tiny bit, the thing would probably end up exploding. In fact, it was definitely already expanding.

"Uhh..."

Lily looked at Lafine, already on the verge of tears. Seeming to put together what was going on, Lafine paled.

"Oh no. Hm. Don't tell me... You can't put that thing out?"

Lily shook her head, pouting. So distracted by the tense situation that she did not even notice that her words had gotten through to Lily, Lafine shouted, "Th-then *why* would you make something like that?!"

"Um..."

The whole surface of the sphere began to warp, wobbling all around.

Oh no! No no no no no! It's gonna blow!

Mr. Nanooooo!!!

Honestly, Miss Lily, your lack of common sense is nearly as remarkable as Mi—someone else we know.

There was a deep sound, and a small section of the orb ruptured. A gout of pale orange flame rushed out from it, scorching across a part of the grasslands like a dragon in flight. The power of the flames was awesome.

"Lily?!" Lafine screamed.

Waaaah!!

Let's just shoot the rest of that up into the air. Um, why don't you try imagining dropping it into the sky? Quickly, please. One, two!

Dropping it...into the sky...?

"Wuhuhh!"

Lily could not picture this, so instead, she imagined throwing the ball of fire. She thought about jettisoning the sphere into the air, as hard as she could.

There was no doubt this was her self-preservation instincts kicking in. Similarly, no one had to tell the rest of those assembled to drop to the ground immediately. Even the bandit leader, leashed to the carriage, fell flat. For a moment, everyone was blinded.

That day, the recorded time of the sunrise came far earlier than usual in the Kingdom of Tils—though, despite the fact that the orb in the sky resembled the sun, its actual form was not quite the same...

Didn't I Say
to Make My Abilities
Average in the
Next Life?!
Lily's Miracle

CHAPTER 3 |

The Birth of a Hero

I T HAD BEEN roughly a month since Lily first set foot in the capital of Tils. In that time, she had begun to learn the connections between voice and words, sounds and letters, from Lafine.

A lack of intellect had never been a problem for Lily, who had been unable to speak only because she had been unable to hear. In fact, because she had once spent all of her waking hours reading books, she had perhaps a surplus of knowledge, which was now bearing fruit. By now, Lily Lockwood was equipped with faculties of language similar to any other typical girl of this time and place.

A cart overtook Lily as she walked, a basket full of bread in her hands. The sounds of the metal horseshoes on the cobblestones and the turning wooden wheels were different here from how they had sounded running through the grasslands a month prior.

The light of the sun above did not give off any sound, merely shining down upon her. Yet Lily was becoming used to the very many other sounds that emerged whenever the sun was shining. Even the voices of men and of women were different. Men's voices were low and heavy, women's high and light.

Lily would never grow tired of it. Just as that young mage told Lily that night, the world was full of far more sounds than she could ever imagine.

"Take this, Lily dear!"

Lily turned around at the sound of a hoarse, thick voice, to see an apple arcing through the air. She swiftly put the handle of the basket between her teeth and caught the apple in both hands. The apple had come from the old man who ran the produce stand.

"Thank you!"

She deftly let the handle of the basket slip down to the crook of her left arm, held the apple in both hands, and took a bite. The tangy flavor and fresh fragrance were overwhelming.

Having spent the bulk of her life locked away in the mansion, Lily had had no idea that the outside world could be this much fun. How amazing her life was! Every moment was such a thrill!

"Ha ha ha! Gonna eat it right now?"

Crunch crunch. The sound of the apple crunching between her teeth was a joy to her ears.

"Huh? Should I not?"

"It's fine! It must be tough for you, looking after that Lafine."

But in truth, it wasn't. Lily had fun almost no matter what she was doing. Still, it was notable that Lafine's reputation preceded her even here in the capital, Lily thought.

"She vanished from this city without a trace several years ago and then showed up again out of the blue last month. Gotta wonder if she's a bit off, considering she never comes out of the house. I swear..."

"I mean, she's a really nice person!"

The shopkeeper's eyes narrowed warmly.

"You really do love everyone, Lily. I'll bet you've been through a lot."

"I guess so..."

When their carriage had been ambushed, Lily would have been lost without Lafine. Furthermore, seeing how capable Lafine had been that night, Lily thought it was something of a wonder that she should be thought of as a bit unreliable here in the capital, from whence she hailed.

From what Lily could gather, Lafine was once an incredibly skilled hunter. Now, she never left the house—but she didn't need to, thanks to the payment they had received from the Flaming Wolves following the aforementioned incident. Not that the sum was enough to support them *forever*.

Incidentally, the Flaming Wolves had made an impassioned plea to the pair that night, asking that, should the two ever become hunters, they think seriously about joining up with the Wolves. However, Lafine had merely scowled at them with a deep disdain, told them to, "Get lost," and kicked them to the curb.

For her part, Lily had thought the proposal quite an appealing one. After all, the majority of her storybooks involved adventurous main characters—like hunters—who always did the right thing.

It would be, she imagined, just like in the tales of Miami Satodele. In those books, there were special personages, known typically as "heroes," who spent their days vanquishing evil and protecting the weak. It had always spoken to her, even when she was younger—though at the time, when she could not leave her room, all Lily could do was aspire to such quests.

If she became a hunter, though, could she take one step closer to becoming a hero?

"Ee hee hee!" She dashed through the streets and opened up the door of their house. "I'm home!"

"Simmer down. Where have you been, getting yourself all worked up?"

Lafine stared at Lily through weary eyes. It was already near one in the afternoon, but she was still in her sleep clothes. A toothbrush stuck out of her mouth.

"Hey, hey, Lafine!"

"Hmm?"

"Could I be a hunter? I think the Flaming Wolves might let me join them!"

"No way," Lafine snapped.

"Why not?"

"If you busied yourself with being a hunter, who'd be around to make my meals? Let me tell you right now, there's no way I can cook for myself. If you went away on a mission, I might end up so hungry I'd cry," Lafine said, puffing out her ample chest.

"Oh no! That's terrible," Lily said, imagining the woman weeping from hunger. "I would feel awful."

"Y'see?"

"Yeah. Okay, no being a hunter then!"

"That's right. All you need to think about is growing up as my dear little sister while you're still all pure and innocent. Then someday we'll marry you off to some rich man's son or some lesser noble or something, and I'll be livin' on easy street."

Lily shot her hand up in a salute.

"Okay!"

"Oh. You do need to earn some money, though."

Lafine removed the toothbrush from her mouth, took a swig of water from the cistern, and swished it around.

"I guess so."

"You find any jobs yet?"

"Huh? For you?"

Lafine looked up, spreading her hands.

"No, for *you*. I'll have to soldier on here, waiting for you. If you don't come back home, I might get hungry and start to cry, so you need to come back home to me every day. You hear me?"

"Yeah. You're the lonely homemaker."

"That's right. Now, bring me a slice of bread with butter."

"Coming right up!"

Lily was being duped. It would be plain for anyone to see. Even so, Lily smiled happily. Compared to her life until now, she couldn't help but be overjoyed. She was able to hear and speak and walk around as she pleased.

However, there was one thing that troubled her. There was something she'd had in her previous life which she did not have now: her storybooks.

In a world where methods of mass printing had yet to be developed, every copy of every book had to be painstakingly copied from the original by scribes and was thus a costly endeavor. The works of Miami Satodele were in particularly high demand, and shortages were always predicted. Indeed, their publisher, Orpheus, had set aside a substantial sum to account for such things.

She wanted her books. However, there was no way that she could ask Lafine, who had provided her with both a home and a future, to purchase these books for her. She had no choice but to earn some money, all on her own. Yes. She had to find a job. That was the solution.

After lunch, Lily set out again.

"Hm. I wonder how I even find a job."

If she were a hunter, it seemed she would be able to use the guild as her intermediary, but without that help, she would have to find other means of locating work. As she passed by the greengrocer's stall, he was in the process of making a sale to a husband and wife. Once it seemed their business was concluded, Lily approached the man.

"Hey, Mister."

"Hm? Oh, hi, Lily. What's up?"

"Are there any jobs I could do?"

"Jobs?" Briefly, he furrowed his brow. "Ah, I see. I've got just the thing."

He glanced upward briefly and then looked back down, before retreating into the shop. When he returned, he was holding a small hat in one hand.

"A customer who was here earlier dropped this. Could you deliver it to them for me?"

"Sure thing!"

Lily grabbed the hat and then took off running, but was swiftly called back.

"Hang on! I haven't even told you who it belongs to."

"Oh."

The man smiled wryly and said, "You'll find the house right through that alleyway. Just head down and make a right. There's a cheeky little boy named Kram. He's around the same age as you, actually."

"This is his?"

"Yeah, he was here with his mother earlier. They were carrying a lot."

"Okay, I'll take it over."

"Thanks!"

Lily took off once more. This trip wouldn't be long at all. She entered the narrow alley and turned right at the junction, finding just one house. It was a cute little structure, with a red pointed roof.

"Excuuuse me!" she called, knocking on the wooden door. Soon, a woman who had a motherly air about her emerged.

"Hello?"

"Um, here. The man at the produce shop asked me to bring this. For, um, Kram."

The woman, seeming to decipher the situation the moment she saw the hat in Lily's hands, turned and called back, "Kram! Get over here!"

"Huh? What is it? I was eatin'. Who's this?"

The woman smacked the boy on the back of his dark-haired head.

"Oww! Mom, what's your deal?!"

"Don't you *oww* me! Your hat!"

"Oh."

Finally noticing the hat Lily was holding out, Kram snatched it from her hands.

"What's with the attitude?! Say *thank you*!"

"Shut up!"

Smack!

After receiving a second smack to the head, Kram turned back to Lily, cringing. He stared at her face, going slightly red.

"Thanks...or whatever."

Smack!

"Ow! Stop hittin' me! You're gonna make me go stupid!"

Smack!

"You couldn't get any stupider! Thank her properly!"

The woman once again raised her hand. Kram hurriedly shouted at Lily, "THANK YOU VERY MUCH!!!"

"Heh heh. You're welcome!"

This seemed to be a very lively family, quite unlike the Lockwoods. After hurling a few more scolding words at Kram, who scampered back inside the house, the woman offered Lily a wry smile.

"Sorry about that," she said. "Thank you for doing all this just for my idiot son."

"It's no problem."

"Come to think of it, I suppose I've been seeing you around here lately. Where did you come from?"

"Oh, I'm uh, Lily Lo...ck...uhh..." Suddenly Lily recalled Lafine's harsh warning to never reveal her parentage. After all, she had explained, they could never know where the assailants of the Lockwood family might be hiding. And so... "I'm Lafine Alstea's little sister, Lily Alstea."

"Goodness, *that* Lafine? That's a shock. I had no idea that lazy girl had such a capable sister."

Lazy girl?! Lafine, your reputation!

The woman stared at Lily as these thoughts ran through the girl's head.

"Well, I call her lazy, but I suppose she's been through a lot, as have the rest of your family. It's probably inevitable things ended up this way."

"I see."

Lily was curious, but she got the feeling it would be rude to Lafine to ask too many follow-up questions, under the circumstances. Still, perhaps it would help to clarify her situation a bit.

"Well, um, I call myself her little sister, but we're actually distant relatives. A few things happened, though, and Lafine said that I could be her little sister, so now I'm living with her."

This was the explanation that Lafine had come up with for their situation, so as not to raise too many questions. At Lily's words, a tinge of sympathy came to the mother's face, as though something about Lily's story bothered her. Of course, considering the tragedy that had occurred at the Lockwood home, Lily was very much deserving of that sympathy, but this woman couldn't know that.

"Anyway, the grocer let me help him out today, so I could start earning my keep."

The mother looked at her affectionately, nodding approvingly. "I see," she said. "You're a good girl. Looking forward to seeing you around, Lily dear."

"Yeah, me too! And you too, Kram."

Kram, who had been standing behind a post eavesdropping, quickly retreated. Given that his receding footsteps had halted, the sound of his breathing remaining in one place, Lily had been aware of his presence the whole time. As she was always paying particular attention to the sounds around her, Lily's hearing was quite sharp.

"Uh... Y-yeah. See you around, L-Lily."

Kram's footsteps skittered away once more.

"That boy, I swear. Always with the attitude—even when he's being shy!"

"It's fine. I don't mind."

Lily was used to cold gazes. She had always received them

from the members of her family. However, what she did not yet realize was that there was something different here. Kram's gaze was not truly cold. In fact, there was a certain heat behind it.

"I see. Well, I apologize on Kram's behalf anyway."

"I'll be going now. See you soon!"

As the door shut behind her, Lily tittered to herself. It was quite a spectacle seeing Kram scolded, but there was still a gentleness, a cheeriness about this family. Come to think of it, she had never been scolded very often, not by her mother or her father.

Perhaps they did not even care to...because she could not hear them...

She shook her head to banish the dark thoughts. She *could* hear now! So, the next time she met them, certainly...

"Okay! I'll be ready!"

She ran back to the produce stand and gave her report.

"Thank you, dear. Are you still looking for more work?"

"Yes. Do you have anything else?"

"Hm. Can you take this box of cabbages to Canadoyle's place? It's down the main road, third house on the left. It's heavy though. Be careful."

"Okay!"

She proceeded to the third house, made her delivery, and returned to the grocer.

"Got any more?"

"Hmm, well, thanks to you, Lily, my work is done for the day. Here you go. It's not much, but here's your reward for helping me."

"Yay! Thank you!"

Lily accepted the little pouch full of coins, gave the man her thanks, and left the stall behind, heading into an alley. She quickly opened the bag and peered inside to find eight half-silver within. She was thrilled. This was the first money she had ever earned on her own.

However. *However...*

The bread the two of them needed to eat lunch cost two half-silver alone. Adding soup, salad, and butter to that was another coin. And that was only accounting for one meal, so once you factored in breakfast and dinner, they would be blowing through at least nine half-silver a day.

This was not enough to live, let alone go buying books. Of course, she had worked only a short time, but the grocer would only occasionally have extra work for her. Naturally, accepting a few jobs from him every day would not be enough.

Lily looked up to the sky and sighed.

"Ugh, it's no use. Earning money is too hard. Guess I'll have to become a hunt—"

"Yo... Li—er, Alstea," said a voice. Lily turned around to see Kram, leaning against a wall. His gaze was averted, and he was scratching the tip of his nose, cheeks red. The hat she had returned to him earlier was low over his eyes.

"Oh, hi, Kram! What's up?"

"N-nothin' much. Just happened to see you there."

"Hmm..."

Kram lifted the brim of the cap slightly and turned his gaze to Lily.

"You lookin' for work?"

"Yeah, I am. If I don't work, Lafine won't be able to eat. She's older than me, but that's just how things are."

The boy looked befuddled.

"Y-you're taking care of an adult? Huh, I—uh. I don't really get it, but that sounds hard Li—er, Alstea."

"Um, you can just call me Lily."

If he called her Alstea, she would not be able to react very quickly. She had only just started using that name recently, after all. Kram pulled the brim of his hat back down, hiding his gaze.

"So, what's up? Did you want something?" asked Lily.

"I know where you can get some work. Want me to tell you?"

"Wow, really?!"

Kram glanced at the enthusiastic girl out of the corner of his eye and spat, "Th-this is valuable information. N-normally, I'd charge a half-silver for this, but today I'll make an exception. Since you brought me my hat and all, L-Li... *Ugh... L-Lily.*"

"Whoa, thanks!"

Kram whipped a slip of paper from his pocket and jabbed it out at Lily.

"Go to the place written here. You can get jobs without going through the Hunters' Guild. It used to be that mostly kids from the slums took these jobs, but I heard they've been runnin' out of folks to take 'em lately... So..."

"Hmm?"

Lily opened the paper. The directions here pointed her to an area that Lafine had recently warned her specifically to stay away from. However, the word "danger" was not yet a part of Lily's mental lexicon. It wasn't that it had been erased the moment she came into possession of powerful magic—it had simply never been a concept she was aware of in the first place, owing to the fact that she had spent the majority of her life in the gilded cage that was the second story of the Lockwood mansion.

"I'll go check it out. See you later, Kram."

"S-sure. If you're ever in trouble, come see me anytime. Seriously, anytime. Don't hold back, okay?"

"Okay. Thanks. Bye now!"

Without sparing so much as a glance at the tough guy stance Kram had attempted to assume, Lily took off walking, eyes fixed on the slip of paper. There was a little map, and the place it marked was not far at all. She moved from the main part of town into the slums and headed for the center.

From inside the buildings around her, many which were little more than rubble, countless children stared out at Lily as she walked down the road. There were no adults here in the slums. The moment they became adults, the children here always set out from this place and never looked back. Some became hunters to earn their keep, while others fell into banditry or other lives of crime. If they were particularly good-looking, they might become the lover of some noble or wealthy merchant. If they were good with money, they might find employ in a shop, but those who lacked either looks or wits usually wound up doing manual labor.

Even so, anything was better than remaining here in the slums, and as a result, most typically left this place sometime in their mid-teens, bidding farewell to those younger than them... those little brothers and sisters to whom they had never been bound by blood.

Of course, Lily knew nothing of these sad circumstances. She strode proudly and lightly through this town of only children, thinking it strange but delightful all the same. Finally, she came upon a small plaza in the middle of the district, surrounded by rubble.

"Is this the place?"

In the wreckage in the center of the plaza sat a single adult. It was the first adult she had come across since entering the area. He was a man, his age indiscernible. He had ashen gray hair and eyes of the same color, the rest of his face obscured by a cloth mask that hung from his nose to below his chin. There was no one else around. She would have expected to see other job-seekers present, but there were none. It was a bit unnerving.

The man's sharp gaze turned to Lily as she approached him head-on.

"Good afternoon."

"Who are you? You ain't from around here."

It was obvious from how she was dressed. Lily was not wearing the sort of patched and tattered clothing that the children from the slums might wear, though she also was not wearing the dress in which she had left the Lockwood home. She was wearing normal clothing of the sort that would not look out of place for any commoner. They seemed to be clothes that Lafine had worn when she herself was around ten, though they were a bit loose in the chest, the sleeves a bit too long. Still, the clothing was far too fine for any orphan from the slums—and too clean.

Plus, the light in her eyes was different.

The children of the slums lived lives saddled with discomfort, and even their smiles reflected this. Lily, on the other hand, carried an innocence that belied even her nine years. Her smile was like sunshine on a day without a single cloud in the sky. From just a glance, it would be obvious to anyone that she did not belong here.

"No, I'm not. But I was told that I could come here to find work. My name is Lil—"

The man held up a hand, cutting her off.

"Hold it. I don't want to know your name, and you don't need to know anything about either me or your employer. All I do is offer the jobs to you, nothing more and nothing less. Those are the terms of service of the slum agency."

For a moment, Lily was dumbfounded, but a grin soon spread across her face.

"Oh, you sure? Okay, yay! Yes. So, I won't say my name."

To be able to avoid giving her own name was a relief.

The man's brows furrowed at this unexpected response. Yet he did not question her, quickly moving to explain the work, when...

"Oh, but," Lily inquired, "how come I can't ask about my employers?"

"To avoid any unnecessary conflicts. Too easy to get wrapped up when you pry needlessly into your employers or the work. I'm your broker and your negotiator. I receive thirty percent of the money your employers pay. The rest is your cut. Avoiding any contact with them is for the sake of your safety."

Lily seemed to ponder this for a few moments and then nodded.

"So I guess that makes you like the guild, then."

"You could say that."

Judging by the man's voice, he did not seem particularly old, though the gray of his hair gave him the appearance of someone in at least his fifties. Was he actually young?

"So, what should I call you?"

"Names are unimportant. If you really need one, you can call me the Broker. So, you wanna talk about the job or not?"

"Oh, yes, sorry. Go ahead."

The masked man nodded.

"Okay, right. So, I said not to ask after your employers, but there will be occasions when those employers are present at the job site—like when you're carrying things for merchants or making deliveries, for instance. Still, whenever your employer doesn't show themself, or you don't understand the purpose of the job, it's best not to look too deeply into it."

"Why not?" The broker did not reply. *Right,* thought Lily, *no questions.* "Okay, understood."

"Good." The man brought a stack of papers out from his pocket. "Let's see, jobs a little girl can handle... Loading carts is probably out of the question. There's a bunch of courier jobs— what do you think?"

"How much can I get for each delivery?"

"Usually about one half-silver each. Taking my cut, that leaves you seven copper."

That was not much at all. Apparently, the grocer had given her a bit of a bonus on her delivery for him. At that rate, she could work all day and still not make enough. Plus, the cut this man took was fairly large. If this were the Hunters' Guild, not only would brokerage be provided, but they provided for everything for the hunters, from insurance to purchasing materials. This man, however, was only the broker. Thirty percent was absurd.

"Ugh! That won't be enough to eat."

"No one's forcing you to work. Up to you whether you wanna take these jobs on or not."

"Oh, right. I should have mentioned, Mister, that I can use magic. Do you have anything like eliminating monsters or escorting people?"

According to her storybooks, exterminating monsters was where a hero truly shone. You got to look cool, and lots of people thanked you, and you even got something to eat out of it. Plus, it seemed like you could make a surprising amount of money from selling the parts.

"*You* can use magic?"

"Yeah."

"Dunno how good you are, but unfortunately those kinda jobs don't usually come around here. Usually it's through the Hunters' Guild, and if something's too dangerous for them, the Crown gets involved."

"How come? Do they not like you?"

The broker let out an enormous sigh.

"This is the slums, you idiot. There's no way kids from the slums or brats from the orphanage could go around killing monsters. Obviously, no one's gonna come here and ask them to do that."

"Oh. Eh heh heh."

That was obvious. Lily was embarrassed. Any amount of thinking could have brought her to that conclusion.

"Also, it's pretty rare for any herb-gathering jobs outside of the capital to come here. That's something that a G-rank hunter would never be asked to do without a chaperone, and currently, you'd be considered even less skilled than that. Try to stick around here." The man continued flipping through his papers. "How 'bout spending the evening with some pervy noble? You could make a few silver in a night, maybe even a few half-gold if ya play your cards right. Might even set yourself on the road to an exclusive contract."

An exclusive contract—in other words, as a lover.

"Uh, I'll pass on that."

Thanks to her storybooks, Lily had a pretty good idea of how these things worked, and thus she had some idea what might be expected of her in order to earn those half-gold.

"Gotcha. I figure someone like you'd be in pretty high demand, though."

"Eh heh, you think so?"

The man cast a sideways glance at Lily, who was grinning, bizarrely pleased by this, as he continued thumbing through the papers. Just then, he flipped all the way to the last page and stopped, letting out a sigh.

"Look, most of the jobs we get around here are just manual labor, considering this is a place where kids don't usually get much of an education. Ain't many jobs in here that would suit a weak little girl like you. Most of these are better for boys."

"Anything like helping out at a shop?"

Thankfully, during her confinement, Lily had received a broad education from Lafine. Granted, Lafine hadn't been too cheerful about teaching her. Or rather, she had only begrudgingly taught her at Lily's pestering insistence. She always seemed quite bored. But in any event, Lily could do basic arithmetic.

"Obviously not. Think about leaving something like that to some homeless brat from the slums. You'd just end up with things stolen or them eating up all the merchandise."

"I'd never do anything like that!"

The man tapped at his own forehead.

"No merchant's even gonna take my word for that. Those guys are suspicious and stubborn. No one's gonna listen to what any kid from the slums has to say, and even if they did listen, they'd never believe 'em."

"Okay. So there's nothing then?"

The man put the papers back in his pocket and looked up at the crestfallen Lily.

"Well, there's still one thing, though I really don't feel like I should be tellin' someone like you about it."

"What? You do have something?!"

Lily leaned toward the man, her eyes glittering. Annoyed, the man pushed her away and then drew back.

"There's a posting to sit by the city gates from dawn 'til dusk and count how many merchant wagons set out from the city and at what times."

Lily tilted her head.

"What's the point of that?"

"Don't ask. Just think of it as a traffic density study. There are a lot of threats to commerce around the capital—monsters and bandits and all. There are probably folks who have a vested interest in making sure all the merchants are reaching their destinations safely."

Lily's smile returned.

"Well, that sounds great!"

"S'pose so..."

Ignoring how the man averted his gaze, Lily leaned forward excitedly.

"I'll take that one!"

"Roger that. Now, you're gonna be responsible for paying half the damage fees for any breach of contract. That said, it's not like there will be a true contract, since neither of you is gonna know each other's names. If anyone shows up asking questions, you just keep up that you didn't see anything and you don't know anything."

"Whaaat? Um... I guess that's fine. I can keep watch for half a day." Lily clenched her fists, her smile redoubled.

"Hope so."

The man took a quill and paper from his pocket, along with an ink well, and drew a simple map.

"Here's the place."

"Got it. When should I go there? Right now?"

"Tomorrow. I told you that you start at dawn, didn't I? Don't be late. Gonna need to bring your own pen and paper for noting down the times and the numbers. When you're done, someone's gonna come and find you to collect those, around the first evening bell."

"Okay. That won't be you, will it?"

"Nope. I'm just the broker. The collector's gonna be someone hired by your employer. Once that's done, you just go on home. Come back here the next day. I'll have your payment ready. Even after my cut, it should be around five silver."

"Okay! Thanks, Mister!"

Lily gave her thanks to the peculiar man and said her farewells before leaving the slums behind. This job seemed like a one-time thing, but if she could keep coming back and receiving different sorts of tasks, she just might be able to eke out a living. Plus, it seemed like it could be pretty fun—she would get to hear all sorts of things, and exploring the city was way better than sitting alone in the mansion. She truly had to find a way to thank that mage who had healed her ears. If only she could meet her again someday...

Lily was practically vibrating with excitement—which is perhaps why she never noticed the young man whose gaze followed her from behind a half-ruined house...

The traffic density study job was even easier than Lily imagined. The greatest difficulty she encountered was that, thanks to the early morning start, she nearly fell asleep out of sheer boredom. All she had to do was stay near the city gates, count the wagons coming through, and write a memo of the time at which this occurred. There was a bench nearby, intended for those waiting for others, so she did not have to stand the entire time, either.

Indeed, this was a fine job. If there were any more of these, she would definitely take them. Plus, Lily thought, if she could manage to afford any new storybooks, she would have something to make even the time sitting and waiting more fun.

Around noon, the first midday bell rang, and Lily began to nibble the sandwich she had prepared before setting out that morning. She had also prepared one for Lafine, who was still sleeping, and left it on the table. Right about now, she would probably be snacking on the same thing.

Suddenly, Lily realized there was a shadow over her. She looked up.

"Hey, that looks pretty good."

The voice belonged to a young man, standing with the sun at his back. To Lily's mind, he had a very kind-sounding voice.

"Good afternoon!" Lily cheerfully replied.

The young man had close-cropped hair and a sword at his side. He looked to be in his later teens, with a toned, muscular build.

"What are you drawing there?" asked the young man. "A landscape?"

"No, this is my job. It's a traffic density study."

After a pause, the young man asked, "Mind if I sit?"

"Go ahead."

Lily scooted over on the bench. The young man sat down on the opposite side. He took some bread out from his knapsack and began eating as well. Compared to Lily's sandwich, his looked quite unappealing—just bread, with no vegetables or meat or anything. Even so, the young man appeared quite happy eating it. In fact, he made it look so very delicious that soon Lily was dying to try it.

"Hm? Is there something wrong with my bread?"

"It looks so good..." Lily murmured. The young man split the bread in half at once and offered some to Lily.

"Here you go."

"Oh, well then..."

Lily broke off a piece of her sandwich and exchanged it for half of the young man's piece of bread. He then grinned mischievously.

"Ha ha ha, looks like I've just made a profit here, thanks."

"Hee hee! Did you just trick me?" Lily asked, but the moment she took a bite of the bread, her eyes opened wide.

It was good. In fact, it was somehow still warm. When she bit into it, steam welled up from within. It was practically fresh-baked. Sure, there were no meat or vegetables to go with it, but the fragrance of the wheat alone was more than enough. It was wonderful.

"This is *good*!"

"Isn't it?"

"What bakery did you get this from?"

"Ha! No bakery could make it this good. My little sister bought the wheat and baked it herself. Well, I say little sister, but we aren't related by blood or anything—my siblings are all more or less orphans."

Lily felt a pang of empathy. With her own family's whereabouts unknown, Lily herself was practically an orphan, Lafine's younger sister in name only.

"Me and Lafine—er, um, my big sister—we aren't related by blood either."

There was a pause before the young man's face crumbled. "I see. But you aren't from the slums, are you? I've never seen you around there before."

"Nope. I live in the regular part of town."

The young man bit into the sandwich.

"This is good. There's a lot of different things in here, and it's super flavorful. This is very well composed. Is that a tomato sauce with diced onions?"

"That's right!"

The pair looked at one another and smiled.

"I'm Veil. I'm sixteen, and I live in the slums. I'm a C-rank hunter."

"Whoa! You're a hunter?! That's so cool!"

Veil smiled a bit bashfully. "I'm still just starting out, though."

Of course, Lily did not yet know that this young man's name was relatively well known even amongst the C-rank hunters of the capital. At the graduation exam of the Hunters' Prep School, he had bested a man named Gren, leader of the A-rank hunting party the Roaring Mithrils, with his swordsmanship.

(Naturally, it should be noted that the one behind this feat had been none other than Mile, the little mage who had healed Lily's ears. Mile lurked in the shadows of most miracles.)

Either way, Veil was a bit ahead of the curve for a C-rank hunter.

Lily was overjoyed. Here was a real-life hero. A hero, who fought back evil monsters and captured villains, was sitting right before her eyes. And now they were even acquaintances.

"I'm Lily. Lily Alstea, nine years old. Nice to meet you."

"You too, Lily."

Just then, a wagon passed through. Lily immediately made a note of it.

"That for your job?"

"Yeah. I got this job in the slums, actually."

"I see..."

Veil, having finished his part of the sandwich, scratched his head.

"So, um, this is kind of awkward, but..."

"What is?"

Veil put one hand to his mouth, pondering something. Finally, he looked back to Lily and spoke.

"What time do you finish work, Lily?"

"Somewhere around the first evening bell. Whenever someone comes here to collect this memo."

"I see. Are you free afterwards, then?"

Suddenly, Lily realized what was going on. Her heart began beating a little faster.

"Um, are you...hitting on me?"

"Goodness, no. I really just wondered if you might be up for a continuation of that job," Veil replied.

Lily patted her still-flat chest.

"Oh, phew! You startled me."

"So, do you have a bit of time?"

"Hmm. Well, if I'm late getting home to make dinner, Lafine might cry..."

"Didn't you say she was your *older* sister?"

"She is."

"How old is she?"

"She's twenty-two."

"Is she ill?"

"No, she's healthy as a horse! I've even seen her—ah, uh, never mind. Eh heh heh." She was healthy enough to hold a bandit boss at knife point, but of course, Lily could not say that. "It's just that she goofs off a bit too much. She sleeps until noon, and drinks even though we have no money, and never leaves the house, and on bad days she sometimes sleeps until evening. Still, she gave me a home when I had nowhere else to go. She's a good person!"

"A...good person..." A knowing expression spread across Veil's face. "Pft... Heh heh heh. Lafine Alstea? Lives in the main city, right? Gotcha. I'll go and get permission from her directly then, while you're working. I'll bring her some basic provisions, too. That should be enough to excuse you for dinner."

"Whoa! Could you really do that?"

Veil tugged on the chain of his necklace and produced a small metal plate. The plate was engraved with a C, to signify his hunter rank, along with his name, the capital branch of the Hunters' Guild, and what appeared to be his registration number.

"This is proof that I'm a hunter. Once I show most people this, they'll believe me. Of course, that means I can never do anything bad," he said with a smile.

"Whoa, that's so cool!" Lily smiled. Somehow, she guessed that it wasn't just his registration tag that made people trust Veil. In Lily's eyes, he seemed like a very reliable individual.

Veil looked at Lily as she applauded and then stood. "Anyway, if I can't get Lafine's permission, I'll let you know so that you can just head right on home."

"Okay, sounds good." Lily nodded.

"Now then, I should get going. See you in a bit, Lily."

"See you later, Mr. Veil."

Veil grimaced slightly and scratched his forehead with his pointer finger.

"Oh, um, just Veil is fine. Also, don't tell anyone that I was here, all right? It's probably better that the person who comes to collect those memos doesn't know that you were slacking off and chatting on your lunch break."

"Sure, I guess so. It must be hard being a hunter. If the guild found out, would they scold you? Since you're working, too, Veil?"

Veil shrugged.

"Who knows? Okay, bye for now."

"Bye bye!"

Lily watched his sturdy back as he walked away, waving. She continued happily eating her bread as he shrunk into the distance, thinking how wonderful it was to have made her first-ever friend.

As the sun sank and the first evening bell rang, the courier arrived. He was a small-framed man, wearing the same type of mask over the lower half of his face that the broker wore, though he was clearly far older. The man strode straight up to Lily and silently held out his hand. Without hesitation, Lily gripped it, shaking his hand up and down.

"Hi there, pleased to meet you."

After an awkward pause, the man pointed to the memo in her other hand.

"Oh right, there. Eh heh, my mistake."

She let go and handed over the memo. The man took a quick glance over the paper, nodded, and turned his back on Lily at once. Then he took off walking.

"I guess I'm done! And then I'll go back to the slums tomorrow."

She stood up from the bench and stretched.

"All done, Lily?"

"Oh, are you done with work, too, Veil?"

"Nope, just starting."

"Hm?"

"Don't worry about it. Let's go."

Lily jogged after Veil as he took off walking.

"Where're we going?"

"Who knows?"

"Is it a secret?"

"Not necessarily. It's just that I don't know, either."

Lily gazed up at the young man now beside her and tilted her head. Veil was walking out of town, through the city gates. Lily jogged to keep up.

"Hey, Veil, are you a bad guy?"

"If hunters were the bad guys, the whole world would fall apart."

"That's true."

Lily had been wondering if she was being kidnapped again, but that did not seem to be the case. Veil only stared straight ahead as he walked along the road, not looking at her. Lily looked back and then ahead to see a man among the travelers and wagons.

"Oh...!" It was the courier. Veil was following the courier from before. "Wait, what are we doing?"

"There are responsibilities that come with everything we do. All the more so when money's involved."

"Hm?"

"Lily, you need to see with your own eyes what it is that you've done."

As they passed by various diverging roads, the number of travelers decreased drastically. It was obvious that there were few people leaving the city this late in the day. Monsters were far livelier in the depths of night, after all.

Of course, Lily was not afraid; she had Mr. Nano watching over her. Veil, as a hunter, probably was not afraid either.

"If he turns around, he'll spot us," Veil said, slackening his pace and letting the gap between them open up. Lily followed suit, dropping back next to Veil.

The courier walked on and on. Veil followed after with Lily in tow, occasionally taking a moment to conceal them in the shadows. Finally, when they reached a point in the road where neither travelers and merchants were anywhere to be seen, the courier took a look around as if to confirm he was in the clear and then ducked behind a rocky outcropping on the side of the highway.

Veil went ahead, pressing his index finger to his lips and then gestured for Lily to follow, sticking closely to the rocks. Lily approached, deadening her footsteps. She could hear two men talking quietly.

"Did you get the timetable?"

"Yeah, it's right here."

Veil and Lily peeked surreptitiously and ever so slightly out from behind the rock, his head above and hers below. The man who received the memo from the courier skimmed over the three pages it encompassed.

"Heh, perfect, perfect. Here ya go."

The man handed the courier something in a small sack. It landed in the courier's hands with a soft jangling of coins.

"Thanks as always... So, you gonna do it tomorrow?"

At those words, Lily felt a seizing in her chest. She was not stupid. Lily Lockwood may not have known much about the world, but she was by no means a fool. It was merely that something like this had never even occurred to her.

"That's none o' yer damn business. Best way to assure a healthy life is if neither of us knows too much."

"Well, of course."

"If yer done here, then scram."

The courier retreated. Veil tucked Lily, now stiff at her terrible realization, under his arm and ducked down behind the rocks in a spot that would not be visible from the highway. The courier headed back into town, making no sign of having noticed the pair.

Lily gulped nervously and asked, "Hey, Veil? That job that I did...was I helping out some bandits?"

"Probably. The person who hired you was a bandit. There are a lot of people like that who hire through the slums rather than the guild. Based on the departure times from that memo, they can calculate where they're likely to find merchants who decided to make camp instead of sleeping at an inn when the sun goes down."

Lily's heart began to pound. Oh. This was bad. This was a very bad feeling. Someone might end up dead because of her memo.

"This is something you need to know: No job taken in the slums comes without strings attached. The only jobs that it's safe to take there are ones that you're certain you know the source of. Don't trust that broker." Veil cleared his throat and then continued, "Sorry. I just thought that it'd be best for you to see what can happen for yourself, at least once, rather than just warning you.

Lily, you are far too careless. It's not your fault that you were used, but I need you to remember that acting heedlessly can put other people at risk of being harmed."

His words felt far away. Nothing was getting in through Lily's skull.

"I'm going to keep tailing this guy and find the bandits' hideout. Then, I'll go and report it to the guild, and we'll return with an elimination team. This is going to be dangerous, so you head on back into town now. Thankfully, monsters don't tend to come out here, and it's not that far, so you should be fine on your own."

Lily had no reply.

She had been deceived. No, that wasn't it. She had been *used*. It was the first time she had truly experienced the wickedness of a stranger. It was an awful sensation, like evil itself was dragging its coarse tongue along her bare skin. Her heart felt so heavy it was as though it had turned to iron.

Tears welled in her eyes. And yet...

She steeled herself and lifted her head.

"No. I'm coming with you. If help from the guild doesn't arrive in time, some merchants might be attacked tonight because of me. We have to hurry up and let them know."

"No way. I can't bring you along—you aren't even a hunter. If you're feeling responsible and want to make up for this, go to the Hunters' Guild. Tell them my name and what's going on here."

"I can't do that. That's just an excuse to send me back to the capital, isn't it?"

Veil clenched his jaw, lost for words.

The bandits would move, and Veil would follow. No matter how Lily hurried, by the time she got back to the guild to retrieve other hunters and get them back here, there would be no one left around.

Lily might lack common sense, thanks to her extended seclusion, but she was by no means stupid.

"Plus, if we keep dawdling, those merchants are going to be attacked. There won't be enough time to get people back here."

Veil put his hand to his forehead. He was lost. Should he see Lily back to the capital, even if it meant taking his eyes off of the bandit? Lily pointed at the bandit ahead of them, her gaze keen.

"Look, he's already on the move. If you try and drag me back to the capital, we aren't going to make it in time before the merchants are attacked."

The man finished reading over the memo and started off into a field away from the highway at rapid pace, without a glance at Veil and Lily.

Lily hurriedly followed. "It'll be fine. You're here, and actually, I know how to use magic. Hurry up, Veil."

"H-hey! Jeez..."

Veil jogged to catch up with her. Upon reaching Lily, he lowered his stance and pulled her down next to him, whispering, "Keep your head down. Thankfully, the brush here comes up to about my waist. If we keep down, they won't see us."

"Got it."

Lily crouched, as she was told.

"Also, I'm glad you're so gung-ho about this, but try to keep your voice a bit quieter. If you don't do as I say, I'm going to drag you back home by force."

Lily leaned in close to the frowning Veil and breathed, as quietly as she could, "Okay. Now let's—"

"Wait."

Veil seized Lily by the arm as she started to move and held up one index finger, his expression harsh.

"Also, from here on out, whatever I say goes."

"Okay," Lily nodded. "Whatever you say goes."

Veil let out a deep sigh and crept quickly after the bandits, body still lowered. Lily followed behind him.

As they climbed a grassy hill and moved into a thicket, Veil whispered, "This is bad. The sun's down. We're going to lose sight of him. Looks like we'll have to get a bit closer."

Lily tugged on his sleeve.

"Hey, Veil. Can I go in front?"

"Can you see him?"

"I can't, but I can hear him."

"Huh?"

As long as there was grass growing on the ground, she could follow the bandit's sounds. Unlike the drawn-out sounds of the wind blowing across the foliage, the footsteps of living things cut a steady rhythm through the greenery.

"You can *hear* him?"

"Yeah. My hearing's pretty good." Of course, until not long before, Lily could not hear anything at all, but this did not seem the time or place to be explaining that.

"Go ahead then. Just proceed with caution."

"Okay!"

"Your voice."

"Okay!"

If they lost sight of this bandit, a merchant wagon somewhere would come under attack tonight for certain.

Her body still crouched, Lily scurried forth like an animal, keeping track of the difference between her own footsteps and Veil's, and the bandit's. Before she knew it, they were descending the wooded hill.

"Lily, wait." Veil placed a hand on Lily's shoulder. "There."

There was a hazy orange light visible through the gaps in the trees. Looking around, several small wooden structures were visible.

"A settlement in a place like this?" Lily muttered.

"It's no village. That's the bandit camp. They set up in this valley so that they can't be seen from the highway. If it were a real village, they would have at least cut a road through the grass."

"I see."

"This is a tough one. They're a bigger operation than I figured. For there to be three buildings that big means that we could be facing a gang of as many as thirty bandits. I had hoped the group would be small enough for me to handle it by myself, but this is too much for me."

Lily thought back to the incident with the Flaming Wolves. Although she had already forgotten the names of the hunters who had guarded the carriage, she knew there had been *three* C-rank hunters there. Even so, when they were ambushed, they had been forced into a surrender by no more than ten-odd bandits. Veil, meanwhile, was a C-rank hunter, the same as those three men. If he was at the same level of strength, then he was vastly outnumbered.

"If we can at least figure out what merchant they plan on attacking, we can get out ahead of them and warn them. Lily, can you guess?"

"Sorry, I don't know. Even though I'm the one who wrote the memo..."

Even if she knew the surrounding geography and remembered the number of wagons that had passed through the gate, as well as the times they had departed, there was no way of knowing what towns they were headed to. And, of course, it should go without saying that she had no idea whom the bandits intended to target.

Veil gritted his teeth, grumbling, "I figured I could manage if it were five guys or so, but this is impossible."

Nothing was worth sacrificing one's life on a reckless battle. Trampled flowers didn't bloom, and being taken hostage would just cause more trouble for the guild. Being a hunter was a job—it didn't make you a philanthropist. If you were dead, you couldn't spend your wages, no matter how much you had earned.

"Grr..."

"I know you feel bad for the merchants, but I don't think there's anything we can do about the attack tonight. We can at least rush right back to the guild and report this."

Indeed, hunters were not philanthropists. However...

The heroes that Lily admired in the stories that she once read went above and beyond. There may or may not have been money to be had from it, but if there was someone who needed their help, these heroes would always jump into the fray, and if they could prevent a tragedy before it happened, they would stand up to those who would do evil. Why? Because to be a hero meant being an ally of justice. And so...

"Okay, let's hurry back. Lily... Lily?"

She was gone. The little girl who had been right beside him had suddenly vanished. Veil looked straight ahead. Lily was already running down the hill—at full speed, without hesitation.

"*L-Lily?!*" Veil shouted, forgetting to lower his voice. Lily looked back, waving at him with a grin.

"I'm gonna go ask the bandits not to attack anyone toniiight!"

"What...uh?!" A strangled noise emerged from the pit of Veil's throat.

He would never make it in time. Even if he started after her now, Lily was going to make it to the camp before he could ever catch up with her.

"Veil, you wait right theeere!"

But Lily Lockwood knew nothing about the boy named Veil. She knew nothing of what inspired Veil, who'd been born in the slums, to live so earnestly. She didn't know that unlike those orphans who came before him, who came of age and left the slums behind, Veil had resolved to remain there as an elder, looking after the smaller children. And she did not know of the feelings he held for the girl named Mile, who had provided him with training because of the kind of person she knew he was. Of all this, Lily knew practically nothing at all.

"If I leave her here, I could never face Mile again..."

And so, within a few seconds, Veil had reached his decision. After a moment of being stunned at Lily's recklessness, Veil pelted desperately after her.

"Dammit, I can only take on seven guys, maybe eight..."

Lily, meanwhile, having reached the bottom of the hill, rushed right up to the door of one of the buildings and flung it open.

"Excuse me!"

Inside, ten-odd bandits, who had been in the process of gearing up, all turned to look at the little intruder who had suddenly barged in.

"Huh?"

"Hm?"

Just as Veil had surmised, there were roughly ten bandits in this building, in which case, one could reasonably guess there would be around thirty in total. Though this was rather large for a bandit troop, a group this size was by no means extremely unusual.

Lily put her hands on her hips, glaring at all of them, then puffed out her chest proudly and cried, "Mr. Bandits, please don't attack those merchants!"

One bandit furrowed his brow.

"Wha...?"

"........."

"Who are you to—?"

The bandits were bewildered—and understandably so. A little girl had suddenly appeared in their secret hideout, blustering about plans no one should have known about, and moreover, she was declaring that they should abandon their night's labor. To put it simply, they had no idea what was going on.

"Hey, little lady, what's your name? Are you a hunter?"

"Oh, my name is Lily Lo—er...Als... It's Lily! I'm not a hunter, just Lily!" Realizing that it might cause trouble for Lafine if she gave her family name, Lily stopped herself short.

"Have you told anyone else about this attack?"

"N-no, not yet..."

It was not a lie to say that she had not told Veil about the attack, as he had been the one to inform *her*.

"Well, that's good," said the bandit, before asking, "So, um, little lady, you bring anyone else with you? You come here alone?"

Lily thought. She couldn't cause trouble for Veil, either.

"Y-yes, of course I'm alone."

"How many of you are there?"

She'd been found out! How?!

Just then, Veil appeared in the doorway. The bandits all readied themselves at once. Veil muttered, his forehead furrowing, "There's too many of them..." Still, he drew his sword and bravely declared, "No one move! I'm a hunter. Drop your weapons. The guild already has this base surrounded."

The bandits held their breaths, panicked. Both sides stared at one another, trying to gauge each other's intentions. In this world, there was no honor in following one's master to the grave. There was merely defeat. Whether you were bandit or hunter, all you could do was throw yourself upon the mercy of the one who was, objectively, the strongest.

Veil was betting on this.

He would spook the bandits into dropping their weapons, negotiating with them from a position of advantage, and then wait for an opportunity to grab Lily and make a break for it.

Lily, meanwhile, was looking up at Veil, her eyes sparkling with innocence.

"Whoa, Veil, you're amazing! When did you call in the other hunters? Wait, can you use magic, too?"

Veil went pale as a sheet. *Welp, that's the end of us,* said his face. The bandits, by contrast, grinned wide.

"My, what's wrong, boy? If you've got so many friends out there, why don'tcha go ahead and call 'em in?"

"Yeah! We still haven't dropped our weapons—go ahead and call 'em."

"No need to hesitate on our account."

Lily clenched her fists, adding confidently, "Yeah, call them, Veil! Um, Veil? What's wrong?"

"Can you be quiet?" Veil grumbled, his face contorted in a pained expression.

It was then that Lily realized what she had done. Veil had told the bandits that they were surrounded in order to put them at an advantage in the negotiations. As she realized this, she spoke without thinking.

"Huh? Wait, what you were just saying—was that a...lie?"

".........."

"Ah... Ah ha ha... I get it. So that's what's going on here. I see. Okay, okay... Umm! *I'm really sorry!*"

Lily bowed in apology, her hair swaying. *I've done it now! I did something irresponsible* again...

"So!" The bandits approached with axes wielded, interrupting their conversation. "What was it you were gonna do to us, kid?"

In an instant, the edge of Veil's sword crossed the wrist of one of the approaching bandits. Sword swinging, he lifted a leg and kicked straight into the bandit's stomach. Blood spurted profusely from the man's wrist as he flew back, rolling across the floor.

"Guh...! Wha—?! Ow! That *hurt!*"

Veil grabbed Lily by the wrist and pushed her behind him, shoving her out of the door with his back. The small girl had no means to resist and tumbled out of the building.

"Hey!"

"Run, Lily. Get up and run."

Lily looked up at Veil's back from where she still lay on the ground.

"Huh?"

"Hurry!"

There was no honor in death and none in self-sacrifice. But there was someone present who needed guarding, and that made all the difference. If Veil were to peacefully surrender here, he would probably be taken hostage, a ransom would be collected from the guild for his safe return, and he'd be released. Killing a hunter would make any bandit a clear enemy of the guild, which could be quite inconvenient.

However, the same could not be said for Lily. She was a young girl and not even a hunter. If she were taken, only the most dreadful of lives awaited her, whether she was kept for the bandits' amusement or sold off as a slave.

Indeed, the bandit who Veil had wounded cried from the ground, "Gah, ow! This friggin' hurts! Don't let that little girl get away! She's gonna be *mine*!"

"And what about the brat here? Take him alive?"

"Don't bother! If we catch that little girl and shut her up, we can whack the kid, bury him, and the guild'll never know! Long as they don't find the body, they'll just figure he got eaten by monsters!"

Hearing this, Lily frowned.

"You can't do that! No!"

Naturally, the bandits were not interested in her protest. Murder in their eyes, the men rushed the door at once.

"Gaaaah!"

"——!"

There was a metallic sound. Veil shouted as he caught the sword of the bandit at the head of the pack with his own blade.

"Run, Lily!" he yelled again.

As Lily tried to make her way back inside, she was once again forced out as Veil stepped backward, blocking the entrance. Keeping his position at the door limited the number of opponents he would have to deal with at once. Though, of course, this would only work until the bandits in the other structures over-heard the commotion and reinforcements came. Beyond Veil's back, the sounds of blades clashing rang out into the night.

"Veil!"

"I'm fine! Get out of here!"

"Okay..."

Veil caught another bandit's blade, repelling him and shoving the man away with a kick to the gut. From beside him, a massive bandit swung his hatchet down.

"Our axes are gonna break right through that dinky little sword of yers!"

"Damn it." Veil traced the blade of his sword with his fingertip. "Magic Blade!"

At once, the fearsome swing of the man's great axe was repelled.

"Guh!"

There was a roaring sound, and sparks flew...but though Veil was driven to one knee by the interrupted force of the blow, his sword did not break. Rather, the blade of the sword began to shine, appearing even stronger.

"Ha! I learned this trick from a certain infamous mage in the capital. My blade won't break that easily."

"A magic swordsman?! You little bastard!"

The sword was fortified by magic, but still, this stance put Veil at a disadvantage. Before he had a chance to stand, the massive bandit swung wildly at his neck.

"Die!" the man yelled.

"Air Shot!"

A simple type of wind magic. The blast of compressed air that shot out of Veil's left fist crashed into the massive bandit's gut.

"Gwah...?!"

Incidentally, this was the same magic Veil had used against Gren, A-rank hunter and leader of the B-rank party the Roaring Mithrils, at the graduation exam of the Hunters' Prep School. It was one thing to use such a trick against a man like that—but a garden-variety bandit stood no chance against the wind magic. The bandit, struck in his solar plexus by the blast, was unable to even brace himself in time and instead fell to the ground face-down, losing consciousness as a mixture of spittle, bile, and blood spewed from his mouth.

"Pity. I can't do much, but I *can* throw a spell or two."

"Y-you little...!"

The remaining bandits hesitated. In that moment, Veil got back to his feet and again brandished his sword. He was still in this. It was too soon to run. Considering the length of Lily's legs, there was no way she could have made it safely out of range. So, he had to buy her a bit more time, Veil thought, steadying his breath.

"Whoa, Veil, you're amazing! You handled that big guy like he was nothing!"

Lily was clapping her hands casually.

"Wha—?! Wait, seriously—you're still here?! Why didn't you run?! Didn't you say, 'Okay'?! I thought you'd already..." Veil trailed off, losing all steam—because Lily was still smiling innocently at him.

"Well, I mean, this all started because of my mistake, so there's no way I could just run away and leave you behind," she explained. "I'm not going back home unless you come, too. Okay?"

"That's if we still can... Oh, jeez."

Veil let out a long sigh. He could hear the footsteps of other bandits, who seemed to have heard the commotion and were approaching from the other buildings. Before they knew it, their exit was blocked.

"What's with these two? New recruits?" asked one.

"Don't be stupid! They're intruders!"

"Dunno about the girl, but this brat here's a hunter. He's got some magic, too. Be careful."

The bandits, who had been hesitant to attack, returned to full force with the arrival of their reinforcements.

"We can't let 'em get away. They know where the base is now. If the guild finds out, our operations here are through."

"Rebuilding our base again from the ground up? No thanks. Damn it, I'm a bandit, not a carpenter!"

"Ha! In that case, let's handle this like bandits do!"

At this point, there would be no more last-ditch hopes. Veil had made a wager, but Lily had not cashed out by taking the opportunity to escape while she could. Now, any resistance would merely lead to a futile death. Normally, this would be the point at which they ought to surrender immediately. However, the bandits had already made it clear that was pointless by saying, "If we catch that little girl and shut her up, we can whack the kid, bury him, and the guild'll never know!"

They had no interest in taking hostages. Rather than demand any ransom money from the guild, the bandits were electing to stay undercover, which meant that Veil and Lily were fighting for their lives. The only question at this point was really which one of them would fall first.

"We're pretty much screwed." Veil murmured with a heavy sigh.

"We are?"

At the very least, the situation they were in was not something that an independent, party-less C-rank hunter could be expected to handle. Lily, however, could not comprehend this. She had, after all, lived most of her life in a fairy-tale world and believed that most people were fundamentally good. Alas, Lily Lockwood was a very poor judge of character.

"It'll be fine," she said lightly. "Now that all the bandits are here, we can just ask all of them nicely to cooperate."

"Wha...?"

Lily drew in a deep breath.

"Um! Hello, bandits! Please call off your attacks for today! And then, why don't you all dissolve this bandit gang and go find some proper jobs? You'll be able to make some money, and there won't be any worry of getting arrested! It's a really good deal!"

There was silence but for the sound of the night wind blowing. Everyone, Veil included, stared at Lily, speechless.

"With this many of you guys, you could all work together quite effectively! If you can be bandits, then I bet you could be hunters, too!"

"B-but being a bandit *is* a proper job!" one of the bandits shouted angrily.

The others broke out into raucous laughter. They pointed at Lily, jeering.

"Ha ha ha! This is killin' me! Is this li'l brat your mom or something?!"

"I mean at 'er age she'd have to be a little sister! Bwah ha ha, she's too much!"

"Ga ha ha, I'm about to bust a gut! Hee hee, someone help me!"

Lily tilted her head, her expression sincere.

"Oh, does your tummy hurt? Are you okay?"

Veil slapped his hand to his forehead. As the bandits simmered down to giggles, one of them pointed at Lily and asked, "You really think you're in a position to tell us what to do?! You do realize that negotiation can only come about when both sides are on equal ground, right?"

"Huh, really? Thanks for telling me!"

"Little lady, are you slow or something? Maybe you should just sit down and let us capture you. It'll be way less painful for everyone involved."

If we were on equal ground, they would listen to me, Lily thought. *Well then, that's simple enough.*

Lily let out a thought pulse all around her.

Mr. Nano, are you here?

Yes, Miss Lily, I am everywhere. Can I help you with something?

How much power would I need to challenge these bandits?

WELL, THERE ARE SOME SLIGHT VARIATIONS AMONGST THEM, BUT IF WE WANT THEM TO CONSIDER NEGOTIATION WITHOUT KILLING ANYONE, STRIKING ONE OF THEM IN THE SIDE OF THE HEAD WITH AN ABSOLUTE MINIMUM-STRENGTH FIREBALL SHOULD AT LEAST BE ENOUGH FOR THEM TO START LISTENING.

What? But that sounds really painful.

IT HAS TO BE ENOUGH TO DEMONSTRATE YOUR STRENGTH. ALSO, TRUTHFULLY, THE TRICK TO NEGOTIATION IS NOT TO STRUGGLE AGAINST AN EQUIVALENT FORCE BUT TO COME AT IT FROM A PLACE OF FAR SUPERIOR POWER.

I see. Thanks.

THE PLEASURE IS ALL MINE.

She would need about thirty of her smallest fireballs, assuming that she could avoid killing any bandits. While Lily considered this, the circle of bandits tightened around them.

"All righty now, if we're done here, just go ahead and drop yer weapon, boy."

"No point in that. I'm gonna end up dead either way, so I may as well just let loose, all or nothing."

"Idiot. What are you gonna do against thirty of us?"

Veil adjusted his sword grip and firmed up his stance. Beside him, Lily looked up into the air.

"Um, some fireballs? Thirty, please?"

She radiated the image of fire up into the air. With a *poof*, a ball of flame manifested above her head—just one. Lily knew nothing about traditional fireball spells. She could only imagine what she thought they must be like, based on the name. Thus, she defaulted to the only type of fire spell she knew. An image of something like the sun came into her mind, only this time far smaller—about fist sized.

Poof, poof.

It was as the second and third orbs appeared that both Veil and the bandits suddenly noticed this new source of light piercing through the darkness. The bandits pointed at Lily, again roaring with laughter.

"Huh? The hell is that? A little kitchen spell? I'm surprised you can use magic, but are you about to cook us a feast or some-thin', little cutie?"

The bandits—and Veil, for that matter, assumed that Lily had summoned a flame-type spell, used primarily for cooking.

"Lily...?"

However, that was not what this was. The heat contained in each orb was nothing to scoff at. After all, this was Lily Lockwood's special fire magic, made in the image of the sun that appeared in Miami Satodele's books. It was not the real thing, of course. If it were the real sun, the heat would be radiating constantly outward, but Lily knew nothing about emissions. These flames boiled only inwardly with heat, its temperature climbing over time until it reached an apex. Naturally, she had not imagined nuclear fission for this false sun, so technically speaking, it was just a regular fireball that happened to be unusually hot.

Poof, poof, poof.

The flames above her head continued to increase in number.

Poof, poof, poof.

"Ha ha ha, ha ha...ha...?"

The bandits' laughter slowly petered out, and their brows began to furrow. No matter how weak this low-level fire magic might be, being hit with that many fireballs at once would mean getting burned.

"Oy! Girl! You stop that!"

A bandit stepped out to grab Lily by the collar, but Veil moved forward to block him. The tip of his sword was aimed at the bandit's chest. Ignoring all of this, Lily continued to manifest more flames.

"Oh, I think I'm starting to get the hang of this."

Poof, poof, p-p-p-p-p-poof!

"Ha ha ha, this is actually kind of fun!"

The balls of flame above her head increased even further. Now, there were roughly thirty. They began swirling in a circle around Veil and Lily, as though to protect them. Standing at the center, Lily looked back to the bandits.

"Um, so, bandits, if I hit every single one of you with one of these, will you consider negotiating?"

"The hell we will! I don't care how many you've got, you couldn't possibly strike us all down with those tiny little things!"

One of the bandits slashed his sword at the eddy of fireballs.

"Hi-yah!"

The instant the bandit's blade touched one of the balls of flame, the metal began to glow red, liquefying before melting entirely and splattering across the ground.

"Wha...?"

The metal that had once been a sword was bubbling on the ground, and the flame ball, which should have dissipated, still floated in the air, unchanged.

"Eep! M-my sword!"

The bandit who had swung at Lily stared at the remaining half of his beloved sword and lost all will to fight, stumbling back onto the ground.

"H-h-how?! Th-those are just some cooking spells! Or like, some fireballs!"

"Should I hit you with this now?" Lily asked innocently. "There's a lot of these, so it's a little hard to control th—Aah!"

Two of the flame balls smacked into one another, warping. Then, they both exploded, unleashing a dreadful wave of heat on the area. That instantaneous explosion alone was enough to singe the hair on all the bandits' heads, the surrounding grass looking as though it had been struck by a bomb blast.

"Gyah!"

"It's *hot*!"

Lily scratched her head, smiling bashfully.

"Ah, sorry. Magic is really tough. I better make more of these... Need enough for everyone."

Poof, poof. Two more appeared.

"Now then, shall we?"

Lily lifted her right pointer finger, swinging her arm up into the air. However, before she could swing her finger back down,

CHAPTER 3
THE BIRTH OF A HERO

one of the bandits hurriedly abandoned his weapon, dropping to his knees and bowing his head to the ground.

"Wa-wa-wa-wa-wa-wa-wa-*waaait*! If you hit us with that, we'll all be dead before we can even negotiate!"

Immediately, all of the other bandits followed suit, dropping their weapons and raising their hands. This was no longer merely a question of superiority of strength. There was not a single soul who would not bow before such power, the likes of which even most mages in this world could not aspire to summon. Even a court magician might find this impossible.

"Huh? Wait, this would kill you?"

"Yes! *Yes, it would!*" a bandit screamed. "That thing's so hot it melted a metal sword in an instant!"

"P-p-p-please stop this!"

Well, goodness! Lily thought peevishly. *That* would *kill them. You lied to me, Mr. Nano.*

WHAT? THIS ISN'T MY FAULT. I *DID* TRY TO REMIND YOU TO HOLD BACK. BUT, HEY, IT LOOKS LIKE THEY'RE READY TO NEGOTIATE WITH YOU.

"W-we get it. We're breaking up the band, starting today. So, please! Please spare us our lives! We've got families! W-we're only doing this for them! Please, we'll leave the country even, just let us go!"

"Families... I see..."

The bandit who had spoken grinned to himself, face still to the ground.

This number was sensible for a gang of bandits, but they could not possibly all band together as hunters. Here in the base was a mountain of all the food and money they had amassed. After this little mage and the C-rank hunter were gone, they could just gather it all up and vanish from the capital region, starting up again near another town somewhere else in the country. It was hard to assess the hunter, but the mage was clearly clueless. It would be fine. They could deceive her.

However...

"What should I do, though? I don't know how to get rid of this spell..."

"Huh?"

The bandit lifted his dirt-smeared face.

"Oh, I've got it. You won't be using those anymore, so I'll just toss it into them."

Lily swung her arm down, pointing to the three buildings behind the bandits.

"Hi-yah!" she said with pretend innocence. And the thirty balls of flame that had been swirling protectively around her and Veil rose up, following her finger. Then, once they had reached a certain temperature, they took off like shooting stars, raining down around the valley. Lily gasped in awe at the glowing trails they left behind in the night sky. "Whoa! Pretty!"

Impact. Explosion. Blast. Inferno.

The flames rose as the area began to glow brighter and brighter with an orange light, gravel scattering everywhere, the heat contained within the spell spreading swiftly along with a black smoke.

The mood had completely shifted; the camp was now a portrait of Hell. The bandits' screams, already swallowed up in the heat waves and the roar of the flames, morphed into cries of anguish as they were blown back, consciousness fading.

It was a massacre.

The three buildings were burnt down without a trace, or really, they were annihilated, the land scorched barren and even the grove on the other side of camp turned to ash.

Lily froze, still pointing. A bead of sweat dripped down her cheek. The power that had been released from each of those tiny suns was nearly as much as there had been in the much-larger single orb she had thrown. And there had been thirty of them.

What happened, Mr. Nano?

YOU MADE THE FLAMES SMALL, BUT YOU ONLY SHRANK AND COMPRESSED THEM. AS A REACTION, THIS MADE THE BLAST FROM THE IMPACT ALL THE MORE POWERFUL. UNLEASHING THIRTY OF THOSE AT ONCE IS ENOUGH TO ALTER TERRAIN. THANKFULLY, YOU DID NOT FIRE THOSE TOWARD THE CAPITAL.

And so, in an instant, the bandits lost their horde of cash, loot, and supplies, along with any means of escape. Thus, Lily closed the curtain on the frequent merchant-wagon disappearances that had been happening around the capital.

It should go without saying that Veil was shrewd enough to drag two of the unconscious bandits back with him to the capital in order to collect a reward.

A reward that he split with Lily.

This was how Veil, a C-rank hunter and one of those people who had been party to the incident, told it:

"I was concerned about someone who appeared to be in danger accepting a job from the slum broker without having a sense of the potential danger, and so I tailed her, but..." He paused, clearing his throat, and looked at Lily beside him. "Well, in the end, it really turned out that she *herself* is dangerous. Considering this incident, I have determined that I need to keep a close watch on Lily from now on."

Lily looked up at Veil, protesting, "But I'm *not* dangerous. Not any more than anyone else."

Lafine massaged her temples, as though trying to stave off a headache. They were in the Alstea family home, and Lafine, Lily, and Veil were sitting in chairs with a simple table between them. Lafine was in the process of questioning them about what in the world had happened to keep them out all night.

Lily had not come home the night before, after going out to look for work early in the morning.

On top of this, the capital was in an uproar.

Something had happened in the forest near the capital last night—some kind of natural disaster or elder dragon attack or who-knew-what. Whatever it was had lit the night sky over the slumbering capital like the dawning sun, even sending out tremors. Everyone living within the capital was shaken awake, flooding from their homes to stare up at the burning sky. Now, this morning, it was all that anyone in the capital was talking about... except for Lafine, who had had a very, very bad feeling about it.

"I see. So, this was *your* doing..."

"Yeah, I kind of messed up."

Lafine stood from her chair, grabbing Lily by the ear.

"What the hell were you wandering around doing?! Do you not think *anything* through?"

"W-w-well..."

Veil stepped in to assist.

"I-I was surprised as well, but thanks to Lily, a lot of lives were saved, so I think you should forgive her."

Lafine glared at Veil.

"Your name is Veil, right? You haven't yet made a report about this to the Hunters' Guild, have you?!"

"N-no, of course not. Actually, I don't really know *how* I should report this. I guess we can say that a meteorite came down from the sky and just happened to strike near where the bandits' base was located..."

Lafine sighed, sitting back down. "People will see through that. It's too implausible." She leaned her elbows onto the tabletop, burying her face in her hands.

"I-I'm sorry I let this happen," said Veil.

"Whatever. Let's just count it as lucky that no one else has found out about Lily's magic."

"Thanks."

With that, Veil and Lafine came to an agreement, leaving the culprit herself entirely out of the loop. A thick silence settled across the Alstea household which situated in an out-of-the-way corner of the part of the city occupied by commoners.

Veil cleared his throat and then looked at Lily.

"By the way, Lily..."

"Hm?"

Lily looked up at Veil, who sat beside her.

"I know this is a bit sudden, but have you thought about becoming a hunter? With your magical skills and a bit of training, I think you could be really good. Naturally, you'd still run the risk of forgetting to hold back, but I think that hunting would provide you with the perfect opportunity to master your skills."

Lafine's face was still buried in her hands, and before she could open her mouth, Lily had answered, her response practically exploding out of her.

"No way."

"Why not?"

"Because I'm going to be a *hero*."

Both Lafine and Veil went slack-jawed at this odd, unfamiliar word. Lily, by contrast, was smiling as innocently as she always did.

"You see, in the stories written by my favorite author, Miami Satodele, there are always these super amazing allies of justice. They're strong, and kind, and they save adults and children and men and women—well, everyone!"

"Is that what a *hero* is?"

"Yeah!"

Lafine's shoulders drooped, her expression skeptical. "Okay, but while you're off doing that, who's going to be bringing home the bacon?"

"Uh..."

Once more, Veil threw Lily a lifeline.

"I've got a proposal to make. If I could have Lily's help with more jobs like the one last night, I can pay her handsomely."

"Hm?"

Holding up a hand to stave off Lafine's objections, Veil continued. "There would be terms. The first being that you agree to never take any more jobs from *that* place."

"You mean the slum broker?"

Veil nodded. "Yeah. I'm sure you've already guessed, but only the worst kinds of jobs go through him."

Lily nodded back. "I figured. But then, what am I supposed to do from now on?"

"Basically, I'll accept jobs through the Hunters' Guild and then you'll help me with them. Depending on the work you do, I'll give you a percentage of the money I receive from the guild. That way, we can keep you—and that dangerous magic of yours— under my watch, *and* you'll be able to work."

"But I'm not dangerous! I'm normal. It's not like I'm gonna bite someone!"

Ignoring Lily's protests, Lafine stood up from her chair and clasped Veil's hand in her own. Her eyes sparkled—no—*glinted* with hunger.

"Will that really be possible? Um..."

"Veil. I'm a C-rank hunter."

Lafine nodded.

"C-rank. All right, yes, sounds good, Veil. Ah, but I do have one condition myself, if I'm gonna be lending Lily to you."

"Lending...?" Lily muttered.

Ignoring her once more, Lafine jogged into the bedroom, returning with a mask-like item, something that would hide only the eyes. Without waiting for Lily's approval, she affixed it to the girl's face.

"Wh-wh-what?! What are you doing?"

The mask was a bright purple and looked like a strange butterfly.

"Just shut up and wear it! I don't care if you make money as a hero or a hunter, but anytime you do work for someone, you're gonna wear this! And don't tell anyone your name! Not Lily *or* Lockwood!"

The moment she uttered these last words, Lafine covered her own mouth with her hands. Nervously, she looked to Veil, who was looking back at her, creases forming on his forehead.

"Lockwood...? Like the Margrave Neiham Lockwood?"

She had messed up. Lafine slapped her palm to her forehead, face falling. Seeing this, Veil frantically shook his head.

"Oh, no, um, no need to answer that... But, well, I see. So that's why you want to hide her identity."

Veil pondered this. As far as anyone was aware, the Lockwood family had two children, but neither of them was named Lily. Perhaps Lily was the child of some mistress Lord Neiham had picked up in town.

"As I am a hunter, allow me to at least make one thing clear. Lafine, you are not allied with those who attacked the Lockwood manor, are you?"

"O-obviously not! What are you *thinking*?! Let's get this straight—I used to work for the Lockwoods!"

Veil looked to Lily, questioning. Lily nodded. "That's right. She's been with my family for a long time. She's famous among the servants for not doing much work."

"Why you little—you shut your mouth already!"

As Lafine put her hands around Lily's neck, shaking her back and forth, Veil watched pensively. If Lily was the daughter of a mistress, and it had been necessary to conceal the very fact of her existence, she had surely had a difficult life until now.

Of course, Veil didn't quite have the full story, but neither Lafine nor Lily would ever tell him that. Having come to his own conclusions, he nodded.

"It's fine, Lily. Though they don't come from as important a place, there are a lot of kids where I live in the same position as you. No need to worry. I'll help you hide your identity."

"...Thanks?"

So, the three of them came to an agreement. Lily would get to be an ally of justice. Lafine would be able to benefit from the money she earned, while still ensuring Lily could hide her identity. And Veil would be able to keep an eye on Lily, who, he insisted, was an exceedingly dangerous person. Their goals aligned, the three of them shared a series of firm handshakes across the table. And thus, a mysterious masked hero was born—one that was soon to be seen all over the capital of the Kingdom of Tils.

"One more thing," Lafine added. "You were out all night, but nothing *happened* between you two, right?"

An awkward silence spread throughout the room. After a few beats, Lily tilted her head curiously at Lafine. "What do you mean?"

Meanwhile, Veil was frantically shaking his head. "It didn't! It wouldn't!"

"Then we're all set."

Lafine stood up on the seat of her chair and planted one foot forcefully atop the table, her long brown hair draping across Veil's face from above. She lowered her voice, curving her spine to bend down as she smiled coldly, and then whispered, "Because if Lily somehow ends up damaged goods, I *will* kill you. She has the makings of one of the most powerful mages in the world, and one day, I'm going to marry her off to a prosperous noble or a wealthy merchant. Actually, if all goes well, I could probably get her betrothed to a royal. Heh heh heh... I'm sure you understand why she is *not* to be touched by the likes of some two-bit C-rank hunter!"

"I-I'm telling you, I *won't*! M-my heart already belongs to someone else!"

Lafine lifted her head, her long hair sweeping back behind her. Her face had already returned to its usual bored expression— though she was still standing on the table.

"Okay. That's good, then. Make sure you look after her."

"I will..."

"Hm?" asked Lily Lockwood, nine years old.

She stared back and forth between her two protectors, totally oblivious.

CHAPTER 4 |

And Now, an Explosion

IT HAD NOW been two months since Lily and Lafine had arrived in the capital of the Kingdom of Tils. This was more than enough time for even a girl who lived as tumultuous a life as Lily to begin to establish something of a routine.

In the morning, she had a simple breakfast alone, prepared a lunch for Lafine, who slept until noon, and headed out for work. In the evening, she came home to make dinner for the two of them. Her work, of course, depended on the day. Some days Veil would request her aid on his hunting jobs, and some days she just helped make deliveries for the local grocer. However, unlike she had been a month prior, Lily was now working not as Lily Alstea, nor even Lily Lockwood, but as the mysterious hero with the violet butterfly mask—Hello World Mask.

At this particular moment, Lily had just collected her pay after a busy day of seven grocery deliveries.

"Thanks as always, Lily."

"Lily? Now who could that be? I have nooo idea what you're talking about," grinned Hello World Mask, refusing to turn around.

"Oh, right," the man corrected himself. "Miss Hello World Mask, could I ask for your help again tomorrow? My back's been strained lately, so honestly you've been a huge help."

Hello World Mask pivoted around. She gave a thumbs-up, just like the main characters of the stories she read, and nodded emphatically.

"Yes, anytime! After all, I'm an ally of justice! Whenever you're in need, just let me know! *Hu-hup!*"

She bounced up and took off, her feet pattering away.

"I don't get this game..."

Lily knew the old man was grumbling behind her back but pretended that she did not hear him. As long as her true identity continued to be protected, that was all that mattered... Though, of course, *she* was the only one who was convinced that this disguise of hers was effective.

Lily pulled a note from her pocket and gave it a once-over.

"Um, let's see, the next job is... Oh, nope, that's all for today."

Most mornings she did odd jobs around town, and most afternoons she helped Veil. Though she had yet to achieve a particularly cushy life, she was now making enough that she should be able to not only provide for her and Lafine's living expenses but also purchase one storybook every month as well—even if she had far less time for reading now than she once did. Still, she was having fun every day. She was fulfilled.

The first noon bell rang. Lily ran boldly through town, the butterfly mask still on her face, toward the park located near the city square. She stopped by a cart along the way to purchase a double orc cheeseburger and a drink for her lunch.

She sometimes thought about making her own lunch in order to save some money, but deliveries were not the only thing she did in the morning. Sometimes she helped unload carts, or had to go crawling around searching for lost pets and such, so it helped to be carrying as little as possible when she left the house.

"Ugh. I really wish I could use storage magic..."

WELL, CAN'T YOU?

In a rare turn, the nanomachines were the ones to initiate conversation.

"Huh? What?!"

Lily turned around in shock. An older woman walking down the road called out to her, "Everything all right, Lily dear? You seem surprised."

"Eh heh, I'm fine!" she said and then gasped, realizing her mistake. "Oh, no! Wait. My name is—"

"Ah, right, right. You're Hello World Mask, the ally of justice, aren't you? Thanks again for helping me clean out my gutters."

Lily put her left hand behind her back, flexing with the non-existent muscles of her right arm and nodded importantly.

"It was my pleasure! After all, I'm an ally of justice! Whenever you're in need, just call my name!"

"Ha! How lovely. You're adorable."

Incidentally, "Hello World" was a phrase that Lily had taken from one of Miami Satodele's books. The stories often involved various terms related to "science," the otherworldly magical system that appeared across all of the author's publications, and no matter what particular branch of "science" was involved, it seemed that the first, most basic spell invoked was always a set phrase: Hello World.

Ever since she had first read it, Lily had liked the ring of the words. It was a fun phrase, one that she couldn't help but feeling drawn to. And thus, she had named herself Hello World Mask.

After waving to the elder woman and watching her go, Lily replied to the nanomachines via thought pulse.

But I can't use storage magic. I could try imitating it, but I wouldn't even know how. I've never even seen it done.

AH, I SEE. MI—ER, THE OTHER MAGE—COMES FROM A STRANGE PLACE, SO SHE WAS ABLE TO PICK UP ON IT RIGHT AWAY. THE CONCEPTS MIGHT BE DIFFICULT FOR SOMEONE BORN INTO A WORLD WITHOUT THE SAME FOUNDATIONS OF KNOWLEDGE. IN REALITY, STORAGE MAGIC IS A RATHER RARE ABILITY.

Lily tilted her head. Who was this "other mage" they were talking about?

THOUGH, TO BE ACCURATE, WHAT SHE USES IS NOT TECHNICALLY STORAGE MAGIC.

I have no idea what you mean. Don't just sit there talking to yourself, Mr. Nano.

I THINK IF YOU CAN FIND A MAGE WHO USES

STORAGE MAGIC AND HAVE THEM TEACH YOU, YOU SHOULD BE FINE. I'M CERTAIN THAT YOU WILL BE ABLE TO REPLICATE IT WITHOUT ISSUE, MISS LILY.

It was then that Lily remembered that she *had* seen something like storage magic once before. When she was left all alone at the Lockwood manor and those four girls arrived, the smallest of them had used it to produce food and water, and saved Lily from starvation.

The spell that that girl used when she saved my life—was that storage magic?

THAT WAS NOT STORAGE MAGIC, AND IT WOULD BE IMPOSSIBLE FOR YOU TO REPLICATE. IT'S AN INCREDIBLY UNUSUAL TECHNIQUE, MORE AKIN TO "SCIENCE."

Whoa! What? Mr. Nano, you actually believe in "science"? Come on, that's just a thing from fairy tales!

Even Lily knew that "science" was a term coined by the novelist Miami Satodele. It was a pseudo-magic from another world, totally fictional.

NO. SCIENCE DOES, IN FACT, EXIST. EVEN MY OWN EXISTENCE IS SOMETHING AKIN TO SCIENCE. ELSEWHERE, THEY SAY THAT ANY SUFFICIENTLY ADVANCED SCIENCE IS AKIN TO MAGIC. BUT YOU DON'T HAVE TO WORRY ABOUT THAT.

I don't get it.

YOU CAN THINK OF "SCIENCE" AS AN INCREDIBLY UNUSUAL KIND OF MAGIC.

Unusual?

YES. FOR EXAMPLE, THAT PSEUDO-STORAGE MAGIC
UTILIZES A PLANE WHERE THE TIME-SPACE CONTINUUM
IS FROZEN, BUT SUCH CONCEPTS ARE UNEXPLAINABLE
BY EVEN THE GRIMOIRES OF THIS WORLD.

*Wha...? Wait, so the person you keep talking about is the girl
that saved me?*

I AM RELUCTANT TO ANSWER THAT QUESTION.
I HAVE NOT OBTAINED THE PERMISSION OF THE PER-
SON IN QUESTION HERSELF. AND SINCE SHE WISHES TO
LIVE AS A NORMAL, AVERAGE GIRL, I DOUBT THAT SUCH
PERMISSION WOULD BE GRANTED.

*I see... Well, that's a shame. Why would someone so amazing
at magic that she was able to heal my ears want to be a normal girl
like me?*

If Lily were that powerful, she thought, she would definitely
become a hero.

UH... MISS LILY, DO YOU NOT UNDERSTAND WHAT
THE WORDS "NORMAL" OR "AVERAGE" MEAN?

Lily still didn't know for certain if the mage the nanomachines
were referring to was the same girl who had rescued her, but she
hoped that she could meet that girl again someday and properly
thank her. Alas, she did not know her name, and thanks to the darkness, she had not seen her face well. All she'd been able to make out
through her hazy vision was that the girl was incredibly adorable.

Speaking of people whom she wished she could see again...
she was still worried about her family. She had asked Lafine about
them, but the woman insisted that she knew nothing. Were her

brother and sister doing okay? Were her mother and father in good health? Just who *were* the brigands who had attacked the Lockwood manor that night?

Lily felt her chest tighten, but she shook her head, determined to cheer herself back up. There was nothing that worrying could accomplish. So she ran along, chewing on her double orc cheeseburger, until she finally arrived at the plaza in the slums. There, she found Veil.

"Sorry I'm late!"

"No worries. We just got everyone assembled."

Beside Veil were ten children around the same age as Lily, some perhaps even younger. They all stared at her with wide, innocent eyes.

"Um...?"

"Oh, these are all orphans from the slums. They're basically my little brothers and sisters. We're going to take them out to gather some herbs today. They're all associate hunters."

"Whoa, that's awesome! All of you?"

"Don't look down on us just because we're G-ranks," one of the boys beside Veil grumbled indignantly. "You aren't even a hunter at all, are you? And what's with that weird mask?"

"Knock it off, Chimley."

The redheaded boy, Chimley, turned his head with a pout. Veil grimaced and continued, "Anyway, this is Hello World Mask, the mage who's been causing a stir lately."

Lily held out a hand proudly and declared, "I'm Lily—er, oh, uh, no. I'm Hello World Mask. Nice to meet you all."

Unsurprisingly, everyone assembled easily guessed that "Hello World Mask" was actually Lily.

"Our masked friend here isn't going to be helping with the gathering but with guarding everyone else as they work. We'll be venturing outside of the capital, where there are all sorts of monsters, like orcs and jackalopes."

Chimley, the redhead, spat angrily, "Come on, Big Brother! We don't need a brat like her. You can just guard us on your own, like always. She's not even a hunter—she's just gonna slow us down."

Veil looked at his shoes, scratching his head.

"Sorry, Mask. Please don't be mad about this."

Lily giggled. Her name was getting shortened into nothing, but she didn't really mind.

"It's fine! I'm not interested in being a hunter anyway!"

What she hoped to be was a *hero*.

Chimley scoffed. "Well, that's nice. You keep thinkin' that. Pretty little thing like you can probably end up the mistress of some rich old dude anyway. Then you'll be on easy street. Lily, was it? You should thank your parents for birthin' you with such a pretty face."

"Chimley!" Veil scolded, but Chimley just averted his gaze, clicking his tongue. Lily smiled back and shrugged.

"I have no idea if I'll be a mistress, but I am thankful to my mother and father! They helped me be born into a world full of so many wonderful sounds!"

Chimley knitted his brow, as if offended.

"The only people on my side are the folks here in the slums. None of us know anything about our parents. Clearly, you've lived a charmed life. Don't come walkin' all over us just so you can play around and make a little pocket change. We don't need you."

"That's enough!" Veil shouted.

"...Tch."

Veil was already aware that Lily's true surname was not Alstea but Lockwood. He was also aware of the tragedy that had occurred at the Lockwood home some months prior. Though there was no telling whether Lily's true father, Lord Neiham, was safe, it was a fact that he'd left Lily behind at the manor and not returned to find her. In other words, it was very likely that either both of Lily's parents were dead or that she had been abandoned. Whatever the truth, Lily was certainly not *blessed*. She was as good as an orphan.

And yet, Lily Lockwood was still smiling. Grinning, actually, with the corners of her mouth perked up and her pearly whites flashing as her eyes shone.

"That's so *stupid*," Chimley spat. "Who'd ever thank their parents? For what?"

Veil stepped over to Lily and whispered, "Sorry, Lily. Chimley's not like me or the other kids here in the slums. He was just abandoned here recently, so the wounds are still fresh for him. His parents..." Veil trailed off.

Whether she had been orphaned or abandoned, Lily was carrying a greater burden than Chimley. Veil could not possibly ask her to take pity on him. Yet she seemed to pay no mind to the other boy and his attitude. As far as she was concerned, every-thing about this world was still "fun." Even the fact that she was simply able to hear and talk to people meant that her world was much wider than it had ever been when she lived alone in her room in the Lockwood manor. She was moved by everything around her. All that she saw, all that she heard—it made her heart leap.

"It's okay, Veil. I understand."

"Let me make it up to you."

"No need."

How would Lily feel if Lord Neiham was still alive and had yet to come to find his daughter? She couldn't be sure. However, right now, she was thankful. This was not a lie. Still, who could say what the future might hold? It was possible to imagine that one day, even she might come to hate her parents as Chimley did—her parents who had taken only her siblings and left her behind, who had locked her away in her room simply because she could not hear. But for now, she could only pray for their safety. That was enough for her. She felt this from the bottom of her heart.

Perhaps having gotten all that he wanted to say off his chest, Chimley was now calmly talking to the rest of the orphans.

"Now then, let's get it together and get going," said Veil. "I'll be going up ahead, so you take the rear, Mask."

"Okay, got it."

Veil started walking, with a sword hung from his side, but the other children were equipped only with small gathering knives and baskets on their backs, and canteens on straps around their necks. Chimley also had a wooden sword in hand. By comparison, Lily was carrying nothing at all.

She intended to be back in the capital by evening, so there was no need for food. She was not a swordfighter, so she needed no sword. She did need water, but if she just sent out a thought pulse, Mr. Nano would bring her some.

Lily gently propped up the basket of the girl walking in front of her from the bottom, just enough that she would not be found out. The girl was so small that it looked like it must be difficult for her to carry. The baskets weren't heavy, but after walking around for a while, it would start to feel heavier, and in fact, the girl already seemed fairly winded. Yet the moment Lily lifted the basket up, the girl immediately looked back.

"Huh? Oh, um, thanks."

"No problem."

She had been found out. But that just meant that Lily could help openly, even lifting the basket slightly off the girl's back.

"U-um..."

"Hm?"

"I'm...Mel," the girl said, her voice small and faltering.

"I'm Lily."

"I know."

"Of course. Oh, but that's a secret right now. I'm H-H-Hello World Mask."

Mel put her hand to her mouth, tittering.

Gosh, this girl is adorable, Lily thought. Just then, she sensed a piercing gaze and looked up to see Chimley, who was walking second in the line, glaring at her.

"Uh—I..." she stuttered.

Uh-oh... Lily thought. *If I start being friendly with Mel, I wonder if Chimley will pick on her later...*

As Lily puzzled over this dilemma, Chimley stopped walking and calmly approached the girls. A drop of sweat fell at the base of Lily's neck as he glared at her hand holding Mel's basket.

Lily frantically withdrew her hand.

"Um... This... Well, I... Eh he he..."

In her mask, Lily looked very suspicious.

"Hmph. You okay, Mel? I'll take that. Gimme your basket."

Mel's gaze wandered between Lily and Chimley.

"Um. But..."

"Just give it to me!"

Chimley ignored Lily, snatching the basket away, wearing it on the front of his chest opposite his own basket. And, with that, he scurried back to his spot at the front of the line, immediately behind Veil.

Mel called after him, "Thanks, Chimley!"

Chimley only waved at her, not looking back.

Lily's cheeks relaxed. Somehow, she got the feeling she had just witnessed something beautiful. It was a good feeling.

"U-um, Miss?"

"Hm? What's up?"

Mel turned only her head back, hiding her mouth with her hand, and whispered, "Please forgive him... The way he acts, the things he says... That's just how he is, but he's not a bad person."

"No worries! I'm not mad."

With Lily at the rear, smiling a mysterious smile, the party separated from the main highway, heading into the grasslands. They would have to continue a while farther before they reached the grove where Veil and Lily had confronted the bandits.

Veil pushed through the tall grass, looking all around them. Chimley, with his baskets and his wooden sword, imitated him, surveying the area. Shortly, the two of them returned. Veil stood before the orphans and said, "It doesn't look like there are any monsters around here. Go ahead and start your gathering, everyone. Me and Mask will be keeping a patrol, so if you see any sign of a monster, you let one of us know right away, okay?"

"Okay!" all the orphans replied.

Well, all except for Chimley.

"Veil, brother, let me in on the patrol team. I could take down a jackalope myself. I can protect the others," he said.

"No." Veil shook his head. "There are limits to the sort of quests you can undertake based on your hunter rank. You're only nine years old, so you're still a G-rank, a guild associate. You're only permitted to do chaperoned gathering. In a year, when you're F-rank, you can start dealing with monsters."

Chimley pointed at Lily and shouted, "Well then, what about *her*?!"

"M-me? Huh?"

"How old are *you*?!"

"I'm nine," Lily replied.

"She's the same age! This isn't fair!"

Veil stepped in. "Stop it, Chimley. Lily already said she isn't a hunter."

"That's right," Lily declared immediately, "I'm a *hero*. I'm an ally of justice."

"Not now, Lily."

"Er... Sorry."

She shuffled back.

Turning back to Chimley, Veil continued, "Lily, who is not a hunter, receives no protection from the guild, or any pay. She's working at her own risk. But it's not like that for you. You receive regular work from the guild, and you get paid, too. So, if you violate the terms of the guild, they'll take away your badge, and you can never work as a hunter again."

"Grrr..."

"Just keep your eyes on the prize and hold out a bit longer, okay?"

Chimley irritably took up his basket and disappeared into the grass. Veil put his hand to his forehead, letting out a long sigh.

"Phew..."

"He seems pretty tough."

"I swear..." Veil shook his head, but he soon cheered up, clapping his hands and turning to the orphans still standing around them. "Come on, everyone. Let's start gathering."

The remaining orphans picked up their baskets and scattered around the area.

"Lily, I want you to guard the perimeter. I can only pay you out of my own guard fee, so it won't be much, but please look after all of them."

Lily flexed both her arms and grinned.

"Just leave it to me!"

"Oh, also, if you use any magic, limit it as much as you possibly can. That's an order."

"Y-yeah... Of course!"

"What's with that reply?"

"Nothing! Everything's fine."

But as Veil turned away, Lily raised a hand to her chin. How exactly did one go about *limiting* their magic?

The orphans had fanned out within a radius of a few dozen steps, crouching down to pick out anything that seemed like an herb and shoving it into their baskets. Veil was resting on a rock set at just about the center point of the group, cleaning his sword and occasionally glancing around, while the empty-handed Lily continued circling the outer perimeter. Once finished with his sword maintenance, Veil began to assist the other children in gathering, but even if Lily had wanted to help as well, she had no idea the difference between a weed and an herb, which meant she was in no position to be of assistance.

She threw her arms up, stretching out her spine.

"Mmm!"

The sky above the plains was clear, dotted with rolling clouds, and a pleasant breeze blew. Keeping watch was a bit of a tedious task, but it was not so bad to just take things easy now and then. Whenever Lily closed her eyes, she could sense all sorts of sounds. That alone was enough to stave off the boredom.

The wind blowing in from the direction of the capital rushed through the grass with a soft rustling but seemed to linger in one spot, with a sort of swirling roar. Lily opened her eyes and noticed a boulder in that direction.

"Hmm."

She closed her eyes again. From somewhere there was the faint sound of running water. Judging from the distant aquatic smell, it was probably upwind of her. She opened her eyes and spied a small stream, far in the distance.

"Heh heh."

This was getting fun. She was surprised to find how many things she could detect without even opening her eyes. Most likely because she had been born without one of her five senses, Lily Lockwood's remaining four had grown that much sharper.

Shff, shff, shff. That was probably the footsteps of the orphans, moving from place to place. *Flap, flap.* That would be the birds, flying out of the grass as they heard those footsteps. The gentlest footsteps were Mel's. Lily had already memorized the sound as the girl had walked in front of her in the line on the road. She knew Chimley's thumping step as well, and Veil's sturdy, steady rhythm.

As Lily stood still, her eyes closed, facing the distant sky, Mel approached her. "What's up, Mel?" Lily called out, not even blinking open her eyelids.

"What? Huh?"

Now, Lily opened her eyes to find Mel's surprised face before her. Lily had startled the girl.

"Miss, how'd you know it was me?"

Lily smiled broadly.

"Heh heh, I wonder."

"Magic!"

"Nope. I could tell by your footsteps and your smell."

"Huh?" Mel began sniffing her own clothing. "D-d-do I stink? But we all just had our regularly scheduled baths, and I've been taking good care of my hygiene..."

Lily shook her head.

"Oh, no, it's not a bad smell. You smell sweet, like fruit. It actually smells pretty tasty."

"Wh-wha...?"

Mel took several steps back, looking alarmed. Lily frantically redirected the conversation.

"How, um—how often do you have baths scheduled?"

"Um, well, someone taught us that staying clean would help us get jobs through the guild and from merchants, instead of through the slums. She's someone that big brother Veil really looks up to. Veil said that he's working his hardest as a hunter so that he can be a suitable match for her one day. He wants to be an A-rank."

"Wow, really?"

Of course, Lily had no idea that said person was, in fact, also her own benefactor. She turned her gaze to Veil to see him picking herbs and tossing them into the orphans' baskets. So as to keep things fair, he seemed to be favoring the baskets of the children who were falling behind the others.

Everyone here was part of the same party, and they would be paid by the guild as such. In other words, each child would receive the same reward, even though some children picked more.

"I should keep picking," Mel said, "so I don't slow everyone else down."

"Oh, let me help you then. Mel, can you show me which of these plants are herbs?"

"Sure! I'm looking for ones that would be useful for making medicine for *noo-trishenell suppelmints*, so that's these ones. When you eat these, it gives you lots of energy. It might even keep you up all night." Mel pulled an herb from her basket. Lily stared at it, memorizing the leaves. "Oh, but only ones about this size, Miss Mask. When they grow too big they get too *fighburr-us* and they get hard to process. So, leave those ones alone," Mel explained, pointing to some tall grasses.

Apparently, the grasses were all nutritional herbs that were overgrown. In front of them, Chimley was busy with his own gathering.

"Got it. Thanks, I'll go have a look."

"Okay!"

Yet as she turned, Lily felt someone's gaze on her back and turned to see Chimley glaring at her again. She had only been looking at the grasses beyond him, but apparently, he had interpreted this as Lily staring at him. Now, he was giving her the stink eye.

"Uh... Nope, okay, just smile, just smile. Okay."

Lily smiled back at Chimley, waving. The boy averted his gaze, unamused, and vanished into the tall grass.

"Gosh..."

She had thought that smiling could alleviate some of the tension between them, but apparently it had had the opposite effect. Human relations were a tricky thing.

Not realizing that Chimley had moved away from the group, Veil continued helping the other children with their gathering. Lily wondered if she should call for him, but given that his departure was clearly her own doing, she thought better of it and followed after the boy instead.

"Sorry, Mel. Can I give you a hand in a little bit?"

"Sure. What's the matter, Miss Mask?"

Lily pointed to the grass into which Chimley had disappeared.

"Looks like Chimley's wandered away. I'm going to go find him."

"Oh. But no fighting, okay?"

Lily certainly had no plans to do any fighting, but in truth, it would be up to her opponent. Still, she could not possibly say no to the adorable child looking up at her.

"Fine. I'll do what I can. Could you go and tell Veil, though?

And in case I end up going in the wrong direction, just yell for me if Chimley comes back."

"Okay, I can do that. Will you be okay by yourself? We're far away from the highway, and there's sometimes monsters out here."

"I'll be fine. I've got magic. Plus, I *am* a hero of justice, after all."

"Gotcha. Be careful, okay?"

If anything, the main difficulty would be not unleashing an excessive amount of magic. Lily couldn't risk burning any of the herbs they were here to collect. But she didn't need to worry about that anyway—not unless any monsters actually showed up.

Mel set down her backpack and ran over to Veil, but it wasn't as though he could go after Chimley. The other children were still here, after all. Leaving them alone would be failing in his duty as a guard. Lily would have to bring Chimley back on her own.

"See you in a bit!" She waved to Mel and rushed into the tall grass.

After a minute, Lily peeked back behind her, but everyone was already out of sight. The grass that she pushed through had leaves of the same type as the herbs Mel had shown her. Apparently, these were all overgrown specimens. Lily separated the grasses with her hands. They were strong and fibrous, and even if she trampled the shoots down, they popped right back up. This was proof enough of how effective they must be as an energy supplement.

"Ugh..."

Still, the fact that they were so tall meant that it was impossible to see Chimley. The field was practically a labyrinth. Thanks to the grasses growing up from the ground, she could not track his footprints. Plus, due to Veil's suggestion that the orphans maintain their hygiene, she could not track him by his bodily odor either.

Lily closed her eyes.

She listened for the boy, but the happy, productive sounds from the others back in the clearing overwhelmed all other noises.

"No use. I'm not getting anywhere."

She parted the stalks with her hands, stepping forward with her high, laced boots as she proceeded alone into the field. She could not see a thing. It was nearly as bad as moving through a deep, dark forest. After proceeding some distance, Lily stopped, strained her ears, and listened.

Her vision was obscured by the grasses, so even if she had happened to pass by Chimley, she might have no idea.

"Maybe I should head back?"

Just then, faintly...

She closed her eyes and held her breath, straining her ears even further. There, beyond the rustling of the vegetation and the cries of insects was the harsh, distinct sound of something running wildly through the grass.

She confirmed the direction and took off running. About fifty paces ahead, she tumbled right over something.

"Eep!"

There was a red liquid splattered over the roots of the grass. Blood. Surrounding the corpse of a single-horned rabbit. This was apparently what she had tripped over.

"A jackalope...?"

She may have had little sense of danger, but this was clearly a monster. And though it was dead, there were no cuts anywhere on the animal. Instead, there was a large dent in one part of its body, as though it had been beaten to death. Its pelt would probably be worth a great deal in this condition.

Chimley had a wooden sword. There was a good chance that this was his doing.

"What? Huh?!"

Shfshf-shfshfshff!

Lily heard the sound of something running through grass. No, more than one thing. Some*things* were running all around the area in an erratic manner, front to back and side to side.

"Chimley?" she called. Just then, something suddenly came flying at Lily from behind, bowling her over onto the ground.

"Gah! Ow!"

Before she had time to resist, her face was pushed down into the dirt after the rest of her. A large figure blustered over Lily with terrifying force.

"What're you doing?! Get up!"

"Huh?"

Someone wrenched her up by the hand, and she began running, legs scrambling.

It was Chimley. He was pulling her by the hand and running.

"Chim—?"

"Quiet! Damn it! *Damn* it! There shouldn't have been anything..."

At a distance of several paces, the grass on both sides was rustling, as though something was chasing after them. Even Lily could tell that they were being pursued by a horde of some kind of creature. Large monsters were hiding behind the grasses. As they ran, she caught glimpses of them. They were immense, with heads like wild boars and large, sturdy hooves for hands.

"Whoa—pig-heads! Are those orcs?! Wow! I've never seen an orc before!"

One orc leapt forward, as if to gobble Lily up, even as she shouted in carefree excitement. Chimley yanked Lily by the arm, swiftly changing directions.

"This way!"

"Whoa!"

The orc's large hooves struck the ground with a terrifying series of thuds. It tore into the earth, sending rubble flying. Even the sturdy grasses were wrenched up, roots and all, collapsing upon the ground.

"Erm..."

If something like that were to come down on her head, it would definitely splatter her brains across the ground. Apparently, Chimley had rescued her just in the nick of time.

He ran desperately ahead with Lily in tow. There was no direction now that was safe. They ran forward and back, left and right—any way that would take them away from the orc's approaching hoof-steps. At this point, even Lily had no idea what direction they had gone from their original location. Chimley, pale-faced, had likely lost sight of their return route as well.

Still, Lily thought gratefully, he was not letting go of her hand. That had to mean he wasn't a bad person.

"Damn it! If I just had a real sword..."

His wooden sword was probably what had taken out the jackalope, but now it was splintered and bent, as though it had already faced off with the orc's special weapons. At this point, it wasn't obvious whether it could still ward off an attack, and Lily thought she'd rather not find out.

Lily ran on through the grass, Chimley dragging her by the arm. Her breath was ragged. Her feet were beginning to hurt.

"Hff, hff...ugh..."

"Hey, no slowing down! We gotta run!"

Lily was a young girl, who had spent eight years of her life locked up in her room. While the nanomachines had unlocked phenomenal magical powers for her, she was almost totally devoid of physical strength.

"Chim...ley..." she huffed.

"What?!"

As Chimley turned his head back, Lily looked at him pitifully and murmured, "I'm...gonna puke..."

"Could you hold out for two freakin' seconds?! Puke if you need to—just do it while you're running! Don't stop moving! Also, if you get any of that on me, I'm seriously gonna kill ya!"

If setting the whole area ablaze was an option, warding off the orcs would have been simple. However, both Lafine and Veil had told Lily again and again that she had to avoid using overly powerful spells. If she altered the terrain around the capital any more than she already had, this might escalate into a military incident.

Even so...

The orcs were not easing up, continuing to mow down the herbs with their clublike hooves. At this rate, those same hooves were going to come down upon their heads before long. No one had yet taught Lily how to use healing spells, and if she were the one whose head was smashed in first, then there would be no chance of doing so anyway.

"Crap! Where'd Veil and the rest of them go?!" Chimley muttered.

It was then that Lily suddenly recalled—she had never seen anyone use healing magic, but she *had* seen the magic that Veil had used against the bandits. That Air Shot spell or whatever it was. She had asked him about it later, and he had explained it as a simple physical spell, in which he summoned the image of compressing air and then fired it.

Chimley was still holding her right hand, so Lily imagined the sensation of grabbing the air with her left, while she sent out her thoughts toward the nanomachines. In her tightly squeezed fist, she could feel the sensation of holding something solid and powerful.

This...this could work.

Just then, the grass parted right before their eyes, and a single orc came pelting toward the pair.

Its weapon-like hooves were already reared up high above their heads, ready to strike down upon them when the moment was right.

"Bring it!"

Chimley at once brought up his wooden sword. It caught the blow, but the wood splintered apart at the center, leaving him just barely enough time to avoid being struck by the orc's powerful hooves. Now, the sword was gone. The creature's goggling, furious gaze landed upon the pair. Chimley held his breath.

"Ee..."

Lily let go of his hand, aiming for the moment when the orc once more reared its hooves, aiming the bullet of air that was in her left hand straight into its shoulder.

"Take that!"

In an instant, the air exploded.

Firing the bullet in a certain direction and actually having it pierce the enemy were two separate things. In this case, the air in question had exploded on impact. However, it ruptured only for the orc, not Lily.

For a moment, Chimley could not believe his eyes or ears.

There was an ear-burning bursting sound, and then a hot wind suddenly blew down the sturdy grasses all around them as the orc vanished right before their eyes.

"........."

Of course, the orc had not actually vanished. Its huge frame had just been blown aside by an invisible force. Its body plowed through the grasses, striking into the ground and bouncing away somewhere into the brush.

Bits of meat and orc limbs rained down from the air all around them.

"........."

"........."

Finally, from behind Lily, who stood speechless, drenched in blood, Chimley timidly asked, "Was that...uh...some kind of... special...technique?"

In truth, what Lily had done didn't *look* much like magic. No matter how compressed, air is invisible. The more compressed the air, the higher the temperature grows, but naturally, heat isn't visible, either. In fact, all Chimley saw was Lily stepping forward and striking the orc in the shoulder with her left palm. Then, the orc had exploded, its body sent flying.

Lily, despite being soaked in the monster's blood, smiled— though the blood dripping down her mask made her smile a bit more eerie than usual.

"I can't do anything like that. I did tell you I was a mage, though."

"Um..."

Chimley withdrew his hand from Lily's outstretched hand.

"........."

"...Ee..."

As a somewhat tense moment passed between the two, the grass behind Chimley parted, and another orc appeared.

"Watch out!"

"Eek!"

Chimley put his arms up to cover his head as the orc's hooves came down. Lily, however, was already in motion, planting her boot in the space between Chimley's feet and thrusting her arms out on either side of him, plunging compressed air into the orc's guts.

"Hi-yah!"

Once again, a terrifying wind erupted, blood and spittle and innards spewing out from the pierced orc as it was blown backwards. Still caught in her stance, Lily muttered to herself, "Whoa, that's super useful."

This magic seemed to have become something entirely separate from the spell that Veil had thought up, but being able to blow an opponent away with a touch, practically without a thought, was far more convenient. Of course, Lily still lacked the means to control her power levels. As such, this was probably not something that she could use on a human opponent, she thought, even as she blew her third orc away with her bare hands.

Chimley, on the other hand, was utterly dead inside. He had just watched this girl, the same age as him, blow three orcs into husks bare-handed, sending them flying as though it was nothing at all.

"Ha ha ha! That was a cinch!"

Furthermore, she was wearing a blood-soaked mask upon her face and laughing...

Then and there, Chimley determined that what he truly feared were not the orcs that had just threatened their lives but the incredibly unsettling girl who went by the name of Hello World Mask, standing before him cackling, bathed in the blood of her enemies...

A set of knuckles came down twice: first, atop Chimley's head and then, atop Lily's.

"Ow!"

"Ouch!"

The pair looked up, annoyed, to see Veil glaring down at them, teeth bared. Needless to say, he had not been thrilled when they returned to the field where the others were gathering.

"B-big Brother, I'm sorry..."

"Why are you hitting *meee*?"

Veil folded his arms in front of his lightly armored chest and scowled. "Because you made me worry." He was flushed.

"Aw ha ha! You really are a sweet big brother, Veil."

"Well, obviously." Veil sighed in irritation and knelt down before them. "Chimley, why'd you go off on your own like that? Spit it out!"

"I-I... I wanted to prove to you that we didn't need to rely on this commoner girl who's not even from the slums. I was going to show you that I could at least take down a monster by myself..."

Veil's knuckles cracked down upon Chimley's head once more.

"Stop being such a brat. I always say that it doesn't matter where any of us come from, but you would be wise to remember that Lily isn't the family that abandoned you!"

"..."

"Instead of such ugly behavior as taking your anger out on other people, you should be thinking about everyone's continued survival. *Grow up*, Chimley."

Chimley hung his head, cheeks burning with shame.

"I'm sorry..."

"I'm not the one you need to be apologizing to."

Still looking at the ground, Chimley mumbled an apology to Lily, who was sitting beside him, "I'm sorry, Big Sister. Thanks for saving me. You might be a little shrimp, but you're really strong."

Big Sister? Weren't they the same age? And wait—had he called her a little shrimp?

She was not entirely certain which part of his words she should be focusing on, but either way, Lily felt a weight lift from her chest. It was tough to be hated by someone. Even if the only result of today was that she and Chimley could get along, that felt like a victory.

Then, Veil pointed at her.

"Now, Li—er, Mask!"

"Y-yes?"

She paled in the face of Veil's glare.

"You ran off after Chimley and didn't tell me. What were you thinking?"

"Um, I thought that if I didn't hurry after him, Chimley might get into trouble... And I mean, either way, everyone else was still back here, so one of us would've had to stay, right? Plus, I was the one that Chimley hated, so I thought I should take responsibility..."

The moment she said the word "hated," Chimley's shoulders began to tremble. His cheeks flushed even more deeply with guilt.

"Chimley didn't hate you," Veil sighed. "He was just lashing out. He doesn't know where to direct his anger, and you ended up being the target because you seemed so happy. Isn't that right, Chimley?"

"I mean... Y-yeah. I'm really sorry. I just feel angry all the time."

"I know."

Veil moved in front of Lily, who was hanging her head, as even she couldn't muster a smile. Again, he raised his hand. Lily bowed her head and closed her eyes.

But it was not his knuckles that came down upon her but his palm.

"Huh?"

Veil moved his hand atop her head, ruffling her hair.

"You really were a big help. Thanks for saving my little brother. As far as I'm concerned, you're a hero to all us poor orphans here."

Her cheeks flushed warm with happiness. It was the first time she had ever experienced this joy—of receiving not just payment for her services but a true *thank you*. A confirmation that she was needed. In all her days locked away in her room at the mansion, she could have never imagined this. This world was exciting, and joyful, and fun.

Plus, she had witnessed something wonderful. Though the orphans of the slums were not bound by blood, they were brothers and sisters who truly cared for one another, and even had a big brother who would earnestly scold them. She now knew what a beautiful thing that could be. Raised in confinement, Lily had never been praised or even scolded. In fact, she only ever saw her family a few times a year. The only person she ever shared a meal with was Lafine.

And so, she realized: This is what it's like to have a family.

Which made her wonder: What *had* been her idea of a family until now? People who left her behind in a dangerous place and never came to find her? Even in the books of Miami Satodele, she had never read about a family like that.

Her smile faded slightly. "Eh he heh."

"Still," Veil continued. "I don't need to have you making me worry. If anything like this ever happens again, you're going to tell me right away. As your employer, I'm going to demand that in the future."

Lily, who had kept her head bowed through all of this, now lifted her face.

"Thanks for worrying about me, Veil."

Until this moment, she had assumed he was only worried about Chimley.

"Well, of course. But now that you get it, don't ever do that again. Promise me."

He was almost more like her real family, Lily thought, than her true parents. If she had an older brother, he would probably scold her like this. So, she nodded, heartfelt and sincere.

"Yeah. Next time I'll tell you right away."

Veil smiled, satisfied, and put his hands on his hips. "Good. Now that we're done here, let's get you all over to the stream."

"Huh?"

Veil pointed at Chimley's backpack, which was bulging with the orc parts that they had been able to salvage.

"We're gonna process that. We have to finish letting the blood and divide it into edible and nonedible sections. If you'd killed them a little more cleanly, we could've sold them in town, but in this state all we can really do is eat 'em. Still, it would be a waste just to throw it all away."

Blood dripped from between the weave of the basket and onto the ground.

"Rejoice, kids! We're having an orc feast tonight, courtesy of Mask here! We can't just leave all this, so everybody eat your fill!"

Mel raised her hands and shouted, "Whoa! Yay! Thank you, Miss Mask!"

That started a chorus of voices, all shouting their thanks at Lily. Veil held up a hand, interrupting them. The clamor silenced at once.

"All right, now, let's divvy up the tasks. I'm in charge of the butchering team. Report and cooking team, you head back to the capital with Mask! Report team will head to the guild and turn in these herbs, and cooking team will go back to the slums and start the dinner preparations! Everyone, roll out!"

The children seemed to have been assigned these roles beforehand. They all sorted themselves neatly into their teams and began moving. Chimley followed after Veil. Mel took Lily's hand.

"Let's head back, Miss Mask! I'm on the cooking team, so I hope you'll be joining us for dinner!"

"Oh, I would love to. But Lafine..."

She would be waiting for Lily at home, hungry. She might even cry.

As Lily fretted, another orphan took her by the other hand, tugging.

"C'mon, Miss Mask, hurry up! The sun's gonna set, and we'll end up cooking in the dark."

"O-okay. Sure thing."

Lily walked forward, the two pulling her ahead and more children shoving her from behind. Her troubled expression turned into a happy one, and she smiled again.

If she brought Lafine back a souvenir of orc meat, surely she couldn't complain about Lily staying for supper.

CHAPTER 5 |

A Plot Unfolds

Lafine Alstea sat on top of the kitchen table in a boorish posture, pouring ale from a bottle down her throat. Outside the window, the moon floated in the sky, and moonbeams crept into the darkened room. The house was silent. All the city had already gone to sleep. The only thing to be heard was the sound of the wind.

She sighed.

Lily had not come home.

She set the now-empty bottle down beside her on the surface of the table and then looked out at the night sky. She saw the moon and the stars. There wasn't a cloud in sight.

"Guess she finally ran... Heh, well, that's fair..."

Lafine had always hated seeing that smile of Lily's, ever since the first moment she laid eyes upon her.

Lily had been born deaf, abandoned by her parents, essentially left for dead all alone in that room in the mansion. And seeing the girl's blissfully ignorant smile pointed her way made Lafine want to puke.

In her own childhood, Lafine had looked up to her father, a man who was strong and sincere. Though he came from common stock, he had taken up a sword and served his country as a soldier. One by one, he accomplished great feats in border skirmishes all around the kingdom—driving out monsters, rooting out bandits. When he was finally granted a knighthood by the king, their whole family had been there to celebrate.

Knighthood, incidentally, was only a quasi-noble rank, lasting but a generation. If he were to continue gaining such renown, though, there was a chance of his winning a peerage, which could be inherited by his children.

Lafine's father saved the weak and battled the strong. He wielded his sword in the name of what was right and was praised by peasant and royal alike. As a young girl, she was proud of him. She learned the art of the blade from him. She wanted to be just like him. He probably thought of her aspirations as nothing more than a child's fancy that had outlasted its time, but still, he put everything he had into teaching her.

Lafine was ten years old when she learned that her father had died.

One day, when she returned home, she had found her mother, weeping in front of one of her father's comrades. They had no idea who or what had killed him.

A knighthood could not be inherited. The family lost their status and returned to their lives as commoners. The extended family, who had been making their presence known in light of Lafine's father's rise to prominence, all seemed to vanish without a word. Granted, they had been commoners to begin with, and even after the knighthood, they continued living in the same home, so on the surface, nothing changed for the family. However, with their sole breadwinner violently ripped away, the Alstea family fell into ruin.

One day, when Lafine returned home, her mother, who had always been there to greet her, was nowhere to be found. She had simply vanished into thin air. For Lafine, it was just like the day she lost her father, except this time there was no one left.

It was then that she felt a shattering deep within. A shattering that could only be her heart.

She had no idea if her mother was alive or dead, nor did she care to know. And since that day, she had believed that this was just how family was. Soon, she cared about nothing. Everything in the world was terrible, and thus, none of it was of her concern.

Still, she did have to eat. So, she put her skills with a sword to use and lived for some years as a hunter. This was the first time that it occurred to Lafine that her sword skills, inherited from her father, were nothing like the knightly techniques the nobles employed. Her technique was not that of the stately, orthodox schools of the knights but a practical one honed in the throes of real life-or-death battles. As a result, her skills far surpassed other hunters of the same rank.

She was savage, ruthless, and indiscriminate. Whether she was up against monster or man, she would strike them wherever a blow could land. Legs, eyes, ears—she slashed them all. Killed all kinds of creatures. Artlessly. Watching her was like watching a beast or monster fight, said her fellow hunters, albeit with more of a sense of chivalry.

Morals aside, Lafine's skills grew rapidly, to the point that within a few years, she had earned herself a reputation. And it was then that the Margrave Neiham Lockwood took her on.

She had never truly wished to be a hunter. Offered a chance at an easier life, she accepted it without a second thought. At first, she had assumed that she would be his exclusive bodyguard. Apparently, she was wrong. Neiham saw her for nothing but her sex. In fact, when she was instated as a servant of the Lockwood house, her sword was confiscated, and she was made to wear a servant's uniform.

He often touched her. It was unpleasant. However, as long as she was safe, Lafine did not care.

The days went on like this, until one night, late at night, Neiham came to Lafine's room.

Yet Neiham's wife, Ivanna Lockwood, was sharper than most noble wives. So much so, in fact, that you might say Neiham could only acquit his duties as margrave thanks to her help. And the night that Neiham came to Lafine's room, Ivanna was already there with her, drinking tea. Lafine had thought the woman's visit an annoyance, but when Neiham arrived, Lafine pieced it all together. Ivanna was protecting her. Or, at the very least, she was protecting her own dignity as Neiham's legitimate wife.

The way that the half-dressed margrave had paled when his wife glared at him still made Lafine laugh.

After that, Ivanna forbid Neiham all contact with Lafine, but rather than drive her out entirely, she put Lafine in charge of her daughter, bowing her head to Lafine despite their difference in status.

"Please, take care of my Lily," she said.

Lafine wanted to puke.

What was the point of protecting a daughter they had already cast away? Was this an act of love or some way of assuaging Ivanna's guilt at abandoning the girl? Or perhaps just a facade—a feigned love that they could parade in front of anyone who knew about the child? Regardless of the Lockwoods motivations, being tasked with such a lowly, hypocritical duty put Lafine's teeth on edge.

Still, Lafine was now under Ivanna's protection, and so she decided to remain in the Lockwood home as a servant who did no housework. That was her right. She had been hired as a guard, not a servant, after all.

She grew distant from the other servants. She was the target of jealousy, even hatred, but that did not bother her. What did she care what the others thought of her? What did she care if she got fired?

However, years passed, and still, Ivanna did not dismiss her. Until, one night, tragedy struck the Lockwood home.

By the time any of the occupants were aware of what was happening, brigands had already infiltrated the mansion. Neiham and his wife took their son and their second daughter, Lily's brother and sister, and fled in their carriage. Only little Lily was left behind.

But, of course, that was just how family was, Lafine thought.

All of the remaining servants, save for Lafine, surrendered. Typically, bandits did not kill anyone who cooperated with them. They knew that killing people would bring down the might of the kingdom upon them, whereas a simple thievery involving breaking and entering would be more easily overlooked.

That said, it was not a happy fate that would await any good-looking female servants of marriageable age, and Lafine had other plans for herself. She had no concerns about maintaining her own chastity, but she also despised the thought of serving the men who had just disrupted her tranquil life, and so she hid.

The truth was that Lafine had not returned just to protect Lily that night.

From the bandit's perspective, there was no reason to think anything of value might lie in a child's armoire. So she had headed to Lily's room to hide from the bandits and dragged Lily into the armoire with her.

Lafine had done it all for her own sake. She *had* to hide Lily to protect her own life. And, just as she had intended, once the bandits determined that Lily's room belonged to a child, they had left the armoire alone.

Sometime after the bandits were gone, Lafine had left Lily, who was sound asleep, and slipped out of the now-abandoned mansion. Like the Lockwoods—and like Lafine's own mother, who had abandoned her—Lafine cast Lily aside.

She felt no guilt. That was just how this cruel, cold world had raised her.

And yet. And *yet*. When they were reunited, that little girl had *thanked* Lafine for saving her. This girl, who had walked an even more desolate path than Lafine, had given her *thanks*, of all things, with a cheerful smile no less.

How could she smile that way?

She put a bitter taste in Lafine's mouth, that Lily Lockwood. She filled her with an unnameable dread, as though she were some entirely alien creature. Lafine hated it. She was creepy.

And so, she decided to use her, this stupid, carefree girl, this irritating daughter of the Lockwoods. Now that she could hear, she had many uses. It was quite lucky that she had gained the ability to hear when her parents had abandoned her. She had good looks, and in just a few years she would probably be quite beautiful. And, as it turned out, she was possessed of an immense magical talent, of all things.

Lafine had no doubts that she would grow into a young woman that any noble or wealthy merchant would desire. It mattered not if she was main wife or mistress. Lafine would marry Lily off to someone rich and then leech off of her for the rest of her life, in return for the debt she was owed in saving her.

All that the world had taken from her, Lafine would take from this girl.

Or, so she had thought.

Lafine looked dazedly up at the moon from atop the table.

"Guess she finally figured it out..."

Lily might not ever come back. After all, the only other time she had not returned before the city was asleep was the day she had been deceived by the bandit gang.

Somehow, the quiet, empty house felt lonesome. It was the same house in which Lafine had spent her childhood with her beloved father, but now it felt terribly cold.

She put the empty bottle to her lips and tipped it up again. What was she to do with herself? Something ached within her chest—the same way that it had the night that her mother departed.

Finally giving up on the empty bottle, Lafine, still atop the table, wrapped her arms around her knees. This whole evening had been no good. She was definitely going to have a hangover in the morning.

Just then, the door slowly, quietly opened.

Frantically, Lafine lay down, right on top of the table, the bottle still in her hand. She squeezed her eyes shut and breathed as though she were sleeping.

"Ugh, it stinks in here. C'mon, Lafine, what're you doing sleeping on the table? If you roll over in your sleep, you're gonna fall and hurt yourself."

Lily's hand was on her side, shaking her, but Lafine stubbornly kept her eyes shut. There was, of course, a reason for this—one which she could not bear to have found out.

"I'm just gonna take this bottle, okay? It'll be dangerous if it falls and breaks."

"Mm..."

Lafine feigned a half-awake reply as the bottle was taken from her hand. Lily's footsteps pattered quickly away and then returned. Something blanket-like was packed under her armpits. Perhaps this was a bit of protection to keep her from falling. Lafine nearly laughed at this half-hearted safeguard but carefully suppressed it. Then, a cape was draped over her stomach.

"Okay, that should keep her from falling..."

The cape was still warm, so it was probably one that Lily had been wearing while out of the house. It carried a faint smoky smell, as if she had been eating meat somewhere. It now occurred to Lafine that she had not eaten anything since lunch.

"Good night, Lafine," said Lily's voice gently. "There's a gift for you on the kitchen counter. You can go ahead and eat that when you wake up."

"Mm..."

A warm fingertip traced over the corners of Lafine's half-closed eyes...wiping away the tears that she had been trying to keep from falling.

She'd been caught.

Lafine Alstea had been crying all night, just as she had the night that she realized her mother had abandoned her.

"You don't have to cry anymore. I'm sorry I was late. I'll always come home every night, so neither of us has to be alone. So, don't go crying just because you're hungry," Lily half-whispered, half-sighed. It was a gentle voice, like Lafine's mother's in days long past.

Lafine gritted her teeth, holding back a tremble.

Stop it.

Stop it. **Stop. It.**

There was the sound of Lily washing her face. Then she left the living room, and a door could be heard closing. Lafine sat up and wiped her tears with her sleeve.

"Why? Why are you always like this?"

Lafine did not yet know. She had no idea what to call this feeling that was bubbling up from deep inside her chest. She huddled into the still-warm cape, her head hung.

I really hate that little girl, she thought to herself.

The next morning, Lily awoke and washed her face, as usual. Her hair was a mess, and she was still a bit tired this morning, after staying out late playing with the kids in the slums.

Lily quickly changed and headed to the kitchen. She had to make breakfast for herself and lunch for Lafine, who would wake up at noon. There was still plenty of the leftover orc meat, so perhaps she could put that on some bread for her with some roast vegetables, Lily thought. However, as she opened the door, her eyes went wide.

"Morning."

Lafine was awake.

No way, Lily thought. *I must still be dreaming. Okay, okay, I better actually wake up now.*

"Wait, hang on! Why're you closing the door and going back into the bedroom?!"

"What?! This is actually happening?! I'm not dreaming?!"

"Need me to smack the sleep out of you?"

Stranger still, Lafine was not awaiting her breakfast. She was already frying orc meat in a pan. And now, she was asking whether Lily needed to be hit with said pan. On the table, there were already scrambled eggs and a fresh vegetable salad—*two* portions, one for Lafine and one for Lily.

"Um... Who are you? Where is Lafine...?"

"Excuse me?"

She had even changed her clothes already. She was usually in her pajamas until lunch at least, oftentimes going the entire day without changing out of them.

Was this the Twilight Zone?

"L-Lafine, are you going out somewhere today?"

"For a little bit."

With a gasp, Lily put it all together.

A date. With a man. That had to be what was happening here. There could be no other explanation for such behaviors as waking up in the morning, changing her clothing, and making breakfast—behaviors that were exceedingly normal for anyone else but totally aberrant for Lafine.

This was troubling. Lily would have to cancel all her jobs today and tail her. She gulped audibly. Having been raised on storybooks, in some things she had knowledge beyond her years.

"All righty!" Lafine served the fried meat onto both of their plates. "Eat up."

"O-okay."

She was certainly in a good mood. Lily had no idea why, but she was sure of this. Perhaps now she might get some answers out of her. Lily pushed her salad around with her fork.

"Hey, Lafine."

"What? If you've got somethin' to say about the cooking you can just make your own."

"No, it's good."

"Oh, okay."

Lafine averted her gaze, looking a bit bashful.

"Can I ask you something?"

"Depends."

"Do you know where my family is?"

For a moment, Lafine froze, fork in hand. But then she continued moving as though nothing had happened, rolling up a thin slice of orc meat and shoving it into a sliced bread roll.

"No clue."

"None?"

"No. I have no idea where they are *right now*."

Lily blinked. Was it notable the way she had said the phrase "right now"? Perhaps she simply meant that she had some idea of what direction Lily's parents and siblings had headed in on the night of the attack on the manor. However, after that, they had moved out of her sight, and she had lost track of them? That was probably what had happened.

Lily got the feeling that would be all the answer she was getting.

"I see. Thanks."

Lafine continued eating, not even bothering to nod. She seemed to be packing her food away in an unusual hurry. When she was finished, she quickly took up her plate and moved to the counter to wash it.

"Guess you finished all the chores."

"Yeah..."

"Thank you."

After she finished washing her plate, Lafine ran her fingers through her hair and tied it in a ponytail at her neck. Then, after securing a leather belt to her waist and taking hold of a shortsword she had picked up from somewhere, she headed to the front door.

"See ya."

"See ya!"

What did she need a sword for? Wasn't she going on a date?

"Ugh. This is so annoying. Why me?" Lafine muttered to herself as she left, a foul expression on her face. If she kept making that face, Lily was pretty sure there wouldn't be a second date in Lafine's future.

Lily quickly stuffed the rest of her meat and vegetables into her bread, shoving the whole thing into her mouth as she stood. She crept quietly to the front door and opened it—then froze in place. Lafine was there looking down at her, arms crossed beneath her large bosom.

"Don't follow me."

She'd been found out.

"Ayff hahweh..."

"And don't talk with your mouth full."

Lily swallowed.

"He he he. Sorry! I just wanted to see this boyfriend of yours."

Lafine's brow wrinkled, but then she relaxed, her gaze drifting up toward the sky. "You can't see him." She spat, looking vexed.

"Oh! So it *is* a date?"

"Yep. It's an adult date, and you're not ready to see that kind of stuff."

"Wha—?! A-an *adult* date?!"

"That's what I said."

Lafine bared her teeth, waving her hands as though trying to shoo away a wild animal.

"W-will you be home late then?"

"Depends. If I don't get back on time, just leave me some dinner. I don't need any lunch today, since I'm gonna eat out. But I'll be using some of your money."

"Oh. Okay."

Lafine turned to leave.

Lily raised her fist in a cheer. "Go get 'em, Lafine! I'll be rooting for you! Let me know if you need a few more coins for your date!"

"...Are you my mother?!"

Lily suspected that now that Lafine knew she might be tailed, she would definitely try to give Lily the slip. Clearly, something was going on here.

Ever since the night that they were attacked by bandits en route to the capital, Lily had suspected that Lafine could not have been any ordinary servant. Was that a dagger she had taken with her? A shortsword? Either way, she had her own weapon, and swords were not cheap. If a normal person who had no need to fight ever had a weapon, at most it was typically the sort of knives that noble women carried, should they ever need to end their own lives when spirited away by bandits—not a blade bigger than a kitchen knife!

What Lafine wore was a *sword*, however short it and her leather belt might be, and she seemed quite accustomed to carrying it.

"Hmm, wonder who it could be."

Having blown her cover with Lafine before she could even attempt to follow her, Lily donned her mask and set out for her morning work as usual. She had a favor to ask the grocer, and so first, she stopped by his shop, a rolled-up poster in her hand.

"Good mooorning!"

"Oh, hello there, Lil—er, Hello World Mask. What's this?"

"Um, it's a poster I made. I was going to ask if I could hang it up on your wall here."

She handed over the rolled-up poster, which the man quickly unfurled.

"Hm, I see. 'From shop deliveries and courier services to culling bandits and monsters—you name it, I can do it, all for a reasonable fee, paid on completion. Hello World Mask, ally of justice, at your service.' Ha! You drew that mask really well. Ha ha ha, *aha ha ha*! This is...this is..."

The grocer folded the poster in half twice and put it into the garbage.

"Trash!"

"Whaaat?!"

Lily put her hands on her hips indignantly, pouting at him.

"This is way too dangerous. Plus, you can't do that kind of false advertising. If you're gonna do business, your reputation is key. You're only nine years old, right? Lily, if you want to really be an ally of justice, you need to become a hunter and rise in the ranks."

"But it's not false advertising... And I'm not Lily..."

"The same goes for Hello World Mask."

Of course, the man did not know that Lily had already disbanded three separate bandit gangs, destroying two of their bases without a trace.

"But I worked so hard on that poster!"

"I'm sure you did. Okay, hang on..."

Perhaps feeling guilty at the sight of her crestfallen expression, he plucked the poster back out of the garbage, took an ink pot and quill and crossed out the "eliminating bandits and monsters" line in dark lines.

"I'll hang it up like this. You should add that you can locate lost items and pets. But then I'd also include something like 're-sults not guaranteed' on the last line. Most lost items never turn up, after all."

"Oof..."

Lily slumped over, dejected. However, she supposed that he could not risk tarnishing his reputation by displaying a poster that made false promises. She understood at least that much.

It would be fine, Lily thought to herself, perking back up. She knew in her heart that if she could just do every kind of job she could, soon enough she *would* be known as a hero.

She would earn herself a sterling reputation! It was time to fight!

"All right," she said. "Go ahead and add that!"

"Sure thing."

The grocer quickly penned the additions and tacked the poster to the wall of the shop.

"Looks good," he confirmed. "This should be good for both of our businesses, Lily. Definitely works in both of our favors."

"Yeah, thanks! Also, I'm not Lily! You're too young to keep getting my name wrong!"

"Okay, okay. Now, you should probably decide on some rates. How many silver will you charge for deliveries based on weight and distance? Better to agree on a charge in advance than argue about it afterward, right? It's tough out there, so if you set a low rate or let other people decide, no one's gonna cut you a break."

"I guess you're right. I don't really know anything about market rates, though. Do you think the Hunters' Guild would be able to help with that?"

"They might. But you aren't a hunter. As far as the guild would be concerned, you're a business competitor."

Lily's face fell. "Hmph."

"Why don't you let me help you? Don't worry, I'm not gonna ask for a commission or anything. If your business starts booming, that'll bring in more customers for me, too."

"Whoa—really? Thanks!"

Lily clapped, leaping for joy as the grocer looked on, his eyes kind.

With the poster now hanging over the grocer's counter, Lily began her usual routine of running around the capital, delivering fruits and vegetables.

Come afternoon, it was time to head to the slums. Thankfully, the gathering jobs that F-rank hunters did were typically daily tasks, so nearly every afternoon, Lily could accompany Veil and the younger kids on their excursions.

She headed right to the slums, so as not to be late. As she passed through the plaza, she caught sight of a familiar figure out of the corner of her eye. Almost reflexively, she ducked behind a building.

"Lafine...?" Lily whispered to herself.

Lafine was standing in one corner of the plaza, her arms crossed. Even from a distance, Lily could tell that she was talking to someone. Who was it? Her boyfriend...?

She giggled to herself. "Hee hee. Found you!" Slipping behind a pillar, Lily peeked out to see who Lafine was with. "Uh... N-no way...!"

It was *him*—the masked man who had tricked her into taking the bandit's job counting carriages. The slum broker.

Lily was shaken. *He* was Lafine's boyfriend?

But neither he nor Lafine was smiling. The man was flipping through his bundle of memos. This did not, in fact, appear to be a date.

What was she doing? Was she looking for work? With this dangerous man? Lafine, of all people?

"I wonder if I should say something..." Lily muttered, but as she stood there waffling, Lafine turned and left. Of course, Lily could follow, but she knew it was unlikely that Lafine would tell her anything. If she was going to be questioning anyone, she may as well try the broker. Lily approached the man. "Hello."

"What's with that mask? You some kinda pervert?"

"Oh." Lily removed her mask.

"Ah! You're the little lady from before. You want yer money? Kinda dragged your feet coming to collect, huh?"

The man put his hand into his breast pocket. However, before he could withdraw it, Lily said, "I'm good. You didn't get paid by those bandits, did you?"

The bandit gang that would have given him the money was now dissolved—by Lily herself. Presumably, this meant the broker hadn't been paid.

"Oh, figured out they were bandits, did you? How unlucky. It seems someone wiped them out before they could provide the payment."

The *someone* in question wore an uncharacteristically fierce expression. "Maybe," Lily said, "it's *lucky* that you didn't have to deal with any bandits."

"Not a fan, huh? That why you didn't come here before now to collect your pay?"

Naturally, the fact that the bandits' base had been destroyed had been reported by the guild to the Crown and was now common knowledge. The broker must have been surprised to learn this.

"Well, obviously! Why would I want to earn money from people like that?!"

The man withdrew his bony hand from his pocket.

"There's no such thing as dirty money. It all spends the same. Anyway, I'm surprised a soft and dumb little brat like you figured out who your employers were all on your own."

Well, to be fair, she had not figured it out all on her own. If Veil had not put the pieces together for her, Lily would have never been the wiser. She might have even ended up working for the bandits again, doing the same kind of job. However, she got the feeling that mentioning Veil's name here would only cause trouble for him.

"Don't condescend me. I'm Hello World Mask—the hero of justice who's been making a stir in the capital."

"Never heard of ya."

Lily's shoulders slumped.

"But seriously though, take your money. You did the job I gave you like a pro. Fair work gets fair pay. If you don't need the money, just give it to the kids in the slums or somethin'. They'll be thrilled."

Lily grumbled softly but accepted a few silver coins from the man and shoved them into her pocket uncounted.

"Stop bringing people jobs like that."

The man raised an eyebrow.

"All I do is pass on jobs to the people who want them. I've got no interest in either the clients or the people who take the work. I provide people with a livelihood. This business saves lives here in the slums."

"But it's dangerous!"

"Dangerous? There was nothing directly criminal about the job that *you* accepted. If you hadn't gone sticking your nose into things, you would've never ended up in any danger at all, would you?"

Lily frowned. "Well, that's true, but if I knew what the job was for, I would never have taken it! *I* might've been safe, but the information I gave those bandits would've put *other* people in danger!"

"And that's none of my business. Or yours. Now, are we quite finished here? I might not be very busy right now, but I'm not a fan of noisy little girls. So if you're done here, then I'd appreciate you getting lost."

Lily did not know what to say. She wanted to give the man a piece of her mind, but considering what she had just observed between him and Lafine, she decided to hold back for now.

"What were you talking about with that woman who was just here? Did she take a job? Another bad one?"

"Let's take these one at a time. One, that was an old acquaintance of mine through work. Two, she didn't take any jobs. That's not what we were discussing. And three, you have to stop with this 'bad job' nonsense. You don't know what you're talking about."

"Well then, what was she doing here?"

Even with half of his face obscured by his mask, she could tell that the man was smiling, ever so faintly. He held one finger up in front of his mouth.

"You know how this business is. I don't offer information about my clients on either side, nor do I try to find out too much about anyone. What you don't know can't hurt you. I told you before to get that through your skull. What's that woman to you, anyway? You know her? If she's just some stranger, you don't need to go butting into her business."

"I'm her family!"

The corners of the man's mouth lifted, this time so sharply that the mask moved with them.

"Family. *Pfft.*" A shiver ran down Lily's spine, but the man continued. "Gotcha. So you're worried about her."

"Y-yeah."

"Don't worry. I already told you, she didn't take any jobs. She just came here to buy some information."

"Information? You mean—"

As if anticipating Lily's question, the man held his finger up in front of his mask again.

"In a gray area like the kind I work in, there's something known as confidentiality. If I ever lose the trust of my clients, I'll lose my life, too."

She was at another impasse. He was not going to tell her a thing.

"If that's all your business here, then scram already. If you need work later, come back then. You're gettin' in the way of business," said the man. With that, he resumed flipping through his memos.

As Lily started to protest, an arm reached out from behind her, and a hand covered her mouth.

"Mmh?!"

"Oh, it's Veil."

Veil?!

Lily swatted the hand away and turned around to see. Sure enough, Veil stood behind her. Ignoring the man, Veil turned to Lily and said, "You shouldn't talk to this man anymore. I told you that, didn't I?"

"Y-yeah, but..."

But Lafine, she started to say, before closing her mouth. If the man was to be believed, Lafine had come to him to purchase information. She was concerned about what sort of information this might be, but at least she was not putting her life in danger just by buying a few tips. In fact, Lily thought, it might be more dangerous for Lafine if Lily were to mention her name in conversation with Veil here in front of this man. Though, apparently he considered her a familiar face...

Lily nodded. "Okay, yes."

"You were late, so I came to find you. Let's go."

Veil shoved Lily from behind and started walking, turning his back on the man and his memos.

"Sorry I was late, Veil. I was worried about something."

Veil didn't make eye contact with either Lily or the man in the mask. "Just how long are you gonna keep this up?" he spat. "Or hadn't you noticed? The slums are different now, thanks to the Crimson Vow."

The man did not reply. He simply flipped through his memos, ignoring Veil's words.

Veil let out a deep sigh and picked up his pace. Lily trotted along beside him, chewing her lip anxiously.

Once the pair was out of sight, the man let out a long sigh and slipped his memos into his breast pocket. He hadn't actually been reading them. He merely had not wished to meet the gaze of that steadfast young man.

He sighed again and then let out a whisper so soft that even the gentlest breeze might have swept it into oblivion.

"So...that's the secret eldest daughter of the Lockwood family. I'd heard that she couldn't hear, but clearly that's not the case. Hmm..."

There would not be any more customers today. He stood up from the fallen pillar that served as his chair and brushed off the rubble from his backside.

Somehow, he sensed busier days ahead...

Mel, Chimley, and the other children were scattered around a field, gathering herbs. Though they stood in the middle of the group, Veil spoke softly, his words for Lily's ears alone. "So Lafine left the house armed and bought some info from the slum broker? That is a bit concerning."

"Yeah."

The two of them had their backs to one another as they spoke, keeping watch in opposite directions. In order to properly chaperone the gatherers, it was crucial that they never let their guard down. After all, monsters could appear from anywhere.

"Veil, do you know that guy?"

"I do, yeah. Don't know his real name, though. For the past few years he's been coming to the slums, recruiting poor kids and orphans to do his jobs. As you're aware, he casts a pretty wide net, which pulls in both honest work and...less savory opportunities."

Lily tilted her head.

"But when I was there the other day, there weren't any other kids there besides me. And today I didn't see anyone besides Lafine. Who is taking those jobs? How does he stay in business?"

Veil scratched his cheek with his finger.

"Well, there's a bit of a story there, actually. I helped clean the orphans up a bit, so that they could get better work. I gave them clean clothes and helped them start bathing. Then, they were able to do the better jobs that kids in the orphanages usually did. It's cheaper for employers to hire the urchins from the slums, after all."

Mel waved at them from where she was gathering. Lily waved back with a smile and said to Veil, "That seems bad. Didn't that cause conflict?"

"It did. All I wanted to do was create a better life for my brothers and sisters, but I ended up making trouble for the kids at the orphanages. However, just when fights were starting to break out, a C-rank hunting party called the Crimson Vow stepped in to intervene and helped make peace between both sides. Thanks to that, we were able to find a peaceful compromise, instead of having the city break out into a full-on turf war."

A C-rank hunting party, the Crimson Vow. Lily had heard this party's name around the city. She hoped that she could meet them one day... (Little did she know, she had already met them, before she ever came to the capital.)

"Oh! So that's why you do so many gathering jobs."

"Yeah. All the urchins who are qualified as associate hunters have been allowed to take on these daily tasks, instead of taking jobs from individual townsfolk. That way their work doesn't overlap with the jobs the kids at the orphanage usually take."

"Don't they want to be hunters, too?"

"Some do. But still, they don't take each other's jobs. There's no set number of individuals who can do these daily tasks, though of course, if *too many* people went foraging, the market price of herbs would probably fall. But if that happened, they would probably get a rank promotion, or go mine ore or something."

A chaperone was necessary for associate hunters to take these gathering jobs. That, Lily now understood, was why Veil had not joined a party—despite being a full-fledged C-rank hunter—and why he never took jobs very far from town.

"I can't thank the Crimson Vow enough. The urchins have been able to get proper work, and the orphanages have received more funding from the Crown. Those girls are really amazing. They're on a completely different level from normal people like me."

A distant look in his eyes, Veil murmured, "I wonder if I'll ever be able to catch up with her..."

Lily grinned, flashing her pearly whites.

"I have no idea who you're talking about, but the way I see it, you're already pretty amazing yourself, Veil."

"I am? How's that?"

"Well, you've been looking after all of these orphans by yourself. I've tried working, so I know how hard it is to earn money. It's difficult enough on your own, but you have all these kids to watch over, too. That's pretty amazing."

"Ha ha, well these kids are my family, after all. Helping each other out is just what family d—"

Veil stopped short, falling silent for a moment. The wind blew across the grasses. The sound of the orphans' cheery voices tinkled in Lily's ears.

"I'm sorry. That was insensitive of me to say."

Lily Lockwood had been abandoned by her family. Either that, or her family was gone from this world. Neither could be considered a fortunate situation.

Even so, Lily replied cheerfully, "It's fine. I still haven't given up on my family. If they are out there in trouble somewhere, I'll go and save them, no matter where they are. But for now, if Lafine is trying to do something dangerous, I'm going to st—well, I don't think I could actually stop her, but I can at least maybe go and help her? She's my family, too."

Backs still facing one another, Lily and Veil looked over their shoulders, sharing a smile.

"Well, when the time comes, I'll help out as much as I can. Just let me know. Whether it's the Lockwoods or Lafine, I'm your guy."

"Thank you. But there's no way I could afford to pay you."

Lily felt the warmth of Veil's back shift slightly against her own.

"Ha ha ha. Well, Lafine is one thing, but when it comes to the Lockwood family, I think I'd just ask for payment from the margrave himself. Plus, the guild might even pay some reward, depending on the circumstances. But if I get nothing, I get nothing. As long as you keep helping us out here in the slums, that's all the payment I need. It really is hard for me to look after all of these kids by myself."

"Well, then—it's a deal," Lily said. "I'll look forward to it." The pair smiled at one another again. "You're a good person, Veil."

"I don't need to hear that from someone who got swindled by that broker."

Lily grimaced. "You're still going to give me a hard time about that, huh?"

Veil cleared his throat and pulled away. Joining the nearest group of orphans, he started to help with their gathering. Lily went over to Mel, peeking into her basket. Perhaps because Mel was the youngest of the children, she had made little progress. She always seemed to be falling behind. Somehow, she reminded Lily of herself, back before she could hear.

"All right. Lemme give you a hand, Mel."

"Thanks, Miss Mask!"

When she thought back to all the time she had spent locked away in that mansion, it was nearly impossible to fathom the enjoyment she took in her new life. There could certainly be worse things, she thought, than to continue living this way.

Contrary to what Lily had feared, Lafine returned home before the chiming of the second evening bell. The moment their eyes met, Lafine grumbled, "What? I told you to go ahead and eat. You didn't have to wait for me."

"Food tastes better when you eat together."

Lafine cringed visibly.

"Eating alone or with someone else doesn't change the taste of the food. And besides, it's tastier to eat something when it's hot and freshly made."

The lamplight swayed. The food sitting on the table had not been touched. Lily had started cooking around the first evening bell, so the meal had already gone thoroughly cold. Lily bounced to her feet.

"Well then, I'll just reheat the soup! It'll probably still taste good."

"Okay."

Lily lit the flame beneath the pot of soup.

"You're home late, Lafine."

"And you've been late before, too."

"True. I guess we're in the same boat," Lily giggled.

"Got a bit caught up," Lafine shrugged. "Couldn't get home until now." She shed her overclothes, letting out a big yawn.

"How come?"

"Well, because I was on an adult date."

Ah, so Lafine was going to lie to her. Even after buying that information from the slum broker. It made Lily a little sad. If something was bothering Lafine, she should have told her right away. Couldn't she rely on Hello World Mask?

"Really?" Lily stirred the soup, not letting her worry show on her face.

Lafine sat down at the table.

There was a long pause. Then: "What's with the quiet? I expected you to try to pry every single little detail out of me. I don't suppose you saw me while I was out?"

"N-n-nope, I didn't see you."

There was another long pause. A very long pause.

"Hmm..."

Lafine narrowed her eyes, her gaze almost painfully sharp.

"Lily."

"Mm-hmm?"

"What kind of work is it you're always doing with that hunter boy Veil? And where? In the afternoons, that is. I saw that weird odd jobs poster up at the grocer's shop, so I know you do that in the mornings. But that can't be earning enough for the both of us."

"Oh, I help Veil's younger siblings out with their gathering, and I serve as a chaperone to protect against monsters. They need the extra help."

"Monsters, huh? Depending on the type, I guess that's a lot better than you fighting bandits."

"Well, I say monsters, but it's only been orcs and goblins and jackalopes, so it's not that dangerous."

Lafine slumped over the table, letting out a deep sigh.

For some reason, Lily's heart was racing.

"Well, I guess that's all right. An opponent like that doesn't stand a chance against you. Just don't go doing anything too dangerous."

Lily poured the warmed soup into a wooden bowl, hands trembling faintly.

"Lafine, were you...worried about me?"

Lafine whipped her head up. "I'm not worried about *you*. I'm worried about my own future. You, as my little sister, are going to get married to a noble or a wealthy merchant someday. I won't forgive you if you go do something weird and mess that pretty face up."

Marriage, huh? Lily couldn't even picture it yet.

"I see... I'll be careful."

"You'd better."

Lily set down the bowls and sat across from Lafine.

"Plus, if you get hurt, who's going to take care of me? Let me make this clear: We would probably both starve to death."

"But the breakfast you made this morning was sooo good!"

Lafine turned her face down to the salad on her plate as if to escape Lily's gaze, a pained look in her eyes.

"W-well, obviously. Nothing I made would ever taste bad."

"Of course!"

Though Lafine's face was turned down, when Lily looked closely, Lily could see her expression was soft. As soon as she noticed Lily's eyes on her, Lafine's expression hardened swiftly.

"Just eat already," Lafine barked. "I'm sure you're hungry."

"I am."

And then, the scene at their dinner table was the same as it always was. Lily monologued happily about all that had happened that day, and Lafine ate in silence, nodding every now and then. Lafine never shared any thoughts about the food, but she ate up all of Lily's cooking without fail. Sometimes, she even went back for seconds.

For some reason, this made Lily Lockwood almost happier than she could bear.

The next morning, Lafine woke before Lily and made breakfast again. Like the day before, she was making preparations to go out. But, of course, she would not say what she was going out for. After she saw Lafine off, Lily left the house as well. And so, she had no idea that, shortly after her departure, a group of mysterious men in hoods and robes arrived at the empty house.

In a practiced fashion, the hooded men shared a series of hand signals and then unlocked the locked door, slipping easily inside. After checking all the rooms to confirm that no one was home, they looked to one another, shook their heads, and left without touching a thing.

Lafine, who stood in an alleyway watching this unfold from start to finish, returned to the house as soon as they had left, checking every corner of every room. After finishing her cursory check, she wiped the sweat from her cheeks.

"Looks like we may've opened a can of worms here."

Tailing Lily and watching the house for some time had paid off. To think she'd witness thieves breaking into her own home! The men had left no traces behind, either. There was nothing missing, and naturally, nothing new. Politely, they had even left the sack full of silver coins that she had purposely set out in an obvious location. They were not thieves, and clearly, they weren't deliverymen.

She put a hand to her mouth. "This is bad…"

In fact, it would have put her at ease if they *had* stolen something. The fact that they had taken nothing meant that they had some business with one of the two members of this household. It was unlikely that they were mere bandits. Of course, the fact that they had managed to pick the lock flawlessly also meant that they had likely done so before.

Lafine could only imagine what this meant: that this had something to do with the Lockwood family—and that meant that the men who had attacked the manor that night had not been after money.

Neiham Lockwood was an influential noble, a margrave who possessed both the reputation and the experience to be entrusted with safeguarding the borders of Tils. He may have been a worthless man who was ruled by his controlling wife, but there was no question as to whether he deserved his title. He was not a duke or a marquis, merely a margrave, tasked with protecting the regional areas from other lands—a task well within his capabilities.

So, if Lafine was correct that the thieves had not been after money, then this was most likely tied to someone who felt that the margrave and his family were a nuisance. It could be some other powerful noble within Tils who had his eyes on the margrave's lands, or if not, someone on the other side of the kingdom's border. In other words—spies from the Albarn Empire to the south.

Lafine sighed and put her head in her hands.

No matter what, this was already too much for a mere former hunter to be dealing with. However, if it turned out their enemies were international spies, that became an even bigger issue. She couldn't do much about something that should rightly be handled by the Crown. There was probably little they could do besides disguise themselves and run away. Moreover, there was a fairly strong chance that it *was* the Empire they were dealing with. After all, if it were a matter of internal rivalries, the noble in question would have already put their name forward as inheritor of the margrave's still-unsecured lands. There was no reason that the king would leave such a crucial border unguarded in perpetuity.

"So the Albarn Empire is behind this..."

This was something much bigger than Lafine had ever imagined. Her heart was beating so fast it hurt.

At first, she had simply been acting on a whim, beginning the search for Lily's family in a bit of out-of-character frivolity. But now, she had come upon something far more outrageous:

the revelation that the Lockwood manor had been attacked, in the dead of night, by agents from the Albarn Empire, of all places.

How had they found her now? There should have been almost no one who was aware that Lafine Alstea was concealing the eldest daughter of the Lockwood family: only Lafine, the girl in question herself, and Veil.

"That boy! *Him...*!"

Lafine didn't know anything about the boy or his background, other than he was a C-rank hunter who hailed from the slums. It was Lafine's own fault for letting it slip that Lily was the sole remaining Lockwood, but it was even more foolish of her not to have kept a closer eye on the boy.

She was letting strangers get too close to Lily.

Lafine grabbed the sack full of coins and hung it at her side. For now, she would set out post-haste, and she would make Veil talk. Depending on how many people knew what, Lafine and Lily might have to abscond from the capital.

"All right."

The moment she stepped out of the front door, she came face-to-face with one of the hooded men. He flashed a sneer.

"Are you Lily Lockwood?"

"...?!"

For a moment, Lafine's face froze in shock, but then, she simply smiled. "Do I look that young to you?"

"Oho! Sounds like you actually know her."

Crap. She'd gotten carried away.

At least, Lafine was quick to react. Quicker than the hooded man.

She clicked her tongue, drawing her sword and swiping at the man from the side. The sound of steel rung out as the man caught Lafine's shortsword with his own blade just in time.

"You little bitch..."

"Out of my way!"

She kicked the man away with a foot to the gut.

"Whoa!"

As the man stumbled backward, Lafine clicked her tongue again and took a quick step back into the house, violently kicking the door shut. She bolted the door from within, though she knew this would provide little obstacle to the men who had already broken in earlier that same morning. Next, she ran to the bedroom, leapt up on the bed, crossed her arms over her chest, and hurled herself through the window. She landed in the alleyway and immediately took off running.

Soon, she heard a shout. "Around the back! Don't let her get away! She's not the girl, but we can probably use her as a hostage!"

With the sounds of many footsteps rounding the house, Lafine pelted down the alleyway, nimble as a stray cat. She jumped over piles of refuse, turning corners and slipping through the gaps between houses, using back alleys to make her way to the slums.

In terms of swordsmanship, Veil was well ahead of the curve for a C-rank hunter. Still, his reaction was nothing short of miraculous.

As he and Lily walked through the slums toward the outside of town, leading their gathering troop, a shadow suddenly appeared overhead. For a moment, he wondered if a cloud had moved in, blocking out the sun.

Even Veil had no idea why he drew his sword in that moment.

Yet some instinct made him act, withdrawing his sword from his belt as he simultaneously shoved Lily back and then caught the flashing steel that came cutting down from above, slicing through the air.

"Wha—?!"

"Found you!"

Lily stumbled backward and fell on her backside. Her eyes went round—Lafine had just leapt out of the air behind them, her unsheathed sword bearing down on Veil. They locked blades, before Veil shoved Lafine back with his superior strength. Lafine fell several steps backward and shouted to Lily, "Lily, get away from him! He's with the enemy!"

"Huh? What? Lafine? What?"

Lafine moved to shield Lily, who was still too disoriented to move. She kept her guard up, the point of her blade still leveled at Veil.

The other orphans were startled and confused, their eyes wide.

Lafine was sweating, shoulders heaving with ragged breaths. Across from her, Veil was lowering his blade with one hand, holding the other arm out as a counterbalance.

"H-hang on now, Lafine! What do you mean 'I'm with the enemy'?"

"Don't play dumb! You sold Lily out to the Empire!"

Lafine dashed forward, slashing her blade diagonally. Veil deflected the blow, retreating.

"I have no idea what you're talking about!"

Lafine kept on him with one blow after another, steps nimble and erratic as a wildcat, Veil catching every blow with practiced precision. As he sliced down to repel another one of her diagonal slashes, Lafine continued in one fluid motion, turning about and redirecting the energy of her swing to ward him off.

"Whoa!"

The blade scraped at the surface of his skin, leaving a faint scratch on Veil's forehead. Then, Lafine came twirling at him again, her skirt billowing.

"Hold on!" Veil cried. "Just listen to m—gah!"

Veil halted her blade and then knocked it right into the ground, stepping on the flat of it with his heel and burying it into the dirt.

No less than a moment later, Veil found his chin struck—by the toe of Lafine's boot.

"F-footwork?! So you're not just good with a sword..."

Without hesitating, Lafine took this opportunity to free her sword. She pointed the tip right at Veil, kicking low off the ground and aiming for his thighs.

Lafine's sword fighting was not characteristic of the chivalric technique used by knights. It was a wild, unpredictable art she had learned from her father. There were no set stances here, nothing that would pass for common sense. Should the need arise, she even knew how to throw her own sword and fight empty-handed. To any normal knight or swordswoman, this would be utterly nonsensical.

Even so, Veil held his own. He repelled her unpredictable motions with speed and accuracy. Still, he was sure that, had he not been able to practice with a certain absurdly fast and powerful member of the Crimson Vow during his school days, he would not have been able to stay on his feet.

Sparks and the sounds of ringing steel filled the air.

"Lafine, stop it!" Lily shouted, but her voice was drowned out by Lafine's.

"This morning, my home was attacked by brigands involved with the margrave incident! They were looking for Lily! They wanted to abduct or assassinate her! Besides us, *you* are the only one who knows about her!"

"Just calm down already! I haven't said anything to anyone!"

Veil took the smallest hop backward, avoiding a low blow aimed for his ankles. If he left too large of a gap, the next moment would probably see him dismembered.

"Liar! There is no one else with a connection to both myself and Lily who knows her true identity!"

Lily, who had been trying to move between the two of them, stopped short. Veil gritted his teeth, avoiding the tip of Lafine's blade with a twist of his body.

"Fine! I guess I've got no choice!" Veil shouted as he gripped something in his left hand. "This might hurt a bit. Please don't hate me!"

It was just an air bullet—a simple spell. But although it was nonlethal, it was also invisible, so it was nearly always effective against an opponent who had never seen it before, even if that opponent was a skilled A-rank hunter.

"I'm the one who should be saying that! Once I've got you pinned, I'll make you talk!"

Lafine, meanwhile, drew a long, needle-like weapon from her boot with her left hand, still wielding her sword in her right. This hidden defense had been the ace up her sleeve during quite a few battles against other humans during her time as a hunter. Like Veil's air magic, it was very effective against an opponent who had never seen it before—hence, the reason for her keeping it concealed.

Both sides kicked off the ground, when Lily's voice rang out.

"There is! There is someone else!"

Both pitched forward, losing their balance.

"That broker knows me, and also you—doesn't he, Lafine?!"

Lafine looked puzzled.

"By broker, do you mean that guy in the slums?"

Lily, now becoming annoyed, balled her fists and shouted, "Yes!"

"How'd you know I was buying information from him?"

"Because I got a bad job from him before! The one that Veil rescued me from! And also, I was watching when you met up with him! Although, he wouldn't tell me what it was that you wanted information about."

Veil let out a sigh of relief and slipped his sword back into the sheath at his waist.

"Phew... It looks like we've found the culprit."

"But he shouldn't have known there was a connection between me and you," said Lafine. "Nor should he have known your real identity. I didn't let anything slip to him. I may as well tell you now: I was trying to get information about the whereabouts of the Lockwood family—but there was no way that alone would've been enough for him to figure out the connections between you, me, and the Lockwoods."

"Yeah, well, but after that, I was worried about what you were doing, so I went to ask him! He wouldn't tell me, but... Oh, I see. That must have been enough for him to figure out who I was..."

It was all coming together. Lafine slapped a hand to her forehead, sheathing her own sword. A cold wind blew past them as she folded her arms over her ample chest and looked sheepishly to Veil.

"Ah, um..."

She had launched a surprise attack and actually tried to kill him based on a false assumption, but Veil, the target of this violence, only stood with his own arms crossed, a troubled expression on his face. Lafine, on the other hand, looked as though she was practically about to cry, as she balled her fists and put them to her mouth, turning her upper body away demurely.

"V-Veil... Mr. Veil? I'm... I'm sooo sorry!"

There was no reaction. After several moments, Veil turned back to the orphans.

"Okay, everyone. You *cannot* tell anyone else about what just happened here. People's lives depend on it. Also, we're not going to go gathering today. There's something I need to do."

The children, who had been looking forward to the excursion, groaned in disappointment, but Chimley and Mel pushed the others from behind and kindly herded them away. Then, only the three—Lily, Lafine, and Veil—were left in the corner of the slums.

Just as Lafine was about to apologize again, Veil bowed his head deeply toward her.

"Sorry. Looks like the slum broker made trouble for you."

"Huh?" Lafine was stunned. "No, uh, I mean I'm the one who should be apologizing..."

Lily tilted her head to the side. "Why are *you* apologizing, Veil?"

Veil sighed. "That guy is... Well, he's my big brother. Me and the other orphans here."

As previously stated, once people in the slums reached a certain age, they tended to disappear. Some young men became hunters and went to live on their own, and some girls became lovers to wealthy merchants or nobles. In other words, there was hardly anyone who chose to remain in the slums after they were old enough to have other options.

Veil's older siblings were no different. Once they became adults at fifteen, they left the neighborhood behind.

Veil had decided to remain in the slums because he didn't want to abandon his little brothers and sisters. He hoped that if he became a hunter, and helped his younger siblings achieve positive things, they could change the face of the slums entirely.

"I had thought that I was the only one from the slums who had the idea to stay here, but apparently I was wrong."

Veil did not know the man's name. In the slums, no one had names unless they offered one up themselves or were given a new one by their fellows. And so, this man was known only as Big Bro.

"He used to be so responsible. This was when I was about five. Though there wasn't any way for all of us to get hunter qualifications or individual work like there is now, until he was fifteen, Big Bro spent all of the money that he earned taking care of the rest of us. We didn't have a luxurious life, of course, but we had at least one piece of bread every day, which at the time we were thankful for. Everyone loved him."

However, once he turned fifteen, Big Bro had left the slums behind, just like all the others. The next eldest, Big Sis, looked after the children, but naturally, the moment she came of age, she stepped into a beautiful carriage and never looked back.

That was just the way it was. Back then, Veil had never even thought to question it.

Incidentally, once the girl known as Big Sis had become the eldest, there was a sudden increase in job requests. In the slums, where they often lived hand to mouth, this was a welcome development.

When the seasons changed, and Brother Dahl became the eldest, he told Veil—then the second eldest—about the slum broker. He was a mysterious figure, his eyes obscured by a hood, his nose and mouth hidden by a mask. His voice was muffled through the cloth so that one could tell only that he was a man. It was thanks to an introduction from Big Sis that Dahl had known of him, and he introduced Veil to the man in turn.

Veil, however, realized something. It was around the time that this broker had first appeared that life started getting better for the orphans of the slums. Thanks to the jobs that this broker offered, hardly anyone was left starving.

Who was he? Veil burned with curiosity about this man.

One day, he happened to glimpse the broker when he had removed his mask. His face was that of the nameless Big Bro, who had left the slums when Veil was only five years old.

Yet even after his identity had been discovered, the broker continued quietly doing his job. There was a not insignificant number of cases where one of the jobs he'd offered brought trouble in its wake, as he didn't distinguish between good work and the bad, but even now, Veil thought of it as an accomplishment on the man's part that the number of starving children had decreased over the years he had been operating.

"Then, I realized something."

There was a way to support the slums *without* leaving them behind. That was why Veil became a C-rank hunter—so that he could keep providing the children of the slums with the means to live through daily work.

Time passed by, and the first thing that Veil did upon graduating from the Hunters' Prep School was to bring new order to the neighborhood. First, he helped the children keep their bodies and their clothing clean. As a result, they would be able to accept jobs directly from the merchants in town. This, however, caused a bit of a conflict.

When the urchins from the slums began setting their sights on the odd jobs in town, they began taking work away from the orphans who lived in the orphanages. This was something that Veil had not predicted. However, the C-rank party, the Crimson Vow, had succeeded in bringing both sides together, and the matter was resolved without incident. Thanks to their efforts, the orphanages began receiving more funding from the Crown, and worries about one group taking work away from the other faded. Additionally, now that Veil had been able to recruit the children of the slums as hunters, they could do daily tasks from the guild, further improving their quality of life.

"Eventually, the children weren't even aware of the broker who had been supporting the slums. Our Big Bro was forgotten by the very people for whom he had stayed here."

Now, the only people who took jobs from the broker were ignorant newcomers like Lily, or those children so young and lacking in physical strength that they could not even go out gathering—though even these young ones could normally live reasonably comfortably on the money their older siblings brought in.

Even so, Big Bro continued to appear in the middle of the slums, with his stack of memos, and would for as long as there was even a single person around to take jobs from him.

"He wants to be the final safety net for the slums, even if it means that he falls into ruin himself. All I want is for him to be free. He doesn't have to keep sacrificing himself for the orph—"

Veil cut himself short. Lily was grinning hugely at him and began to crow excitedly, "He really *is* a good person, then! He's like the hero of the slums! He stays here, supporting everyone behind the scenes! That's so *cool*! The way he's going about it is wrong, but, wow, I really admire that!"

"Y-yeah. I guess you're right. A hero...huh? I see. That's true."

Lafine teased Veil, a devilish smile on her face, "Really makes you look stupid, huh? And here you are, always trying to do the *right thing* to support the slums."

"Uh..."

"No, wait!" Lily quickly added. "I mean, you're like the father of the slums, Veil. The Papa!"

"That still seems like a step down from hero..."

"Also, I'm not that old—at least not yet." Veil smiled softly. "Anyway, I'm the only one who knows the broker's true identity. Not even Big Sis or Dahl knew. So, I'm the only one who can stop him. I want him to get away from this dangerous life. I want to let him know that the orphans of the slums can thrive now, without anyone else suffering."

Lily nodded fiercely.

"I want to help him, too. Plus, we have to figure out this Lockwood problem sooner or later."

"Yeah. This involves us, after all. I'll do what I can to help, both with Big Bro and with the Lockwoods."

"Okay."

Lafine, who had been sitting on a toppled barrel and listening, hung her head and put a hand to her forehead. All she had meant to do was seek out a little bit of information about Lily's family. But now she knew she'd opened a whole can of worms. No matter how desperately she brandished the truth before this pair's eyes, they were unlikely to back down.

Plus, they were still up against the Albarn Empire.

Now that the agents in question knew her name and location, she would never be able to escape this. She certainly could not return home, lest she be spotted and spirited away. She already knew too much. All she could do now was prepare for the worst.

Lafine sighed. "I've determined the location of the Lockwood family. And I know why they've been attacked and imprisoned."

Both Lily and Veil whipped their heads around, taken aback.

"But before I say anything more, I have to ask you: This is going to be incredibly dangerous—do you still want to know?"

It was a pointless question. The pair nodded at once.

"Of course we do."

And so, that was that.

CHAPTER 6 |

Farewell with a Smile

THE CARRIAGE ROCKED along the now familiar road that connected the capital of Tils to the border town governed by the Margrave Lockwood. Lately, a lot of people had been traveling away from the currently unmanaged border town to the much safer capital and other cities. Naturally, there was almost no one traveling in the opposite direction. The only people foolhardy enough to travel to a place where war loomed on the horizon were mercenaries, hoping to make a name for themselves in battle, and those engaged in the sort of shadowy professions that they could not speak about with others.

As such, there were only three people within this carriage: Lily, Lafine, and this time, Veil. It was a bit lonesome, but the fact that they were able to speak about their current situation without reservation was a blessing. Lafine spoke first.

"The night that the Lockwood manor was attacked, the Lockwoods fled the scene in their fastest carriage. Given that they haven't shown their faces since, I had assumed that they were hiding out somewhere, but now it seems they were waylaid by agents from the Albarn Empire somewhere en route to the capital and dragged off to some secret prison near the border."

"Is that what you found out from Big Bro?" asked Veil.

"Yeah, it is. It's pretty rough, but I did get a map, too."

Incidentally, the slum broker, Big Bro, had not shown his face since giving Lafine this information. There were two possible reasons for this: Either he had been taken out by spies from the Albarn Empire or paid off with instructions to make himself scarce.

Veil hoped for the second explanation to be true, although he realized that it was probably unlikely.

"Plus," Lafine continued, "there's some evidence to support this. Most importantly, that the kingdom has not abandoned its border. In fact, it seems the king moved immediately to secure the border, sending his troops out to the unsecured area right away."

"So, a provisional border guard...?" Veil asked suspiciously.

Lafine shook her head.

"No. Defense of the border is already bolstered by a military patrol, around not just the towns, but the plains, the mountains, the coastline—everywhere."

"So they're looking for my mother and father?" Lily wondered.

"Correct. Which means it's possible they'll be locking down the national border, hoping to catch any secret agents from the Empire who might try to exit Tils."

Veil covered his mouth with his hand in dawning realization. "So that means the agents responsible are still wandering around Tils, unable to return home."

"Bingo. Meanwhile, the Lockwoods are their hostages. That's the info that your 'Big Bro' sold to me, anyway. It does seem that he likewise sold the information he got from me and Lily—about the secret eldest daughter of the Lockwoods—right back to the agents, though. What a wild informant, selling information to both sides at the same time!"

"My apologies."

Lafine snorted. "Well, I'm certainly not going to hold it against you. You've been looking out for Lily, and I've already caused plenty of trouble for you... That said, I'll be holding you to your promise to make sure that Big Bro of yours is held accountable, once you find him."

Sitting alone on the bench opposite Lafine and Lily, Veil clenched his fingers atop his knees. Then, he looked up at Lafine, eyes filled with determination.

"Yeah. I'll need some time before that, though. When we find him, can you give us a little time to talk, just me and him?"

Lafine's face tensed. "Come again? Sorry, but right now, your Bro is a traitor to the kingdom. I can't just let that go."

"I know. I just need a few minutes."

As Lafine scratched her head, her mouth twisted as though she had just tasted something bitter, Lily wrapped her arm around Lafine's, admonishing. "It's fine, Veil."

"You little...! Just how soft can you *be*?!"

"*I'm* the one he sold out, Lafine."

Lafine looked all the more bitter but clamped her mouth shut. "Jeez... Fine, do what you want..."

"Thanks."

Then, Lafine yanked her arm free of Lily's. She poked Lily in the nose with her pointer finger, eyes narrowing.

"And you."

"Huh?"

"How do you feel about your parents, the Lockwoods?"

"How? I mean, they're my family."

"That doesn't change the fact that they fled and left you behind, whatever their reasons were. I was there. I know. Your brother and sister aside, do you not at least hate Neiham and Ivanna?"

Lily's eyes went wide.

"You get it? They abandoned you."

"H-hey now, Lafine. You don't have to put it like..."

"Quiet. This is important. If it weren't, we wouldn't be staking our lives on it," said Lafine, holding up a hand to hush Veil. She continued, "Veil and I are the only ones here. Lily, I want to hear how you *really* feel."

"How I...really feel...?"

It wasn't like she hadn't thought about it. No matter how she tried to justify it to herself, on the night of the attack, her mother and father had abandoned her. They had taken her siblings with them when they ran, but they had left her all alone, knowing that she very likely wouldn't have the resources to save herself. That much was certain.

It had been impressed upon her that the Lockwood family had no need for her—by her own parents, no less.

But, perhaps, had they had a bit more time, they would have taken her along, too?

Reality—and Lafine—were not so optimistic.

"Lily, if you're in this to get revenge or tell your parents how much you hate them, then we should stop here. There's no need for you to risk as dangerous a situation as this for some people who are worthless to you. Don't worry about Veil's Bro for now. If you want revenge on your parents, you can leave that to the imperial spies."

"Yeah," said Veil. "I agree. This carriage ride could be a watershed moment for you. I would never judge you if you wanted to turn back now."

Lily stared hazily into the distance. Then she grinned, the way she always did. Or rather, she tried to, but her mixed-up emotions only manifested as an equally mixed-up expression. Finally, she opened her mouth and spoke, her voice trembling weakly, "Is it wrong to love them, when they don't love me?"

Lafine and Veil both gulped, their expressions identical.

"As long as I just don't ask for too much, I'm sure I wouldn't be a burden on them, right?"

Both of the adults' eyes opened wide, their expressions twisting with sorrow before they averted their gazes.

Seeing this, Lily was certain that she had given the wrong answer. So, she frantically added, "A-and anyway, Mother and Father aside, someone has to look out for my brother and sister. They're still too little to know anything..."

Suddenly, something squeezed tightly around her. Lafine had wrapped her strong arms around Lily, who looked as though she might be on the verge of collapse.

"Lily. You really are stupid. More than I ever imagined," said Lafine. "No, far, *far* more than I ever imagined."

"Lily," Veil chimed in, "I won't say that I understand everything that you're going through, but my parents abandoned me in the slums, so I can guess a little bit of what you're feeling. So can I say something?"

Lily nodded weakly from within Lafine's arms.

"I don't think you need to decide anything about your family now. When you see them again, you just need to hit the Lockwoods with everything you feel in your heart in that moment. And when that happens, Lafine and I will be right there beside you."

As he spoke, the comforting sound of Veil's voice vibrated all the way through her chest, and the warmth she felt from Lafine's body seeped into every corner of her own. Lily felt she had known such happiness once, long ago, when she had only just been born, but not since then—not until now.

"Yeah."

As the carriage swayed onward toward the border, Lily smiled happily, listening to the sound of horseshoes and wagon wheels.

The crackling of the bonfire echoed throughout the night.

The three had set up camp in the shade of a boulder out in the fields. Partway to the border, they had paid the driver their fares and hopped out on the side of the road. The moment the driver had received his payment, he turned around and double-timed it back to the capital.

Though they had passed many carts and travelers along the way toward the capital, they had not seen anyone else heading southward, away from the city. An uneasy atmosphere had arisen in the wake of both the attack on the Lockwood manor and now the border blockade—and the people were seeking refuge wherever they could. There were credible rumors among the citizens of the capital that the Albarn Empire would be attacking at some point in the coming days. On top of that, Lafine told the other two, the number of men at the blockade would be proportional to any incoming army. Plus, if any large-scale war broke out, the king would order them all to evacuate anyway.

"...or so I'd like to think," Lafine finished, her hands over her face.

"If we were to take out the agents from the Albarn Empire in order to save Mister and Missus Lockwood, do you think that might pull the trigger?" asked Veil.

"I don't think so. It would be one thing if we were already at war, but for now, both nations ostensibly want to maintain the peace. I doubt Albarn would want word to get out to other lands that they had been sending secret agents into Tils. If our plan succeeds, Albarn will probably just wash their hands of those agents—or even try to write them off as bandits."

"They'd feign ignorance?"

"Yep. At best, those agents will end up indentured in the mines. At worst..." Lafine dragged her thumb across her own throat. "The Empire'll vanish them to keep them from talking."

Lily pursed her lips. "Really? Those poor people..."

Lafine's face twisted. "Listen, kid. Those guys might have killed your entire family. We have no idea where they are right now and what these guys might be doing to them. So don't be such a softie."

"I guess you're right..."

"I'll say this once: While they might be keeping the margrave and his wife as bargaining chips, your brother and sister are worthless as hostages. From their perspective, there's no value in keeping them alive. I need you to understand that. There's no point in pitying the enemy. Got it? You cannot hesitate if we have the chance to strike them down."

As Lily's expression clouded, Veil hastily added, "But they also must be aware that murdering your siblings will put them in danger of much harsher punishments. Even if they can't escape indentured servitude, they'll likely want to avoid execution. So I'm pretty sure they won't be killing anyone pointlessly, even if they aren't useful in the negotiations."

"O-okay."

Lafine glared at Veil.

"Cool it, buddy. Could you not keep blowing her up with all this hot air? If she hesitates, *we're* the ones who are going to end up dead."

"That may be true, but let's remember there's only so much we can reasonably put on a nine-year-old's shoulders." Veil grimaced.

Meanwhile, Lafine took a warm drink in hand and started to sip.

Lily could not help but watch the scene with a smile. What fun this was, being with her two friends, in the midst of an adventure.

As Veil looked to Lily, she grinned wide, all innocence. "It'll be fine, Lafine. I may not look it, but I'm pretty good at negotiating. You already know that all I have to do is show off a bit of magic, and everyone agrees with me right away. So, I'll just hit them with something when we get there. *Ka-boom!*"

Veil raised his eyebrows. "That's not negotiation, that's just intimidation."

Lafine shoved him aside, flexing one arm. The herbal tea in her cup went flying, splashing across Veil's arm.

"Ow!"

Lafine ignored him. "Yes! That's right! You keep up that fighting spirit! If you can avoid a battle, you should always avoid it! The easiest victories are the sweetest!"

"I'll do my best."

"Yep, yep." Lafine nodded. "You just take it easy. Even if we mess up and can't go back to that house, we can just go crash in the slums where the imperial agents won't find us. Ha! This is working perfectly!"

Veil, who was busy blowing on the burn on his arm, looked up at her indignantly.

"Hey, wait! I've already got enough little brothers and sisters to look after..."

Lafine put a hand on his shoulder in an overfamiliar manner and gave a cutesy wink, followed by a thumbs-up. "Thanks a lot, Big Brother Veil! Hee hee!"

It was her patented congeniality attack.

"Y-yeah, you're welcome...Big Sis...?"

"Ugh!"

A painful counterblow. It shook Lafine to her very core.

"Well, I mean, you *are* older, right?"

Lafine grabbed Veil by the throat, squeezing and shaking him back and forth.

"I'm supposed to be your *little* sister! Were you writing me off as some kind of old spinster just because you're young?! Is *that* how you see me?! It's not that I haven't been able to get married, I just don't want to! Don't make assumptions about me!"

"N-no, that wasn't what I... Gah! Why are you like this?!"

"Ah ha ha."

Suddenly, the pair froze.

"Ah ha ha ha ha ha ha!"

Lily had burst out laughing. It was not her usual cheerful giggle but a full-on belly laugh.

Lafine and Veil looked at one another, cracking a simultaneous grin. A gentle breeze blew across the isolated field...and then, the very next moment, Lafine seized Lily's chin with her right hand, so tightly that one could almost hear a crack.

"Ho ho, and just what is *so funny?*"

"Uh? Aaaaaah! I'm sorry!"

Lafine was furious.

As Lily flailed, Lafine pulled her hand away from her. Veil was already reaching for his sword. However...

"Don't move."

Realizing what was happening, Veil froze and hung his head. He was suddenly aware of a knife blade being held to Lafine's neck. He pulled his hand away from his sword and lifted both palms into the air.

They were fully surrounded by a dozen men.

Lafine clicked her tongue. Though they had chosen an inconspicuous spot to camp, it had been foolhardy of them to have lit a bonfire and roasted meat. The scent carried far and wide on the wind. In a flash, there was another blade at Veil's neck, and he was being bound with rope.

"Damn it!" Lafine spat, facedown on the ground with her hands tied behind her back. Her weapons had been seized, and a foot pressed down upon her spine. "Ow! Hold it! Is this how you treat a *lady*?!"

"Idiots! Do you think bandits care about your gender?" asked the offender. "You'd be in a lot worse trouble if anyone else had attacked you."

Lafine glared up at the man from the ground. "Well, thanks for the advice! In that case, are you gonna let us go home quietly?"

"Sure. If you don't do anything stupid. Don't get us wrong, though. We won't go easy on you just because you're a woman. You're gettin' the same as any man would."

In other words, the man was suggesting, if they resisted, they would be killed.

Lafine grumbled, spitting out grit, but she did not speak. There was nothing she could do for now but wait. And Lily, meanwhile...was making a commotion.

"W-w-w-w-wah! B-bandits!"

No one had even bothered trying to restrain Lily. Clearly, they had not even factored her into the equation. Not only was she female and a child, but she was entirely unarmed. Even a mage would normally have had some sort of staff.

"That's right, we're bandits. You just play nice and no harm'll come to ya," the youngish man said calmly and plainly, an almost pleasant expression on his face.

All of the men appeared to be in their twenties or thirties, physiques honed from daily training. Their outfits were all different, but they were each equipped with a longsword. They were clearly well trained, moving swiftly into formation. Strictly divided in their roles, some were in charge of threatening the hostages and some in charge of binding them, some in charge of keeping lookout and some in charge of backup. Furthermore, they worked silently, not even employing hand signs. They kept their conversation to a minimum, their movements sharp and efficient.

"Look for food and valuables," commanded the one who seemed to be the leader. After making sure the hostages were fully immobilized, several of the men began rifling through their things. They took Veil's longsword and Lafine's shortsword, scabbard and all, along with the sack that Lafine had at her waist and the food in Veil's knapsack.

"Lotta food in here."

"Well, that's a relief."

They handily shoved their findings into the leather sacks that they were carrying and then silently nodded at one another.

All of the little group's food and travel funds had now been taken. Next, the men kicked dirt over the bonfire and swiftly left, vanishing into the night. In a lot of ways, they had been lucky. The men had taken only their valuables, food, and weapons, eschewing the snatching away of young women that often happened during such attacks.

The leader, the last to depart, turned around and said to Lily, who was standing stock-still, "Sorry, Little Miss. We gotta work hard to make a living out here, too."

"B-but, that's no reason to go taking other people's things! You're doing something really bad," she replied weakly.

The leader grimaced, taking a few silver coins out of the sack and tossing them at Lily's feet.

"Here, that should be enough to get you all a few days of food."

His voice was flat, so Lily could not tell what he was thinking. And while the gesture seemed kind, then again, those silvers had belonged to the travelers in the first place.

"You aren't that far from the border town. I'm not really in any place to be saying this, but I wish you safe travels."

And with that, the leader vanished into the night as well.

Once he had departed, Lily took the knife that was hidden in Lafine's boot and cut through her bonds.

"Are you okay, Lafine? Those guys were really pushing you around..."

"It's whatever. I'm just annoyed. I'll definitely be getting back at them for this."

Lafine stood and took her knife back from Lily, cutting the ropes binding Veil.

"He he, guess that went pretty well, huh, Veil?"

"Yeah, it did. I'm honestly surprised how quickly we reeled 'em in. Guess Big Bro's info was good."

Freed from his bonds, Veil stretched his wrists and then the rest of his body. Then, he dug under a rock, unburying two unsheathed swords, one long and one short. The weapons that had been inside the sheaths the bandits took were only wooden replicas. They had been whittled to the same thickness as a steel blade, but they were little better than stage props, useless even as practice swords.

"Miss Lafine."

"Thanks."

Lafine caught her shortsword from Veil as he chucked it over, sticking it through her sash in a practiced fashion.

The information that Lafine had purchased from the broker was roughly as follows:

Not long after the members of the Lockwood family went missing and the army of Tils set up their blockade of the border, an enterprising bandit troop had started running amok in the area. Casualties were few, and they hardly ever abducted anyone, so neither the guild nor the military had come after them.

However...

Big Bro had made the conjecture that the margrave and his wife, fleeing danger on the night of the attack, had hidden themselves somewhere between the border town and the capital, but their location had been discovered by agents of the Albarn Empire. They had, he guessed, been captured. However, thanks to the king's swift decision to lock down the border, the agents in question had been unable to return to the Empire.

At this point, the men had two choices: betray the Empire and surrender themselves to the kingdom or take up work as bandits.

Given that they had taken the margrave hostage, even if only for a short time, there was no question that if they surrendered themselves, they would be enslaved. Meanwhile, the Empire would deny all knowledge of these men, abandoning them to their fates. Truly, the only choice they had was to take up as bandits and bide their time until the blockade was dissolved.

With this information in mind, Lafine had suggested, before leaving the capital, that they intentionally camp in the area where the bandit attacks had been taking place, choosing a location that was hidden yet purposely conspicuous. The plan had been a great success, as the so-called bandits had appeared on the very first night.

There was no debating the fact that these "bandits" were agents of the Empire. No matter how you looked at it, there was nothing bandit-like about them. They even conducted themselves with knightly chivalry.

It would be easy to wreak a bit of havoc in a place like this. They could just have had Lily use her magic. However, they still did not know the location of the Lockwoods. Depending on the strength of their loyalty to the Empire, torturing information out of these men might prove impossible. So, instead, they allowed the men to believe they had successfully robbed them and then followed after them.

This plan would have been impossible to implement if the men knew what Lily looked like, but for better or worse, no one even knew of Lily's existence within the Lockwood household. They might have their spies, but even so, these agents were in a foreign land. Even if they were aware the margrave's secret daughter existed, no one would have had any idea of what she looked like.

"Let's tail 'em. Lily, can you really tell where they went? It's pitch-black out."

"I can! The spirits will tell me!"

"Wha...?"

Ignoring Lafine's questioning gaze, Lily closed her eyes and sent out her thoughts to the nanomachines. *Mr. Nano, are you there?*

YES, INDEED. I AM EVERYWHERE.

So you already know what's going on then, right?

OF COURSE. LET'S KEEP THOSE MEN UPWIND...

The wind began to blow, unnaturally, in a different direction from the way it had been blowing just a moment before. Obviously, this was the nanomachines' doing.

So they won't be able to notice me from my smell?

YES.

Are you saying I stink?!

NO IDEA. WE CANNOT DEEM PHENOMENA GOOD OR BAD IN TERMS OF HUMAN SENSATIONS, AS WE DO NOT THINK IN OLFACTORY, VISUAL, OR AUDITORY TERMS. IT'S MERELY, UM, THAT IT DOES APPEAR THAT YOU HAVE AN INDIVIDUAL FRAGRANCE.

"Wah..."

Lily sniffed her own arm.

"What are you doing?" asked Veil curiously, leaning closer to her.

Lily leapt back, screaming, "Wah! N-nothing! Veil, you pervert!"

"Wha?!"

The young man was shocked to hear this accusation—one that had never once been levied against him in his entire life. Lafine patted them both on the back.

"Enough! Just hurry up and follow them! I shouldn't have to tell you all this, but if they get away, there goes all of our food and money!"

"Th-that's true. Um, it's dark, so both of you give me your hands."

"Huh?"

"Why?"

"Hurry up. They're gonna get away, aren't they?"

Without waiting for confirmation, Lily took Lafine's right hand in her left, Veil's left hand in her right, and took off running upwind.

"This way. Just try to keep up."

"O-okay."

"All right..."

For some reason, all three of them were biting back the same grin, but in the dark of night, none of them noticed.

They paused at the crest of a shallow hill, beneath the verdant greenery of a patch of evergreen trees. A faint orange glow illuminated the night sky in the basin below. In a hidden corner of the valley, there were lights. By straining one's eyes and peering through the gaps in the trees, it was possible to catch sight of some kind of structures. The glow of lamps seeped faintly from a building there at the edge of the basin. There seemed to be people moving around, too, though it was hard to judge how many.

"That's probably it."

Lily stopped walking. Lafine and Veil, still holding her hands, stopped as well.

"What is that? Since when is there something like that within Tils?"

"Looks like some ruins. Pretty spacious ones. Could practically be half of a village."

Ruins. So, they were using some undiscovered ruins as their hideout. Lily strained her eyes. She could not see them, but her mother and father, her sister, and her brother were in there somewhere.

"Phew..."

They had run fairly far. Somehow, mysteriously, Lily had managed to keep her breath as steady as the two adults behind her, who had longer legs and were significantly more physically fit.

Mr. Nano, did you do something to me? It's amazing—I'm not tired at all!

I HAVE DONE NOTHING. THIS WORLD CURRENTLY HAS NO EXPLANATION FOR THE CONCEPT OF ADRENALINE, BUT BECAUSE YOUR MIND IS CURRENTLY VERY EXCITED, IT IS TRICKING YOU OUT OF FEELING ANY PAIN OR FATIGUE. INCIDENTALLY, HOWEVER, IF YOU *DO* WISH TO HAVE "SOMETHING" DONE TO YOU IN ORDER TO STRENGTHEN YOUR BODY, I WOULD BE HAPPY TO DO SO. SHALL I?

These were the spirits that had already brought upon a dramatic alteration in Lily's physiology: the restoration of her sense of hearing. If she were to carelessly mention something like body strengthening, she just might end up transformed into a beastgirl or demon. Imagining this, Lily quickly replied, *I-I'm fine for now. Maybe later, okay? If things get dangerous.*

....

Oh no... They seem disappointed. Did they really want to make me as strong as a monster?

I SEE. IT SEEMS YOU HAVE LET OUT SOME THOUGHTS THAT VAGUELY RESEMBLE AN ANXIETY OR FEAR...

No, no! Y-you're just imagining it! I definitely wasn't thinking that you seemed like some crazed mage trying to communicate with a monster or something!

There seemed to be a very long pause.

WELL, THAT'S FINE. NOW PERHAPS IF YOU WERE TO PRAY FOR A WEAPON... THOUGH, OF COURSE, THERE ARE NO GODS IN THIS WORLD.

Huh?

Save for the nanomachines, there was only one being who was aware that this world had been abandoned by the gods—a girl by the name of Mile, who had been reincarnated from another plane. That girl was, incidentally, Lily's benefactor, but she did not wish to let that be known. Though she possessed power second only to an elder dragon, she wanted nothing more than to live as an average girl. In fact, she was the complete opposite of Lily, who longed to be a hero.

Appropriately enough, it would appear that Mile had pushed some small portion of her own hidden, undesired power upon Lily Lockwood, who had been born as a normal girl.

IT'S ALL CAUSE AND EFFECT...

Causanifect? That sounds like some kind of weird medicine.

IT ISN'T, the nanomachines replied shortly. ANYWAY, THERE ARE MATTERS IN THAT VEIN THAT WE WILL BE UNABLE TO EXPLAIN, SO DON'T WORRY YOURSELF OVER IT. JUST DO YOUR BEST, MISS LILY. SHOULD YOU FIND YOURSELF IN PERIL OF DEATH, WE SHALL BE READY TO DEPLOY THE AFOREMENTIONED MEASURES AT ANY TIME, SO PLEASE CALL UPON US AT YOUR EARLIEST CONVENIENCE.

Ready to turn her into a beastgirl or demon...?

Uh, yeah... O-okay...

Anyway, Lily thought, she would try her best, only if to prevent *that* outcome from occurring.

WHAT'S WITH THAT REPLY?

"...Lily are you listening?" Lafine's face was twisted, and she was looking at Lily intently.

"Uh, yeah? Sorry, what was that?"

Lily had been so concentrated on her mental conversation that she had not even realized Lafine was speaking to her.

"Are you really all right? You were spacing out for a good while there."

"I was talking to a spirit. He's the one who's been guiding me. Er, is 'he' right?"

Lafine's expression twisted even further. "...Are you messing with me?"

"I-I'm being serious!"

"Guys, keep your voices down, I'm begging you," Veil interjected. "We aren't out of the woods yet just because we've found their base."

Lafine clicked her tongue, self-satisfied. "Well then, what're we gonna do now? Do we go on in? Go back and report it?"

"Normally, this is where we'd go and call in the royal forces via the guild, but it'd be days before they could make it here. These guys are on the lamb, so there's no telling when they might up and leave. I'm worried about the hostages' safety, and I have no idea about Big Bro's whereabouts. They may have even captured him already."

Another problem: They had no idea what kinds of numbers they were up against. The men who had assaulted them earlier under the guise of bandits were around twelve in number, though one could be certain that that did not account for the full group. They would have had to leave behind enough members at the base to watch over at least four hostages, after all. Once you factored in the particular care necessary in guarding the margrave and his wife, who were key players, as well as more agents to patrol the perimeter of the ruins, they might be looking at least a dozen or more additional people lying in wait.

"There might be as many as fifty here, in total," Lafine muttered.

"If we're lucky," Veil bitterly replied.

"Still a while until dawn," Lafine said, standing.

"What are you doing?" asked Veil.

"Surprise attacks are my specialty. Better to hit 'em in the dark than to fight them head-on. I can preemptively take out as many of their number as possible before they catch on, and you two can just follow in after me. Though I understand this might not be your bag."

Veil was slack-jawed.

"You've gotta be kidding... You may've caught me off guard with that ambush of yours, but after the first blows you were way stronger. Honestly, I was pretty much gambling on being able to keep up with you. I had a trick or two up my sleeve, but once those didn't work I would definitely have ended up on the losing end."

Lafine quirked an eyebrow in practiced fashion.

"Oh? Nice to hear something so encouraging from you for once. But, Veil, you underestimate yourself. I never expected you to be able to guard against that attack. Did you maybe pick up your sword skills from someone who had a unique style, not like your average knight or swordsman?"

Veil's eyes went wide.

"Oh, y-yeah! Back at the Hunters' Prep School I studied with a girl who had no form and relied on her speed and power, just like you." His gaze moved downward in thought. "Yes, okay, I see. So that's why I was able to react and deflect your surprise attack just in time. That was all thanks to her, too."

"Most people trained in proper form are no match for my surprise attacks. It's more like the way a wild animal hunts, or like an assassin's technique. Heh! I'm guessing that, given that you were able to protect yourself against me, that master of yours was considered a bit of an oddball, as far as swordfighters go?"

"Y-yeah. Well, she was pretty much an oddball all around. And actually, she wasn't a swordfighter—she was a mage."

There was a pause.

"Huh?" Lafine knitted her brow.

"Well, she was a mage, primarily. She was a strange girl, ridiculously strong, so much so that she could hold her own against an A-rank hunter with just a sword, but her magic was even stronger than that. As far as I'm aware, there's no one who could beat her."

"Wha...?"

"She never bragged about it, though. In fact, she seemed to try to conceal her abilities, for some reason. She was always saying how she just wanted to be a normal girl," said Veil with a wry smile.

"Well, that'd be impossible," replied Lafine with a strained smile of her own.

"Totally impossible. She seemed to think that she was doing a good job of hiding her strength, but everyone, classmates and teachers alike, realized how talented she was."

Lafine pointed at Lily.

"Just like our little make-believe hero over here?"

"It's not make-believe!"

Ignoring Lily's protests, Veil continued, "Actually, I'd say it's the opposite. In her case, she was a make-believe normal girl."

Lafine grimaced.

"She really was an oddball, huh?"

"If you really want to know more about her abilities, I could introduce you to the leader of the Roaring Mithrils, the man that she faced in a sword battle at the Prep School's graduation exam. Though, Gren is an A-rank hunter and pretty busy, so I'm not sure when you'd actually get a chance to talk to him."

"Gren of the Roaring Mithrils is a pretty big deal, isn't he? How do you have enough of a connection to get in contact with him?"

Of course, Veil had won his own fight against Gren at the graduation exam, though it could not exactly be called a fair contest. Just before their match, Gren had taken a huge beating from Mile, after all. Even under those circumstances, Veil had still claimed victory by only a thin margin, using tricks that were unlikely to work twice. Veil, however, talked around this.

"Well, let's just say we have some acquaintances in common."

Lafine gave a small shrug and pointed to Lily.

"I'm good on the introductions, thanks. Gren would be one thing, but I've got no interest in this master of yours. I've already had my fill of weirdo mages with this little critter here."

This time it was Veil who grimaced. He glanced at Lily and mumbled seriously, "Yeah, we do have one of those right here, don't we? I guess there's more than one in this world."

Of course, the two of them had no clue that the weirdo mage present had essentially been created by the other weirdo mage in question.

"I'm not *that* weird!"

"Sure thing. Keep it down."

Lafine rolled her shoulders.

"All right then, let's see if we can take out twelve or so of them from behind, quietly. Be absolutely sure not to make too much noise."

"Got it. And if it starts to look dangerous, get out of there immediately."

"Roger. And, Lily—"

Lily tilted her head.

"You can't use *any* magic during this secret mission."

"What?!"

"Listen, dummy, if you use that flashy, overblown magic, we'll be spotted and surrounded immediately."

"But then can't I just let off a big *kaboom* once they're all in the same place?"

Lafine poked her in the forehead.

"I already told you no. Don't forget, there are hostages somewhere in there. The agents might use them as a shield. Plus, are you really ready to kill a person—enemy or not?"

It was only as Lafine said this that Lily realized the truth—all of the spells she had used up until now had been extremely lethal. Even that wind ball spell, which she had thankfully used only on orcs, was powerful enough to blow anyone away with a single strike. And if the victim did not perish instantly, they certainly wouldn't be long for this world unless a very powerful healing mage was on hand to stop their bleeding.

"…"

"Until you know how to control yourself, let's keep it to just threats."

"Yes, ma'am," Lily nodded grudgingly. Still, deep down in her heart, she vowed: If either Lafine or Veil ended up in real danger, she would mow down everything in her path, if it meant saving them.

"All right, let's get going."

The three looked to one another and nodded. The next moment, Lafine was practically sliding down the slope toward the hideout, silent as the wind despite the dead leaves underfoot. She grappled along tree trunks, moving steadily downward at breakneck speed.

"Whoa! She really is like a wild animal. I can barely hear

her footsteps or even the rustling of the foliage," Veil muttered, impressed.

After watching for a short while, they saw Lafine raise a hand to them, her back still turned. This was the signal. Veil supported Lily with a hand so that she would not slip, and then they started down the slope. When Lafine gave another signal, the pair stopped, while Lafine went on ahead. They repeated this pattern a number of times as they continued down the slope.

And then, the signals stopped. The two waited a moment.

Lily steadied her breath. Her heart was racing. Then, Lafine leapt up.

There was an agent on patrol. Lafine grabbed the man's neck, the tip of her hidden blade pressed to his carotid artery. Her lips moved against the patrolman's ear. The man stopped moving. Then she strangled him until he fell, unconscious. Keeping an eye on her surroundings, she dragged the man into the grass, quickly covering him with leaves.

"I take back what I said," said Veil. "She's not like a wild animal, she's like an assassin."

"I-I don't *think* she killed him, at least."

The signal for them to halt changed to one of beckoning. They only proceeded a short distance, however, before they were stopped again. Lafine lay down on the ground, holding her breath.

"Huh? Why are we stopping again?" asked Lily, tilting her head.

"There are usually multiple men on patrols like these. She's probably spotted another one," Veil quietly explained.

"I see..."

The pair stood waiting at roughly the spot where Lafine had buried the patrolman in the underbrush. Lily picked up some of the leaves and placed her hand at the strangled man's neck. There was a pulse. He was alive. However, there was a concerning amount of leaves stuffed into his mouth.

"I think he's alive."

"Lily, it's gonna be a problem if he wakes up. You need to leave him be."

"Oh, right."

She diligently covered the man in brush again. She wanted to at least remove the leaves from his mouth, but she got the feeling Veil would scold her. After a brief wait, another patrolman came jogging along.

"Yo, hold up! You could walk a little slower. Jeez, Will, you're always so serious. Er—huh? Where'd he go? Will? Wiiiill? Huh?"

They could only guess that the man lying unconscious at Lily's feet was Will. At the absence of any reply, the newcomer seemed to notice that something was amiss. His face tightened, and he adjusted his hands on the grip of the spear he carried. However, it was already too late. Lafine had snuck up out of the darkness and had her arms around his throat.

"Hyuguh...!"

It was only a few short seconds before the man's limbs sagged, and he was unable to even let out a sound. Once again, Lafine dragged the man along and hid him in the underbrush. It was strange, Lily thought, that she was taking the time to stuff leaves into the man's mouth yet again and grinning all the while. She seemed to just be antagonizing him.

Following her hand signs, they continued down the slope, until finally they arrived at the bottom of the basin.

What stood before them was not merely wreckage, it was *ruins*—of a town, no less, a sprawling ancient ruin filled with structures that had seen the weathering of hundreds, perhaps thousands of years.

"Whoa..." Lily gasped, amazed.

Not a single roof remained intact on any of the buildings. The walls were all half-crumbled and covered in ivy. Trees grew up through the rubble, and the ground was almost entirely covered in foliage. Small streams, which appeared to have once been irrigation canals, were still flowing, but by now they looked almost like fully natural formations. Under the glow of the moon, the scenery was enough to make one's heart dance with imagination.

"It's beautiful..."

"Lily."

She came back to her senses at a hand sign from Lafine and quickly followed behind Veil as they proceeded into the ruins. Veil pulled her by the arm to keep her from tripping on the rubble.

"Thanks."

"No problem. Be careful, and try not to make any sound."

"Okay."

It was a lot easier to walk now that they were not traipsing down a slope covered in dead leaves. Now and then Lafine halted, looking around as though keeping an eye out for a trail. After a brief pause, her signal would come again, and Veil and Lily would stop, too.

Voices. They could hear voices speaking. They could not make out the words, but the sound was such that it had to be more than just one man speaking to himself. Veil let go of Lily's hand and put his hand on the hilt of his sword.

Lafine had crouched down low, half-hidden behind some rubble. She was just starting to peek out when—

"Lafine!" Lily screamed.

A figure appeared atop the wreckage that Lafine was hiding behind. They plunged down from above, striking down toward Lafine's back, a blade glinting in the moonlight. By the time Lafine noticed, it was already too late.

She'd never make it in time!

The moment Lily realized this, a chill ran down her spine. *Lafine was dead,* she thought. A formless fear churned up inside of her. However, a longsword swung in at the last possible moment, deflecting the scimitar that struck down toward Lafine.

"...!!"

"——?!"

Veil's upward swing fought back the slice of the scimitar. The sound of clashing metal rang through the ruins as sparks flew. Lafine dodge-rolled forward, immediately kicking off the ground to reverse direction again. She drew her shortsword, slicing at the ankles of the shadowy figure. The dark, scimitar-wielding form acrobatically evaded her blade, landing softly back upon the ground.

"He dodged *that*?!"

Numerous footsteps came thumping toward them. Either thanks to Lily's scream or the sound of the blades, it seemed they had been detected by the guards—and not just two or three of them, judging by the sound of it.

Lafine clicked her tongue.

"Veil, let's fall back!"

"Go on ahead," Veil replied.

Lafine, who had already started running, froze. "Wha—?!"

Veil was facing the emaciated shadowy figure, the tip of his sword lowered. He should have been able to hear all of the footsteps, but he gazed only at the figure in front of him.

"Take Lily and go ahead, Lafine."

"All right, what's with the cool guy act?"

"Please don't mistake me. I'm not doing this so that you all can get away. In fact, it seems I'm the one who was naively mistaken. I thought that I'd be rescuing my Big Bro. That was stupid to assume." He leveled his blade. "I knew from the moment that sword came toward your back just now that I'd have some things to settle with him instead... Isn't that right, Big Bro?"

Lily gasped.

"When a family member has gone astray, it's up to the head of that family to correct it. So, please go."

When Lily strained her eyes, she recognized the eyes that glowed faintly in the moonlight. The person's face was hidden by a mask from the nose down, but there was no mistaking it.

Both the ashen gray eyes and the bangs that peeked out from under the hood sparkled silver in the light of the moon. It was the slum broker. The one they had thought was a well-intentioned ally, working for the sake of the orphans. But if that was the truth, why would he have made an attempt on Lafine's life? Why was he being allowed to move about freely in a place like this, in the camp of the agents of the Albarn Empire?

There could be only one reason.

The many footsteps grew closer, and voices could be heard.

"I think it came from this way—hurry up!"

"What are the two lookouts over here doing?!"

There was no time left.

The broker's muffled voice sounded from behind his mask.

"You're such an idiot, Veil. It's incredible to think you even made it this far. I abandoned the slums and gave myself up to the Empire long ago."

Veil looked at him, clenching his teeth with a sorrowful expression.

"Why...?"

Before she could hear the answer to this question, Lily was bodily lifted up by Lafine, who slipped past Big Bro and ran.

"We've gotta go!"

"Lafine, wait! What about Veil?!"

"No time."

Lafine took Lily into her arms and removed her from the area by force. The sound of swords could be heard. Again and again came the ring of clashing metal, followed by the cries of men's voices.

"Lafine, *please!*"

Lily flailed her limbs violently against Lafine's grip around her waist, but Lafine only held her tighter. Lily's face twisted in pain.

"Gah!"

"Settle down."

They were getting so far away now. They rounded a stand of trees, and Lily could no longer see a thing. In the nearly pitch black, she could not tell where they had run. Once they were a great distance away, Lafine finally set her back down on her feet.

There was no going back. She had no idea which way they had even come. They had left Veil, her mentor and her precious friend, surrounded by enemies on all sides.

Her heart grew heavy and sank into the pit of her stomach. Her insides felt like lead.

"Lafine, why...?"

"Lily, what did you come here for?"

"...To...save my family."

"That's right. And this is your only chance to do so. Veil is buying us some time. We need to take this opportunity to reach the hostages and free them."

"But..." Lily's voice squeaked out from the depths of her throat. "But Veil..." Her voice was so small, weak, and faltering, it surprised even her. "Veil will die..."

"Lily, what did *he* come here for?"

"Same...as me... To save—"

"His family. Do you think he could turn tail and run when his family is right there in front of him? What would you do if you were in his shoes? Would you be persuaded to run away just because the enemy outnumbered you? If that's the amount of resolve that you have for saving the hostages, then we'd be better off just abandoning this whole operation right now."

Hearing these harsh words, Lily took a deep breath. Her mother and father had fled and abandoned her, but even so, if it had been them and her brother and sister back there...then yes, even if Lafine or Veil had ordered her to evacuate, she would not have heard them.

Lafine continued, "Even if the three of us could have somehow made our way through all of that, the main enemy corps was already aware of our position. They'd probably drag the hostages away or start some big game of tag with us. Naturally, that would mean a far greater chance of harm coming to the hostages."

In other words, remaining with Veil would have been pointless.

"You and Veil are companions on the same path, with the same goal. So you should be able to understand each other's feelings. You don't want to make Veil give up on the thing he came here for just to help you accomplish *your* goals, do you?"

"No..."

"When he told us to go on ahead, that was when you got it."

"Got *it*? Got what?"

Lafine balled up her fist and punched Lily lightly in the chest.

"Hey!" Lily stumbled a step backward at the unexpectedly heavy blow. "Lafine, that hurt."

"Don't you get it? This is the best chance you have at saving your family."

"Ah..."

Gradually, her chest began to fill with warmth where she had been struck. The dull pain turned slowly into heat.

"So, seize that chance. It's not often in a woman's life that she receives the gift of a man putting his own life on the line to help her."

"O-okay."

Lafine paused and cleared her throat.

"Besides, you underestimate the C-rank hunter, the swordsman Veil. He's guilty of underestimating himself as well, but you shouldn't look down on his skills. No matter how you slice it, you have to be fairly skilled to make a C-rank."

Approximately one year ago, when Lafine was still living as a servant at the Lockwood manor, she heard about a group of students that had caused quite the commotion at the graduation exam of the Hunter's Prep School. Among this group were four young ladies and one young man.

"I never did imagine that he'd be talking about Gren of the Roaring Mithrils, of all people..."

There was no doubting it. You could count on one hand the number of people in Tils who could best Gren in a swordfight, after all. That one young man was Veil. And among those four young ladies was the master who had taught him that thoroughly chaotic sword technique.

"Huh?"

"Never mind. I'm just saying that Veil is a lot more talented than either you or even he realizes. That weirdo master of his that he talks about must be really good." Lafine put one hand on her hip and chuckled. "So, well, I'm sure he'll be fine. Before you know it, he'll be trotting along after us. Until then, we need to hurry up and find your family and free them. Then we can all skedaddle together. Sound good?"

"Yeah!"

Lafine turned her back, the hem of her skirt swaying, and began walking briskly. Lily looked back one final time and then started running as fast as she could after Lafine.

In light of the number of opponents he was facing off against, Veil had already applied magic to his sword. The blade would never withstand the fight without it. His hands, gripping the sheath, began to go numb as the sound of metal rang out.

"You little—!"

As Veil used the heel of his boot to force back the man who came bearing down in front of him, he swept back with his blade to mow down the men around him. The tip of his sword scratched against the breastplate of a man who had been approaching from behind, sending sparks flying.

The surrounding enemies frantically opened a gap.

"You come here to take back the things we stole from you? Idiots. And here we thought we could let you off easy without anyone getting hurt."

"Sorry. This is just what a hunter's gotta do."

Hunter. The moment the men heard this word, their faces twisted. However, they soon righted themselves.

"You all need to learn your places."

Stepping back nimbly to evade the naked blades that came pelting onward, Veil repelled the onslaught with an upward swing.

"Guh..."

"Graaaah!"

The men tried to use this opportunity to strike him in the torso, but Veil deflected their incoming attacks with his sword, opening a greater distance.

"Well, you're persistent."

"This guy's pretty good."

"Be careful. Don't go at him alone. Watch each other's backs."

Veil gritted his teeth. This was not easy. If they had come at him as recklessly as bandits did, he would have been able to dispatch many of them, but these were trained soldiers in formation, protecting each other's weak points. Though they had disguised themselves as bandits, there was no mistaking now that these were indeed agents of the Albarn Empire. Of course, they would probably never admit to such a thing, even under torture.

"Phew..."

Veil regarded his surroundings briefly, without time to even wipe away the sweat pouring from his brow. There were seven imperial soldiers. Including Big Bro, that made eight. The situation was bad.

Big Bro had reclaimed his sword and clambered atop one of the remaining walls of a ruined house. He was surveying the skirmish intently, not lending his aid to either side. His intention was unclear, but Veil was glad for the reprieve, in any event.

He was surrounded on all sides, without even a wall to protect his back. He had thought of breaking through this siege and running to get some distance from the men, but frankly, he was not sure if he was strong enough to pull it off. Besides, he couldn't risk the chance of Big Bro, who showed no signs of moving, getting away from him.

"This is bad..."

The moment Veil glanced carefully left, a soldier to his right swung his sword at the ground, kicking up dirt.

"Hi-yah!"

The soldier swung his longsword down at Veil's head from an angle, attacking from a blind spot. As though he was already aware this might happen, Veil avoided the slash with just a twist of his body.

"What?!"

The moment the soldier's blade grazed past his cheap leather armor, Veil pierced the man's sword arm. He then quickly changed stances and went for the tendons of the man's legs. The man had already dropped his weapon and collapsed on the spot, writhing as he grabbed his own legs to hold back the bleeding.

"Gw-haaaah..."

Giving the fallen man a wide berth, Veil renewed his grip. The man had foolishly acted on his own, stepping right into the gap that Veil had purposely created. Thanks to this, he had been able to easily reduce the enemy's numbers by one, yet he was still most assuredly in dire straits.

Just as the soldier behind him lowered his blade, took the fallen man by the hands, and tried to remove him from the battlefield, Veil spun right around and cut through the arteries of the man's arms.

"*Hi-yaaah!*"

"Gwuh?!"

A great spattering of blood and rivulets of sweat soaked into the dark ground. Before the man could even attempt to flee, his face twisted in horrible pain, Veil stabbed through both his greaves with his longsword.

"Argh..."

The man, having fallen on his backside, looked up at Veil. His expression was one of despair.

"Stop!"

However, Veil had already turned away from the fallen pair. He was not going to end their lives. Robbing their legs and arms of movement should be plenty to keep them from coming after him again. Plus, it was simply poor strategy to do anything that might incur the wrath of the remaining five. Speaking of which...

"You coward!"

"Cutting down a man who comes in to provide aid... Have you no pride as a swordsman?!"

"Bastard, you call yourself a hunter?!"

This time a squad of three ran out to drag away the two injured men. Naturally, he did not have the capacity to take all three of them at once. So he turned back and wiped the sweat from his brow, steadying his breathing and focus.

"Bold thing to say when there's this many of you surrounding me, when I'm only one person. How can you shout at me about cowardice or a swordsman's pride when you're nothing but bandits?"

Of course, he was already aware that these men were *not* bandits. However, it was clear that they were, in fact, engaging in banditry. If they were the sort of proper soldiers who had pride in their profession, then it would hurt them to hear themselves denounced in this way. Veil hoped that perhaps, he could appeal to their consciences, make them feel a bit guilty, just break their strides even a little bit... But the men simply fell silent.

Had he miscalculated?

Veil chided himself inwardly. He seemed to have only confirmed what these men thought of him.

"Surround him. Simultaneous attack."

"Roger."

"Sorry, dear little nameless hunter. You're exactly right. However, we're on a mission."

Five blades leveled at him all at once.

Ah, this was bad. In which case, he had only one card left to play.

"Yeah, I know. For the Albarn Empire, right?"

"——!"

All the men held their breaths—while Big Bro, standing atop the wall and watching over the whole scene, continued to look on, frozen.

The man who appeared to be the leader of the soldiers bitterly spat out, "H-how...did you..."

"It's because I'm in charge of protecting the eldest daughter of the Lockwood family. I've done some looking into this incident. My goal is to free that girl's family and reunite her with them."

"The guild knows that we're imperial agents, not bandits? The royal family does?"

The air prickled with tension. Veil decided to lie.

"That's right. I got the guard job through the guild. I'm sure by now that all the information about you all has made it up to the Crown. If the Kingdom of Tils issues a formal complaint against the Albarn Empire, I'm sure that you all will be swiftly dispatched."

Veil hoped that this would be over quickly if he could undermine the men's fighting spirit. However, things were not so simple.

"I see. Well, in that case, there's no more point in talking." The leader shuffled closer to Veil, never loosening his grip on his sword. "Allow me to make one correction, though. Previously, you suggested that we were acting in service of the Albarn Empire. That was wrong. Dead wrong, boy."

"...?"

The five men now held their swords at their sides, almost casually. Sweat dripped down Veil's back. He could feel an unerring bloodlust, far stronger than he had up until now. The leader continued to speak in a calm, steady tone. "We're not working for the Empire. We're working for our families, who are waiting for us back there. Until we detain every last member of the Lockwood family, who are in charge of guarding Tils' borders, we will not be permitted passage back home. Should there be any deserters or traitors, their families will be imprisoned... So, step aside!"

"........."

Of course, this was not unusual. Everyone fought for their families. It only stood to reason that these men had families that they wished to protect. Lily had a family she hoped to be reunited with. And Veil had a brother whose mistakes he had to correct.

In and out. Veil took a deep breath. Inhale and exhale. Then, he spoke. "Whatever you say, I don't think we can avoid this. This world is full of so many unpleasant things."

"That's something I think we can both agree on."

"Ah ha ha."

"Heh heh."

The squad leader began to laugh, and Veil followed suit.

Yet a moment later, there was a sudden shift, as both Veil and the five other men kicked off of the ground.

"Graaaaaah!"

"Waaaaargh!"

Veil swung back to avoid the blade that was swinging his way, striking forcefully at the man he had just been laughing with moments prior.

"Hi-yah!"

"Gwah!"

Both his arms went numb from the fearsome recoil, but he forcefully shook it off. His blade was strengthened by magic.

It could strike against any metal without breaking. The squad leader was blown backwards, tumbling along the ground. Quickly, Veil changed grips, ready to run the man through, but at that same moment, another blade came swinging in from the side. He managed to duck in the nick of time, and the sword swung right over him.

"Nice try!"

"Surround him!"

He jumped up from his lowered stance all at once, dodged the attack that was launched toward him, and reached his left hand out into the night sky, grabbing at the air. The moment he landed, he struck down on the shoulder of the man who was approaching him from behind.

"Air Bullet!"

With a dreadful sound, the man face-planted onto the ground.

"Gwah...?! Guh!!"

"W-was that *magic*?!"

There was a great dent in the man's pauldron, and his arm had been wrenched into a strange angle. Quickly, while the man was busy staring at his own arm in shock, Veil sliced through the tendons of the soldier's legs.

And now, there were four.

"Gwaaah! You brat!"

Veil planted his feet firmly on the ground, blade in his left hand, as he bodily deflected a blow that came toward him with the attacker's full weight behind it. Beads of sweat scattered into the night air.

"Guh...huh!"

"Graaaaah!"

The moment that Veil forced the man back, the soldier's back wrenched, all his power lost as he tumbled forward. Veil slashed at the man's thighs.

Three left!

Just then, a sharp pain ran down his back—Veil's favored leather armor had just been sliced through from behind. There was no doubting if he had waited even a moment to take a half-step forward, the blow would have been fatal. He rolled to escape further attacks, struck the ground, and hopped back up. This was possible only because he was wearing leather and not metal. That said, were he wearing metal, he would never have taken the damage in the first place.

"Hff, hff, hff..."

"Don't let up!"

Gritting his teeth through the pain, Veil took a heavy step forward, striking at the man ahead of him with his blade, now shining with a magical light.

"Ha!"

"...!"

The keening sound of steel rang out, and the man's sword went flying. As the man staggered backward, his face cramping, he turned and called up to Big Bro, still atop the wall, "Oy! No Name! What're you just standing there watching for?! Didn't you convert to our side?!"

Big Bro ignored the man's words and pointed behind him. "Have you really got the time to be distracted?"

"...!"

The man turned back to Veil just in time for an air bullet to crash into his face.

"Argh!"

There was a bursting sound...

The man's neck warped and stretched like it was caught in some violent gale, his body tumbling through the air as though struck by a blunt instrument. As the man fell to the ground, he convulsed a number of times and then fainted, foaming at the mouth.

Two left! This was going surprisingly well.

Yet just as Veil was congratulating himself, the two remaining men came at him from both sides in a pincer attack. He caught the attack coming from his right side with his sword but had to block the left one, painful as it was, with his left forearm.

"*Sh...it!*"

A violent pain ran through him, blood dripping from his damaged leather armguard. The man to his right immediately drew back his sword again, aiming for Veil's neck.

"Hah!"

Veil avoided by ducking, though the blade grazed his cheek. He took some distance, catching the attack from the man on the left with his sword. With his leather armor, Veil had the upper hand in terms of agility but was lacking in terms of protective power. He tried to refresh his grip on his hilt, but he had all but lost the strength in his left hand, his fingers unable to bend. Much worse still, his arm was beginning to numb, so he could not even lift it. His arm hung limp, droplets of hot blood dripping from his fingertips down onto the ground.

Without a free hand, he could not use his air bullets. He could, of course, drop the sword that was in his right hand and use the air bullets instead, but that was too risky. Without a sword in hand, he would not be able to catch or deflect any attacks at all.

There were still two enemies left—three, if you included Big Bro.

Strangely, Big Bro showed no signs of moving. There was no telling what he was thinking. He claimed to have pledged himself to the Empire, but all he was doing was standing by and watching these imperial soldiers perish. Yet for now, that was none of Veil's concern. In fact, it was favorable for him.

Back and forth Veil swung, his sword clashing against the soldiers', no time to even bind his limp arm. The sparks that spouted into the night air lit all three men's faces, mixing with droplets of blood and sweat. Of course, this sort of one-armed fighting was far less taxing than it would have been when taking on five opponents at once. Still, the bleeding was not slowing. If the fight dragged out too long, sooner or later, Veil would be unable to move.

He crossed swords with the men, changing position again and again in order to avoid their pincer attacks. Though five of their allies had fallen, these two showed no signs of letting up.

Of course—after all, their families were being held hostage as well.

"Ugh! This just keeps getting better and better."

He caught the blade that swung down toward him with his longsword, forcefully swinging his paralyzed left arm up to splash blood upon his opponent's face.

"Eurgh!"

It hit the man square in the eyes. Then, the other man leapt out right in front of Veil, who frantically retreated.

"Cha!"

With a shout, Veil evaded the downward diagonal slash of the man's blade, twisting past his side in pursuit of the man who was retreating. The man, blinded, had no means of evading Veil's sword. The tip of the blade plunged deep into the man's right thigh.

"Gaah...!"

Veil kicked the collapsed man's sword away, leaving one final opponent—the leader, currently slashing down at him from behind. Veil caught the leader's blow with his sword, sending the blade glancing off.

"Give it up already. All of your allies have fallen. Please just back off. If you can do that, I'll just leave you all be."

"You know I can't do that. If we want to see our loved ones or set foot upon the ground of our hometowns ever again, we require all the blood that flows through the Lockwood line."

The man changed his grip. He rested his blade on his shoulder and twisted his leg, lowering his body and screwing his torso to the right, so far that his back was exposed to Veil. It was obvious that he was determined to settle this once and for all. This was an all-or-nothing move, one that would leave a huge opening if it was not successful.

The man's cheeks twitched softly with a smile.

"It's probably a bit of an affront to say this, but I've gotta thank you. Sorry... You see, my wife just had a kid..."

Veil's face twisted.

"The Lockwoods have family, too. And I have brothers and sisters back in the slums."

For just a moment, the man's gaze shifted up to Big Bro atop the wall, before it turned right back to Veil.

"I see."

Apparently, that was all the man had to say. He faced Veil and kicked off from the ground. With his body still twisted, back showing, he struck in close to Veil's chest.

"..........!"

It was a killing blow. Still focused on the man's words, Veil stepped back too late. He had no chance to evade the man's attack. He was completely unguarded. However... He could not fall now and leave the others behind. He would not falter.

With the last of the strength in his left arm, Veil caught the blow just before it landed. The edge sunk into his palm, ripping into the flesh and bone and leather upon his forearm, but—before the blade could take his life, it stopped clean.

For some reason, he scarcely felt the pain.

"Looks like I've lost..."

Veil's blade traced the leader's legs as he uttered these words. The man collapsed. Veil removed his own leather gear with his intact arm. He ripped his shirt and tightly wrapped his left arm using his right hand and his mouth.

His makeshift bandages did something to staunch the blood, but it still flowed. Even so, it was unclear how much longer he would be able to stay on his feet without some healing magic.

Veil had to make this quick. He looked upward—to his elder brother, who stood leisurely atop the ruins, the moon shining at his back and a scimitar in his hand.

Lafine and Lily proceeded carefully, keeping themselves hidden. They passed by numerous patrolmen, but Lafine did not go ahead of Lily as she had before. She held on to the girl's hand the whole time. Now that Veil was gone, this was perhaps necessary, to keep Lily from being on her own. Leaving the girl without an experienced hunter at her side would be as good as leaving a sheep alone in a forest full of monsters. Though, of course, if this particular sheep were left unsupervised, she might just turn into a beast herself.

Either way, for now, she must be guarded.

"Lafine, we've been going for a while now. Do you know where the hostages are?"

Lafine followed the retreating form of a passing patrolman with her eyes, her light brown hair swaying.

"I can triangulate it from where we've encountered the guards and their patrol areas. These don't seem like the kind of guys who would go around patrolling areas that aren't important. Chances are high that the hostages are being held somewhere around the center of that big circle they keep making."

"Whoa..."

With every passing day, Lily was seeing Lafine in a new light. Back when she was a servant at the Lockwood home, she seemed like a truly useless, unproductive person. She was supposed to be Lily's attendant, but there was a different servant in charge of cleaning Lily's room and the area around it. Lafine didn't cook for her, either. The only thing she seemed to be capable of was going out to purchase the storybooks that Lily liked to read. Some days, she slept the whole day in the mansion's bay window, or even on the roof. Other times, when things were particularly rough, she went so far as to sleep in Lily's big, fluffy bed. Even when the head butler scolded her, she replied only with a yawn.

And yet, after they had fled from the border town, there was a big change in Lafine. She was making fools of bandits, going sword-to-sword with active-duty hunters, and even cooking breakfast every now and then. Moreover, there were suddenly some implications that she was once a hunter herself.

Suddenly, her slender form seemed so much sturdier and more reliable.

They proceeded stealthily into the crumbling ruins. Finally, they spotted a yawning opening within the ground, which continued on to a set of stairs. One did not even have to peek within to see that it was not dark inside. A faint orange light seeped out into the night. Lafine turned to Lily and put a finger to her lips. Lily nodded obediently.

In this area alone, the grass had been trimmed back, and the exposed ground showed countless footprints. In fact, upon closer inspection, it seemed that the grass had not been trimmed but was so thoroughly trampled down that it no longer grew. There was no mistaking it. Quiet sounds drifted out from the hole as well. Not voices but the gentle *clack, clack* of footsteps.

After taking a look around at their surroundings, Lafine let go of Lily's hand. She peeked inside the hole, took a few steps down the stairs, and paused. She took a few steps more and then beckoned Lily with a signal much like the ones from before. Timidly, Lily snuck down the stairs. She stepped by tiptoe onto the ground, steeling her heart and calming herself with each careful lowering of her heels. Still, she moved quickly. When she caught up with Lafine, Lafine gently stretched out her hand and patted Lily on the head.

"........"

That's good, well done, the gesture seemed to say.

In contrast to the childish way she was just treating Lily, an almost lascivious smile spread across Lafine's face.

Ahead of them was a hallway. Though the men were making use of the pre-existing structures of the ruins, this hallway was clearly being in active use. Here and there lamps were lit, with small flames swaying inside, which made it easy to see.

Though the hall was well maintained, the ruins were still ruins, with countless walls reduced to rubble. For every usable space, there was a pitch-black hole opposite. It was unsettling and eerie. Still, Lafine slid silently into the darkness. Lily followed after, minding her footsteps, waiting for another signal. Finally they began to hear the sounds of human activity. There did not seem to be any doors between them and the voices, so though the sounds were faint, they could hear clearly. There was definitely someone there. There were voices, speaking as softly as possible. Lily still could not tell what was being said.

Lafine walked, and Lily followed. Still holding one finger to her lips, Lafine used her other hand to indicate for Lily to look ahead. She was pointing to a guard, reclining in a chair and dozing. Both his breastplate and sword sat at his feet. Lily looked to Lafine, and they nodded at one another. The two snuck forward—but just as they attempted to pass in front of the man, his eyes suddenly opened.

"Wh-who are y—oof!"

Lafine covered the man's mouth before he could finish speaking, the tip of her shortsword drawn and pressed to his neck. Just before she could pierce the man's throat, Lily grabbed Lafine's arm with both hands.

"Lafine, no!"

"Listen, y—hh!"

The man twisted his body, escaping from Lafine and running deeper into the ruins, shouting.

"Intruders! We've got intruders!"

Countless footsteps sounded from inside. They echoed off the walls and ceiling, making it impossible to tell how many people approached.

"We gotta head back!"

Lafine pivoted, running back toward the entrance.

"I'm gonna hide. If you're with me, they're gonna come after you, too. Go on ahead."

Lily, however, did not move. Lafine stopped and shouted, "Lily!"

"I'll be fine. I'm going to hide myself and wait."

The footsteps were approaching. There was no more time. Even if they ran at full speed now, they would likely be captured before they could ever make it back to the entrance of the passage. Or at least, Lily would.

There was no time to even think about it.

Lafine pounded one of the walls in frustration. Her teeth clenched and her eyes filled with resentment, she glared at Lily and spat, "Fine. I'll draw them off. But you listen to me. I'm not gonna come back in here to save you."

"I know. I'll try my best. Thank you for bringing me this far, Lafine."

"…"

"I love you, Lafine. Even if you hate me, I still love you."

Lafine clicked her tongue, her face twisting horribly, and then ran back down the path by which they had entered, shouting loudly, "Hey, wait! Don't run so fast! Lily! Lily Lockwood!" Not waiting to watch her go, Lily quickly ducked behind a crumbled wall, hiding herself in a small, darkened room. Not a moment later, a number of soldiers went running past.

"Did you hear that voice just now? A woman?!"

"Wait, did she say something about Lily Lockwood?"

"The last remaining Lockwood is *here*?!"

"The fool. Did she come here for her family?!"

"Sure is convenient that she walked right in here to be captured!"

"After them! Do *not* let them get away! We've gotta catch her if we wanna go back to the Empire!"

None of the men passing by took any notice of Lily hiding in the side chamber, and soon they had all vanished, running after Lafine. The moment they were out of sight, Lily proceeded quietly down the hallway.

Now that she was alone, the darkness was incredibly eerie. Her heart was pounding much more fiercely than before. Her palms were slick with sweat, and all of her body screamed for her to run.

There were probably around twelve men chasing after Lafine. If her and Veil's predictions were correct, there would still be more enemies remaining within. Lily's legs threatened to seize up on her, but she forced them ahead. Her family was waiting for her. Her real, biological family. She could not even imagine how she might feel if she were able to find them safe and sound. But they were still waiting—waiting to be rescued. She had to go. She had to be strong. Both in body and heart.

She put her hand into her pocket and took out her butterfly mask, her usual disguise. Even the main characters of the stories she read were afraid sometimes. However, they never stopped moving. As long as there were people who needing saving, they always pressed on. That was what made a hero.

And so, she would transform. That alone would make her stronger...or at least, she hoped it might...probably...hopefully...

"Okay."

Feeling her heart pounding in her chest, she took off running. Thanks to Veil keeping most of the patrolmen occupied and Lafine drawing off most of the underground enemies, there seemed to be no one else around.

A door!

Finally, she reached a single door. It was quickly obvious that this door was not part of the ruins but a wooden one that had been recently installed. Even Lily could infer that this was a clue that she had found the secret base of the agents of the Albarn Empire. She took in a long breath and then let it out slowly. Softly, she pushed open the door. The hinges creaked.

As she slipped inside, three pairs of eyes fell on Lily. Unfortunately, they were not those of her family. They were soldiers, all wearing the same garb as the men who had run after Lafine.

"An intruder...?"

"Just one little girl? And what's with that freaky mask? This some kind of kinky game?! That's disgusting! What're they teachin' kids here in Tils these days?!"

Ugh! This man has no taste!

"Anyway, I guess we'd better catch her. Even if she's got nothin' to do with this, she knows our location, so we can't just let her stroll on out of here. If the king finds out about our position, it's really gonna mess with our plans. Gonna have to keep her here until we can find a new base."

Across from the men was an iron door. This was clearly another new installation. Lily stared at it, imagining her parents and siblings just beyond the doorway.

One of the soldiers moved around her, blocking her path of retreat. Lily thought, these men had not yet realized that she was the remaining Lockwood. Lafine's shouts would not have reached this far. So, they had just mistaken her for a lost child who had come wandering in.

"All right, kid, just be good and you won't get hu—"

The man who had blocked her way suddenly paused; a wild wind had just whipped up within the sealed underground room.

"Wh-what is this?"

Lily stretched out both her hands, seizing the air. The air raged around her palms, whipping up a whirlwind. She had not come this far just to be captured! So, like she had with the bandits, she would show them her strength, and then they would have to negotiate with her. Within the violent, unnatural wind, Lily shouted proudly in her childish voice, "My name is Hello World Mask! I'm an ally of justice protecting the Kingdom of Tils—in other words, a hero! I hear that you have hostages here! *Release them at once!* If you do not, I'll make you regret it!"

For a moment, there was nothing but the sound of the wind. Overcoming their initial surprise, the soldiers collected themselves. Even if this appeared to be a magical wind, it was just blowing around chaotically. So much so that it didn't appear that it would even be able to knock over a single iron sword stood on its end. Clearly, there was no reason to fear the likes of this little girl. Though, child or no, she was still a mage. They could not let down their guard.

The soldiers leveled their swords at her. Lily faltered, taking a step back.

"Stop that magic now. If you don't—"

"I-I *can't!*" Lily shouted, whipping her head back and forth.

"You idiot! Are you saying that that magic will hurt even you?!"

No, no, that's not it. It's not.

Lily shouted, nearly ready to cry, "No! I just have no idea how to stop magic once I start it!! So...do you mind if I shoot it into you?"

Veins bulged on the soldiers' foreheads.

"Of course we friggin' mind! If it's that much of a problem, just shoot it into the wall over there or somethin'!"

"B-but Lafine said that if I destroy the walls, the ceiling of the ruins might fall down and bury this whole underground place..."

"Look, these ruins might be old, but they're not gonna be knocked down by some little breeze like that! Quit complainin' and just let it go! W-w-w-wait, wait, hold on! Don't point that this way! W-we won't forgive you if you shoot that into us!"

The men were wrong. Walls that old and weathered would most certainly crumble in the face of her wind magic. Lily was confident of this. She knew the rotations of this spell were even more powerful than the ones she had struck the orcs with. Even if she tried to hold back the power within the spheres grasped in her hand, violent winds were already seeping out beyond them. Just in case, she called to the spirits.

Mr. Nano, what's going on? My magic seems even more power-ful than before!

THAT IS LIKELY BECAUSE YOU ARE USING YOUR MAGIC WHILE AGITATED, AND YOUR THOUGHT PULSES ARE THAT MUCH MORE POWERFUL. INCIDENTALLY, BY OUR CALCULATIONS, THERE IS A 98 PERCENT PROBABIL-ITY THAT THE WALLS *WILL* CRUMBLE IF YOU RELEASE THE WIND. THE REMAINING 2 PERCENT IS THE CHANCE THAT THE WIND WILL SIMPLY PASS RIGHT THROUGH THE RUINS ENTIRELY.

Purr-sent? That sounds like some kind of cute animal!

Lily sensed something like a weary sigh.

ACTUALLY, A PERCENTAGE MEANS THAT, IF YOU STRUCK THE SAME WALL ONE HUNDRED TIMES WITH THE SAME SPELL, NINETY-EIGHT OF THOSE TIMES, THE WALL WOULD COLLAPSE.

She was crestfallen.

FURTHERMORE, IF THE WALL DOES COLLAPSE, THERE IS AN INCREDIBLY HIGH LIKELIHOOD—78 PERCENT—THAT THE CEILING WILL COME DOWN WITH IT AS WELL. SHOULD THAT HAPPEN, THERE IS NEARLY THE SAME PROBABILITY THAT YOU, AND EVERYONE ELSE DOWN HERE, WILL BE BURIED ALIVE AND PERISH. AS YOUR OBJECTIVE SEEMS TO BE THE RESCUE OF YOUR FAMILY, WHO ARE BEING HELD HOS-TAGE BEYOND THIS ROOM, I WOULD NOT ADVISE THIS METHOD.

The nanomachines' response was calm, but Lily got the sense she had just been told something of dire importance.

What if she had simply asked Mr. Nano to determine her family's location from the start? No, there was no point in thinking about that now.

Waaaah! So it'd be dangerous to hit a person with this, even if they're wearing armor?!

NO, THEIR ARMOR IS QUITE STURDY, SO EVEN TAKING A DIRECT HIT SHOULD ONLY DENT IT.

Oh! Well, in that case!

The soldiers took a step back as Lily pointed her hands toward them.

"H-hey, you little witch, what're you doing?! We told you not to point that at us!"

In a slightly frantic tone, the nanomachines added, WE SHOULD MENTION THAT THE HUMANS INSIDE THAT ARMOR *WILL* BE CRUSHED TO DEATH, THOUGH. QUITE PAINFULLY, AS THEIR BONES PIERCE THEIR ORGANS. ALTERNATIVELY, THEY'LL BE BLOWN BACK INSTEAD AND THROWN INTO THE WALL, WHERE THEIR INNARDS WILL GO KA-SPLAT.

Ka-splat, huh?

She had no idea how high the likelihood of this *ka-splat* was, but regardless, it seemed best that she not pursue this course of action. Lily pouted, pushing out her bottom lip and staring at the soldiers with tearful eyes.

"Umm..."

The fiercely powerful wind swirled in her hands. It was as though a tornado had been compressed down to palm size, which made it all the more difficult to handle. It was something a wooden house would not be able to withstand, made even more powerful by virtue of being highly concentrated.

Not thinking, Lily blurted, "Hey, Misters, can you help?"

"With what?!"

"Putting this out?"

"How should we do that?! Just hurry up and shoot it into the wall and get rid of it!"

She had honestly assumed that at long as she did not use any spell that was like her fireballs—or rather, her pseudo-suns—everything would be fine. Those were dangerous. Underground, with nowhere to run, the men would be burnt to a crisp. However, it turned out that her wind spheres weren't exactly safe, either. She should have refrained from magic entirely, just as Lafine had told her.

Lily looked upward to keep the tears from falling. Yet even as her vision blurred, she suddenly realized something. Wouldn't everything be all right if the ceiling that was going to topple down on them was gone entirely?

Mr. Nano?

YES, THAT SHOULD PROVIDE A MUCH GREATER CHANCE OF SURVIVAL THAN SHOOTING YOUR WIND INTO THE WALL.

Lily's gaze flicked back to the soldiers.

"Wh-what?! You back to tryin' to shoot us with that *thing*?"

"Misters! Please, watch out and get down!"

"Huh?"

Without waiting for a reply, Lily pointed both hands toward the ceiling.

"Uh-hup!"

The air exploded. It would be absurd to even refer to it as anything so ordinary as wind. A powerful wall of air, with Lily at its center, shot upward from the underground chamber. The soldiers, with nowhere to run, were blasted back into the walls. Probably, this was the best-case scenario for them.

There was a thunderous sound. The earth itself let out a shriek. Lily's maelstrom pierced through the ancient underground ruins, blasting the heavy earth that enshrined them into the night sky.

It was like a cold volcanic eruption...

The rubble that was shot high into the air rained down on the ruins like meteorites, once more shaking the earth. Finally, when everything had settled again...

"........."

The rubble that had once been the ceiling tumbled down over the walls, bit by bit. A dense cloud of dust surrounded them.

Everyone in the room, including the perpetrator herself, was flattened to the ground, staring up at the night sky in shock. Where there was once a sturdy stone ceiling, there was now nothing but air. The ceiling was gone. Kaput. Vanished without a single speck. Lily turned slowly to the soldiers, who were plastered to the walls.

"Um, so anyway, could I please ask you to just go ahead and release the hostages?"

The men, still on their knees, only gazed at the girl who stood before them. Yet now, they looked at her in fear.

"Um."

At their lack of response, she once again thrust her hands out toward the soldiers. The soldiers scuttled back, pressing themselves against the walls.

"Please release the hostages. They're my beloved family."

"——!"

"Y-you're Lily Lockwood...?"

She nodded.

"Damn it, no one told us that the other girl was a *mage*!"

"How the hell were we supposed to capture a monster like this?"

The men's faces were painted with despair. One of them, however, rose to his feet.

"Monster? What of it? If we don't capture *all* the Lockwoods, we won't be able to go back home! Do you not want to see your homes or your families again?! Is this not the time to put our lives on the line?!"

The other soldiers looked at one another, fear still in their eyes. Their expressions were clearly bitter, but the next moment they stood, either in resignation or resolve, and opened their mouths.

However, before they could speak, Lily cut in. "No, I don't think that's right. You all can't die here. No one would be able to smile tomorrow if something like that happened. Wouldn't it just make your families sad if you threw your lives away for them?"

The soldiers shut their mouths again, as though they had lost all their vigor. The first man, however, shouted more loudly, "Then what exactly do you want us to do?! We don't have anywhere else to go! Considering that spell you just let off, we're probably gonna die here anyway! But if we run, we'll be executed! And our families will be punished, too!"

"We're in the same boat here, little Lockwood. Our families are being held hostage as well. We never had any choice to begin with. It's better for us to die here." The man pounded his chest with his fist, resolve strengthened. "That said, our deaths will not be in vain! With our deaths here, the Empire will reward our families handsomely!"

In contrast with the man, Lily was smiling sadly.

"I don't really understand all this complicated stuff about your country, but I don't think your families would take that kind of reward. They'd say it was bad and that they didn't need it. Really bad. I'm sure they'd rather see you alive once more, no matter how."

Lily's smile twisted.

"Even someone like me, a child abandoned by her own parents, would feel that way."

The man's face changed. What was once an antagonistic glare was now a look of confusion and pity.

"You...you came here to save them, even though they abandoned you? Is that why your name wasn't on the list of the Lockwoods? Because you were abandoned?"

"Yes. So, I have nothing to lose. But I still don't want to die. I didn't come here to die. I just came to see them. And I want you all to live, too. If you keep on living, then there's always a chance that you might be able to see your families again someday."

Words were so difficult to use. Nothing Lily wanted to say was coming out right. She lacked confidence in her own words. She *could* use them, but it was incredibly hard. She could not express even the smallest part of what she truly wanted to convey. Now that she could hear, now that she could speak, she finally understood this.

The man looked down and spat, "Someday, but when? It's already been two years since we left the Empire and have been wandering around this place. Two *years*... We've fallen so far as to live like bandits, just dreaming of the day we might see our homes again."

Never in her life had Lily seen a grown adult with his face screwed up like a little child's, quietly trying to hold back a more pitiful expression. It was sad. It was scary. But she knew he had to bear it.

"There's nothing more you can do with words." The man picked up his fallen sword in his right hand. "So, please... Just... end me. End *us*."

"All right," Lily softly replied.

The man gave a twisted smile. He chuckled quietly and said, "Thank you, Miss Lockwood."

Then he sighed and bent his body down, kicking off of the rubble-covered ground. He flew toward Lily with his sword in hand and the intent to kill, wholly unguarded.

"Hi-yaaaaah!!!"

For Lily, it would have been simple to murder this man. It would actually be far harder to fell him without doing so. She could not use either her flame sphere or her wind. However, there was one other type of spell that was burned into her memory. Lily extended her right arm, tracing it with her left hand, from her upper arm to her fingertips.

"Magic Sword."

She did not have the power to hold a sword and swing it around. She could barely even manage a knife. She lacked the physical strength required. So, she had no choice but to strengthen something that she could *not* drop. As her arm was coated in a dull glow, she lifted it upward to defend against the raised swing from the man now stepping toward her.

She was prepared for the pain. As she imagined it, the worst-case scenario would be that the magic misfired, and she would lose her arm entirely. However, unexpectedly...there was an impact. Her elbow did not catch the blade. Instead, she felt a heavy blow to her shoulder. There was no metallic sound. But the blade was repelled, as though it had struck something unbreakable.

She still had an arm. She was not hurt. Her clothes were not even cut.

However.

"Ah!"

Her right arm, strengthened with magic, was fine...but a sharp pain ran through Lily's right shoulder. Before she knew it, she had been pitched into the rubble. The difference in physical strength between a grown man and a young girl was immense. Her back slammed against the ground, and she went rolling.

"Uh..."

The man slashed diagonally upward, the tip of his sword scraping along the ground, aimed at Lily's neck. Lily moved the moment before he could strike, pulling her right arm up to catch the attack, but this time she was blown back into the crumbled remains of a wall. She fell to the ground, red staining her vision.

"Uh...wuh..."

She turned only her eyes to the approaching footsteps, to see the tip of the man's sword trained on her, approaching at high speed.

I'm gonna die...

It would be simple. She could just hit him with a fire or wind sphere. If she died now, she'd never see her family again. She would die, never knowing if she loved her family or hated them.

So, would she have to kill him?

No. No, no, *no*. Someone. Someone had to save her. *Anyone.*

VERY WELL, UNDERSTOOD!

The nanomachines' voice resounded in her mind, and Lily was overcome by an odd sensation, as though something was racing throughout her body. A bizarre sense of power bubbled up from every pore. Before she even noticed that her pain had dissipated, Lily's hands began to move. They were striking the ground, bouncing up from where she was collapsed.

She was moving. Her body was moving, just as she had pictured. Just like those people in her stories. The man's sword pierced into thin air as she leapt over him. He looked as though he was truly taking his time.

Lily landed silently behind him and struck the man powerfully in the side with her magic blade-arm, just as he was about to turn around.

"Wha...?!"

The man suddenly disappeared from view, and there was a sound of the right-hand wall collapsing. By the time Lily turned her head, he was already unconscious and buried in the rubble.

An anticlimactic resolution.

Lily was not the only one who was stunned at this result. The other soldiers, now having lost all will to fight, were equally flabbergasted.

The nanomachines whispered to Lily, WE HAVE IMPLEMENTED THE BODY STRENGTHENING THAT WE DISCUSSED PREVIOUSLY. DO NOT WORRY, YOU HAVEN'T TURNED INTO A BEASTGIRL OR DEMON OR ANYTHING. IF YOU ARE CURIOUS, THIS HAS BEEN ACHIEVED BY NANOMACHINES PROLIFERATING IN EVERY PART OF YOUR BODY. IT IS ONLY TEMPORARY, BUT WITH OUR HELP YOU CAN OBTAIN THE STRENGTH OF THOSE HEROES YOU SO ADMIRE. IF YOU PRAY TO BECOME FASTER, YOU'LL BE FASTER. IF YOU ASK TO BE STRONG, THAT WILL HAPPEN AS WELL.

Whoa...

A rare response, even for them.

NATURALLY, THERE ARE LIMITS, AND THERE IS NO

CHANGE TO YOUR BODY ITSELF, SO PLEASE BE AWARE THAT YOU WILL LIKELY BE IN A LOT OF PAIN AFTER THIS BATTLE, AS A SIDE EFFECT.

Side effect?

MUSCLE PAIN, STRESS FRACTURES, STRAIN, AND SO FORTH.

Lily whipped her head side to side.

Nooo!!

WHAT WE'RE SAYING IS THAT IT'S JUST BEST NOT TO ABUSE YOUR POWERS. HOWEVER, YOU HAVE ONLY BEEN FIGHTING FOR A SHORT TIME, SO YOU'LL PROBABLY GET AWAY WITH NOTHING MORE THAN BRUISES. IF YOU WISH TO USE THIS POWER FOR A LONGER SUSTAINED PERIOD IN THE FUTURE, WE WOULD RECOMMEND DAILY PHYSICAL TRAINING.

At any rate, it seemed she was saved. Lily removed the magic from her right arm and brushed the dust off her skirt. Then, she turned to the now-silent men before her and said again, "I'd like you to release the hostages now."

There was no response to these words.

And so, Lily pulled the keys hanging on the wall down with her fingertips and put them into the iron door at the deepest point of the underground chamber. With a little pushing, the door opened, hinges creaking, allowing the little girl inside.

Showers of sparks flew again and again into the night, and a shrill clanging echoed through the darkness.

He's fast!

Veil's skills had grown even more since the intense training he had received under the supervision of a certain girl at the Hunters' Prep School. However, even if you took away the fact that he could only use one arm right now, and that the loss of so much blood was clouding his vision, it was clear that the scimitar-wielding broker before him—Big Bro—was a worthy opponent.

".........!"

He could not fight back Big Bro's attacks with only one arm. Meeting his strength with more strength would only see his own sword repelled. He had to take the blows and let them slide. Rather than fighting power with power, he had to allow the force to flow past him. He had no other choice. Not only was his left arm entirely useless, he could no longer use his air bullets, the ace up his sleeve.

The blows came again and again.

"Please, Bro, stop! Why are you fighting for the imperial army?!"

"It's not for them."

Veil deflected a blow aimed at his thighs just before it struck. Sword slipped across sword, sending a font of sparks flying into the night air. Each time, his opponent's ashen gray eyes flickered in the darkness. The tip of the scimitar whipped a sharp wind over the end of Veil's nose, grazing past his face as he bent backward.

"I'm fighting for the slums. I did yesterday, I am today, and I'll do it again tomorrow."

"What are you talking about?!"

Big Bro turned his body and avoided the downward slash Veil unleashed as he stood again. It was a razor-thin margin, a snap judgment. Big Bro's skill with a sword was fully on par with an A-rank hunter's. This probably should not have come as much of a surprise, considering that he had managed to live this long as a broker of illicit jobs, doing business with bandits. In fact, what was hardest to believe at this point was that this was a man who had ever been gentle or kind.

Still twisted, he unfurled a rope and spun around, launching a scimitar attack at Veil's side with the centrifugal force of his movements. Veil was only barely able to block the blow, standing his sword up with the tip against the ground and pushing his immobilized left shoulder against the top of it. The powerful attack reverberated, and pain coursed throughout his whole body.

Veil bit back the pain, gritting his teeth, and yelled, "The slums have already been saved! Things are getting better now! There's no reason for you to keep sacrificing yourself for them! We don't need you to do that dangerous job anymore!"

The slums *had* been saved. Previously, it was not uncommon to see children dying of starvation, but thanks to Veil's dedication, his resolve to stick around after his fifteenth birthday, and the changes enacted by the Crimson Vow, starvation was now quite rare.

A change was underway. For everyone and everything.

Veil stepped forward, swinging his sword, but Big Bro caught the blow cleanly and pushed him back at full force.

"That's not enough."

"What do you mean?!"

This time, Big Bro took a heavy step forward as Veil stumbled back, right foot plunging between both of Veil's. He was so close now that Veil could smell his breath. So close that he could feel death beside him.

"Can you care for your little brothers and sisters when they're wasting away from illness? Can you shoulder the burdens of the expensive medicines they need?"

His longsword keened as he caught another blow. Or wait— it was not the sword itself that was keening. Veil soon realized it was his own right arm, now starting to go numb. As he noticed this, Veil's body went limp. He had been knocked upward. He was not high off the ground, but both of his legs were most certainly in the air.

Where did he get all that power within such a thin frame?!

Veil put all his strength into his fingers, consciously gripping the hilt that threatened to go flying from his hand. If he lost his sword, the battle would be over.

He landed. His heels skidded backwards.

"Is watching over them as they die your idea of salvation?"

"Guh!"

Veil bent down in the nick of time, avoiding a blow aimed relentlessly at his neck. Before that thrust could turn into a slash, he jammed his ruined left shoulder into Big Bro's side, pushing him away.

There was a gap. Veil's vision was still blurry. He no longer knew if the liquid trailing down his own cheeks was blood or sweat. He was seeing a double image of the man before him. He shook his head.

"Let me explain, Veil. I want to get rid of the slums. I want to erase even the notion of the slums from this world entirely. And so, I had no choice. Just like when I had to involve myself with bandits during my time as a broker."

At this, Veil's expression shifted.

"What do you mean?! What are you gonna do to the slums?!"

"Don't get me wrong. I'm not saying that I'm going to slaughter everyone there or anything. I'm saying that I wish to change the Kingdom of Tils. And for that to happen, it is necessary to utilize the Albarn Empire."

There was a pause of just a few breaths. Then, Veil's eyes opened wide.

"Don't tell me you intend to help the Empire invade Tils? Did this whole thing with the Lockwoods, who are supposed to guard the country's borders—did it all come back to that?"

"Yep."

Big Bro removed the mask covering his mouth and tossed it down at his feet. Veil got the sense that this was how he meant to show he was not lying.

"I made an agreement with the prime minister of the Empire, in exchange for the lives of Margrave Lockwood and his family. When the Empire invades the capital of Tils, only the slums will remain untouched. Then, in the aftermath of the invasion, the children of the slums will be treated as normal citizens."

"Do you really think that promise is going to be kept in the midst of a war?! Plus, the slums are already starting to flourish without you having to do all tha—"

Before Veil could finish speaking, Big Bro shouted back, "Getting a few jobs doesn't change the fact that they're urchins! How can you forgive a royal family who can just turn a blind eye and leave children to suffer? Don't you get it, Veil?"

A crazed grin spread across his face.

"Both the royal family and the urchins of the slums—all of us will live together as equals! What could be a more splendid outcome than that?"

Veil gritted his teeth and yelled back, "But they'll *die*! Even if the orphans aren't caught up in the war, there will be countless casualties, among commoners and nobles alike. Can't you see that?"

"That doesn't matter!"

His bloodshot eyes wide, the crazed smile still upon his face, Big Bro spoke quietly now. "I don't care how many tens of thousands of people fall victim outside of the slums. How many hundreds of urchins in the slums have the royal family and the common people abandoned and left to die? They'll get what they deserve."

Veil hung his head as Big Bro continued.

"Now, it's our turn to abandon them. The crimes cancel each other out. Everyone will be equal—royals, commoners, and urchins alike."

Veil had no words. What could he say to this? He felt only an intense sorrow. To think he would be hearing such things from the kind Big Bro, who had always cared for everyone. It was miserable and frustrating. Somehow, he managed to hold back the tears that threatened to overflow.

"You aren't doing this for the slums. You're just doing this because you want revenge."

"Won't you join me, Veil? Unlike our other big brothers and sisters, who ran away and left the slums behind them, you chose to remain there. You're the same as me. You should be able to understand how I feel."

"Big Bro, I can't..." Veil choked. "There are a lot of people among the commoners who do support the urchins..."

"Reform comes with sacrifices. The people of this country are far too insensitive to the plight of urchins. We need to tear down Tils and rebuild it from the ground up."

Veil could see that it was already too late for him. He was so hellbent on his own revenge that he was using the slums as a tool. His very sense of humanity seemed to be slipping.

Veil looked up at Big Bro meaningfully.

"Lily. That girl, Lily Lockwood, who you tried to sell out to the Empire, said that you were a nice person. She's been lending her strength to help out the slums. All of the children of the slums love her. Would you kill her, too?"

"Well, unfortunately, that girl is still a noble."

He knew. Veil knew that would be the reply.

He wasn't going to be able to get through to him with words. That part of him was already gone. So, there was only one thing left for him to do, as his brother.

"Come with me, Veil. We can liberate the slums together."

Big Bro held out his right hand, but Veil shook his head and steeled himself, longsword in hand.

"I'm going to stop you. If I win, you have to abandon this stupid plan and go somewhere far, far away."

There was a momentary pause. The cold night wind blew languidly around them both.

"Sorry, Veil. Looks like our path as brothers parts here. Still, I'll honor that promise, even though there's no chance of you ever beating me."

He put both hands on his scimitar.

Veil breathed out softly and kicked off the ground. Almost at the exact same moment, Big Bro kicked off as well. They closed the distance in an instant—but just before they met, Veil put all of his strength into his diagonally propped longsword and flung it at the other man's head.

"Raaaah!"

"——?!"

Big Bro just barely stopped the spinning longsword with his scimitar.

"What are you d—"

He was unable to finish that question.

It was but an instant that Big Bro's gaze was trained on the flying longsword, but in that time, Veil had already stepped in close to him, still empty-handed.

He stooped down. Low, very low. By the time Big Bro tried to swing his scimitar, it was already too late.

"Air Bullet."

The bullet of compressed air that shot from Veil's right hand crashed right into the his opponent's solar plexus. His thin body was bent sharply in two. He crashed backward into the ruins with a fearsome force, hacking up blood and bile.

"Guh-guh!"

Veil picked up his sword in a leisurely manner and stood before his now-collapsed big brother. The man glared up at him, his eyes fierce, but then his face slackened as he sighed. Finally, he whispered, "I guess I lose. Kill me."

There was no hesitation.

Veil gave his sword one great swing and plunged it through his sash. Then he said, "No...you're going...to keep your...promise..." His vision was blurring.

Veil swayed violently forward.

"Veil?"

"But...no matter how...far away...you are...our...bond will never...be so easily...broken... I will al...ways be your...little brother af...ter...all..."

Then darkness encroached from the edges of his doubled, blurred vision. There was a sound like something snapping inside of his head, and all Veil's strength left him. He crumbled to his knees, losing consciousness as he fell across his brother's body.

"Hey, Veil! *Veil!*"

It was just like when they were younger. Veil had contracted a grave illness while in the slums, and without medicine, found himself on the verge of death. He now remembered that night, where his nameless big brother sat by him, worriedly calling his name just like this the whole night through.

From behind his closed eyes, a stream of tears finally began to flow.

The hinges creaked. The heavy door slowly opened.

At the end of a narrow passageway, there was yet another door—to make escape that much more difficult. Lily Lockwood's family was beyond that door.

As Lily walked along the stone path, she removed her butterfly mask. The only footsteps she heard were her own, and there were no signs she was being followed. The soldiers had already lost all will to fight.

What should I say first? Lily wondered. *I'm sure they're going to be surprised to see me here.*

"How have you been? I'm here to save you."

"Guess what, I can hear now!"

"I've practiced speaking, too."

"And I can even use magic."

"I've made a lot of friends."

"Why did you leave me behind that night?"

"Was I always just a burden to you?"

"Have the two of you been good little children?"

"Have you been taking good care of Mother and Father?"

"You haven't just been crying the whole time, have you?"

"Did you...even know about me?"

"Did you know...that you had a big sister who has never even spoken to you?"

Her steps began to slow, until finally she stopped dead in the middle of the hallway. Her hand, gripped somewhere around her heart, trembled faintly.

She was afraid. Her legs would not move. This whole time, she had only been plunging blindly forward, thinking of how she was going to save her family. And now, the moment was suddenly right before her eyes.

The trembling in her hands spread to her legs, from her legs to her whole body. She was not cold, but her teeth were chattering.

It was too late to turn back.

Her breath was as ragged as if she had just run a marathon, but she dragged her legs forward. After a short distance, when she was just close enough to touch the door, she stopped again.

She could hear voices. She could hear her brother and sister crying, and her mother comforting them.

They were here. Right on the other side of this one little door. The family who had abandoned her. Her body was soaked with so much sweat that it terrified even her.

Would they accept her? Or would she be rejected?

The moment she put the key to the lock, she was overtaken by the urge to flee.

No, no, no, *no*. That would be far too irresponsible. Veil and Lafine had given up so much to get her here. She tried to put the key into the door with her trembling hands, but it would not fit.

It clacked and clacked, but would not go into the keyhole. She had to hurry, before the soldiers came back to their senses. She had to.

Lily was so wrapped up in thinking that she did not even hear the footsteps approaching from behind her. A warm, soft hand rested atop her own trembling fingers. Then, the key slipped right into the lock.

"...?!"

"Don't chicken out after you've made it all this way, idiot."

Hearing this voice in her ear, all the tension flooded out from Lily's body.

"Lafine..."

She looked back over her right shoulder, to see a woman with light brown hair standing there. She was covered in bruises, smeared with blood and sweat, panting heavily.

"What?"

"Oh, it's nothing. Heh heh."

This time, the key, gripped firmly in both of their hands, turned solidly within the lock. *Ka-chak*, sounded the lock as it opened.

Lily looked over her left shoulder and saw a masculine face, covered in half-dried blood—Veil. He was breathing raggedly as well, as though he had hurried here.

"Veil!"

"Hey there. I got to talk to my Big Bro, thanks to you."

He was alive. He had stayed alive—for her. Thank goodness. Lily felt relief in her core. Then she noticed, Veil's whole body was dyed red, as if he had been bathing in blood. His left arm looked particularly bad.

"You're really hurt!"

"Don't worry about it. Looks like Big Bro tended to my wounds while I was unconscious. Before he left. I think it was magic."

Though he had never once used magic when battling me, Veil thought, smiling bitterly. Still, there was a faint happiness in his smile, as though a weight had been lifted from his shoulders.

His face was pale, but he appeared to be telling the truth. Lily did not see any fresh trails of blood on him. Everywhere it was visible, the blood was mostly dried.

"Plus, it seems like I was able to thwart a huge plot that was about to get underway. But I'll tell you more about that later. For now, there's something you have to do, isn't there? My work is finished. Now it's your turn, Lily. Go on in."

"No need to worry! No matter what happens in there, we're right here. You go and say everything you need to say to that stupid family of yours!"

Lafine kicked the door open, and Veil gently shoved Lily in. She staggered into the cell, swallowing nervously, and slowly raised her eyes.

There, she saw her beloved family, the ones she was supposed to hate. Had her father Neiham lost some weight? His cheeks were sunken. He regarded Lily in shock, his eyebrows knit together. Her mother Ivanna was cradling her two siblings to protect them, while the pair looked up at Lily, eyes filled with a blank wonderment.

"Ah..."

Her voice caught in her throat. No words came out.

"Uh..."

It was like before, when she could not hear or speak. Finally, Neiham broke the silence.

"Lily, is that you...? What...are you doing here...?"

"..."

Neiham's cheeks sagged. "Ha! So you were captured. You were lucky enough to escape the first time, and yet you let yourself be captured without even putting up a fight. You're as useless a half-wit as you ever were."

".........."

The words feel so heavy in my stomach. It's like I've swallowed lead weights. I bet he still thinks that I can't hear.

Both Veil and Lafine wore fierce expressions, but they did not move. They remained hidden on either side of the opened door, pressed just against the walls.

"I'd thought that maybe that explosion just before might actually be someone coming here to save us, yet here before me is a face I never hoped to see again. Looks like our luck has finally run out."

Lily's face slackened. She closed her eyes and then faintly opened them, wringing the sounds from her throat.

"N...no. I brought...myself here..."

Both Neiham and Ivanna's faces shifted in an instant. Their eyes were open just as wide as when the door had first been opened, mouths gaping. Lily put a finger to her ear. She tried to force a smile back across her sorrowful expression, but it was strained.

"I can hear now... I...can hear everything..."

There was a beat.

There was a beat, and then the margrave drew back.

"*Impossible!* You had an illness that even the most expensive healing mages in the capital couldn't cure! Even the court magicians rejected it! So, why now...? Y-you can really hear me...?"

Lily continued, her voice shrill, "F-father! I...can use magic now, too. I defeated all those bad guys, and made it all...the way... here..."

She could not go on. She finally knew it. She knew how her father truly felt.

They really didn't want me. My mother isn't saying a word, and my siblings are looking at me like I'm crazy. I'm just some girl who they've never seen before. They were never even told about me, their deaf older sister.

Her chest was tight. It ached. She wanted to run away wailing.

"Aha... Okay... I see..."

She hung her head. All the strength left her body.

Neiham began muttering nervously. "D-don't tell me you came here seeking revenge on me? Would you really hurt me, your true father, with that magic of yours?"

She had no words. It was not that she could not continue, it was merely pointless. She should have known.

Neiham held his hands out, eyes fearful.

"H-hey! Well, now that you can hear and speak, everything is fine! If you've come here to save us, then we'll happily welcome you back as a member of the family again!"

Her heart quashed every single word that she could think of saying. Every one of them felt wretched.

"Listen! We can just say that we've learned that our eldest daughter, who was abducted as an infant, is still alive and has finally returned to us! You have a happy future ahead of you as a noble! Not only are you fair of face, but you've come back with magic as well! Yes, it's perfect! Perhaps the Lockwoods will even marry into the royal family one day!"

Enough. That was the word she could not bring herself to say.

"I know that you've had an unfortunate life up until now, but from this point on, you can have whatever you like! Now, return to my side, Lily!"

Lily could do nothing but stand there, hanging her head, her shoulders slumped. Lafine pushed her forcefully aside, approaching the margrave.

"Pardon me, Your Excellency."

"Hm? Well, if it isn't Lafine. Glad to see you're safe as we— wh—? Gah!"

Lafine's fist smacked straight into Neiham's cheek. He fell, neck twisting, his face going red.

"Y-you little harlot! My face!"

Lily grabbed Lafine's clothes.

"That's enough, Lafine," she said calmly, smiling purposefully, as wide as she could. "I didn't come here to save them in the hopes that they would love me. I came here because I love *them*. That's what a hero does. So, I'm fine. It's okay if they hate me. Even if it is a little sad to hear. So, please, don't do something like that just for me."

Lafine snorted and shook her arm free of Lily.

"You're way off the mark. Don't get me wrong. I only punched that man because he was standing in my way."

"Are you mocking me?! Do you not recall the debt you owe me for being so kind as to hire the likes of a common girl from the family of a once-knight?!"

Lafine narrowed her eyes, glaring at Neiham.

"I think you'd better shut your filth-spewing mouth now if you don't want me to cut it right out of your face, pig."

"Wha—?!"

Lafine strode boldly past him, staring down at Ivanna, who still clutched her two children.

"Do you have any defense to make to Lady Lily, Lady Ivanna?"

Ivanna softly pushed the two children back to the wall and then slowly stood, puffing out her ample chest. Her dress was soiled, but an air of refinement still hung around her as she spoke with dignity. "I have none. For what should I apologize? My husband and I are members of a noble family, tasked with defending the borders of the Kingdom of Tils. That night, to assure both the preservation of the Lockwood line and the safety of our kingdom, we made the choice that was most prudent, and fled."

"And?"

"Yes. We ranked the deaf Lily below our two younger children, who were strong and healthy. Leading us to the result you see now."

Ivanna stared back at Lafine, resolute and unflinching. But her amber eyes were not looking at Lafine. They were looking at Lily Lockwood herself, who stood dumbfounded beside her. Ivanna walked around Lafine and stood in front of Lily. She folded her hands in front of her stomach and bent forward in a bow.

"I'm sorry, Lily. There is no denying that we abandoned you." She lowered her head. "I suppose if I were to say anything else to you, it would amount to little more than excuses. It's just that, well, the unfortunate way that things ended up—no, even that is little more than sidestepping the point."

Lily looked at her mother through hollow eyes.

"You are free now," the woman continued. "Should you choose to return to the Lockwood home, I swear to you that we will welcome you back as a rightful heir. However, if you are disillusioned with us, and desire to live in the outside world, then we will simply watch over you. The decision is yours to make."

"Wh-what do you think you're doing, Ivanna?!" Neiham shouted. "I am the head of the Lockwood family, and I am the one who makes the decisions! Lily is our wonderful daughter, who understands the principles of magic! We may even be able to join her to the royal family in marriage! She's not going *anywhere*!"

Ivanna's eyes pierced right through him. When she spoke, her tone was low but scathing. "Neiham, be quiet."

"Guh..."

Everyone said that Neiham never would have gotten where he was in life if Ivanna had not become his wife. And now, it was clear to everyone present that the rumor was true. Ivanna once more turned to Lily and smiled at her wistfully, her resolve fading.

"Should you choose to spread your wings in the outside world, I promise you that from here on out, we Lockwoods will do nothing to impinge upon that freedom. That is the best gift that I, a mother who abandoned her own precious daughter, can give you."

Lily looked up. She glanced at Lafine, who quietly averted her eyes. Veil merely leaned against the wall with his arms folded, watching stalwartly.

There were so many things she wished to say. You could have built a mountain out of them. However, most of those words vanished in her mouth before she could ever speak them. What could possibly be left now, inside this empty shell that she had become?

"Hey, Lafine," she spoke.

"What?"

"Thank you for your help. I'm sorry you got involved in something so dangerous."

"Hmph. What're you acting so out of character for? What a drag. All I've done is cause trouble for you since that night, haven't I? And so, what, after all that, that's all you have to say?"

"Yep."

"I see. Well then, just hurry up and get the hell out of here. I'm lookin' forward to getting back to my single life."

Next, she turned to Veil.

"Veil."

"Yeah."

"What happened with your big brother?"

Veil unfolded his arms and gazed at his blood-soaked left side. The wounds were completely closed. He had heard his brother desperately calling his name while he was unconscious. In that moment, Veil was certain that the shady broker had turned back into the Big Bro he knew and loved. And so, he smiled faintly.

"Who knows. He's gone off somewhere far away, now. But I'm sure that someday in the distant future, should we happen to run into one another on some city street somewhere, we'll be able to talk and laugh again as brothers. It's all thanks to you, Lily, that I had this chance. Thank you."

"I'm glad."

"Yeah."

Lily smiled at Veil, and then, she turned back to Ivanna Lockwood. In the corner of her vision, she saw Neiham Lockwood as well. She straightened her back, fixed her posture, and opened her mouth.

"Mother, Father. Thank you, truly, for giving me life. Thank you for raising me for nine whole years, despite my shortcomings. Thank you for looking out for my little brother and sister as well, in that same home," she said. Then she firmly declared, "I still love every single member of the Lockwood family!"

For a third time, a look of awe spread across Neiham's face.

"Lily... We treated you so poorly, but you're still forgiving us?"

Ivanna smiled quietly, opening her arms to welcome her daughter.

"Welcome home, Lily."

With a pained expression, Lafine covered her ears, while a faint smile crossed Veil's mouth. That was the Lily Lockwood they knew and loved, after all. The girl overflowing with such foolish kindness that she would declare her love for everyone and everything in the world, even those who betrayed her.

However, Lily was not finished speaking. She did not rush into her mother's open arms. It was not over yet.

"Right now, I'm the happiest I've ever been. So..."

That day, through a tear-filled smile, Lily Lockwood bid her birth family farewell.

CHAPTER 7 |

Hello World

BY THE TIME Lily and the others finally brought the Lockwoods out of the ruins, the agents of the Albarn Empire had already vanished. It was clear, after that, that they had moved on, based on the fact that the bandits who had been rumored to be plaguing the border region had vanished as well; however, their trail was already cold. Even much later it was unclear if they had returned home to Albarn or if they had found another place to live somewhere within Tils.

Likewise, from that day hence, the broker never showed his face in the slums again.

What began as a major event, the kind that would send ripples through the capital—the unprecedented event of one hunter and two commoners disrupting an invasion by the Albarn Empire—was, in the end, reduced to nothing more than a footnote. The simple disbanding of a bandit gang. It was

Margrave Lockwood's own testimony, and that of his family, that supported this.

Even now, the Lockwoods were unaware that it was a group of agents from the Albarn Empire who had attacked them that night, or so said Margrave Neiham Lockwood. According to him, they were nothing more than a large group of bandits who had kidnapped the Lockwoods seeking ransom from the Crown. In fact, that was probably what the family themselves had been told by the agents.

As far as the young man from the slums, it was a more unfortunate story. Though he had been instrumental in saving the country from danger, the only compensation he received was whatever small reward the guild could provide and one modest prize from the stingy margrave. Of course, said young man, Veil, did not seem to mind. In fact, the one who seemed the most torn up about this was a certain woman who would have a drink and smoke a pipe and bluster about the truth of the incident to anyone who would listen down at the pub.

As far as anyone was concerned, Lafine Alstea's stories were nothing more than the drunken ravings of a woman infamous around those parts for her general slovenliness. It would be a further reach still for anyone to believe the fantasy that *she* herself had been part of the group of just three people who had saved the Kingdom of Tils from danger.

And so, in the end, there was no dramatic change to the three of their lives. Lily Lockwood, however, was still satisfied. After all, the type of hero she wished to be was one who battled evildoers in secret. It was fine if no one knew what she had done. Whatever happened in the past, what made Lily the happiest was to be content right now.

...Still, it *would* be nice for someone to praise her once in a while.

"Hi-yah!"

A hand came chopping down on the top of Lily's head.

"Ow! Lafine, that hurt!"

"It's *fine* if no one knows what I did. I don't *need* anyone to praise me. Sure. I get it. However, *I* need money. You don't have to work. You don't have to get up early. But I want money. I want enough money that I can just sleep the whole day through. I. Need. *Money.*"

Veil muttered, smiling wearily, "Heh! That's just the kind of trashy thinking they talk about. Classic Lafine."

"What?! Who's the one sitting around here eating up *our* food while he's talking trash?!"

"C'mon, Lafine, stop that! Don't shout with your mouth full. It's flying everywhere. You're the one who's making a mess around here."

Lafine put a hand to the back of her head and gave a flirty wink.

"A little girl like you would never understand, but men find that very attractive in a pretty lady. Isn't that right, Veil?"

Veil replied, with utmost honesty, "No. I wish you would stop."

"What?!"

"It's okay," Lily comforted her. "Anyway, we wouldn't be able to afford this food if Veil didn't keep bringing us work. Besides, I'm the one who actually does most of the jobs as Hello World Mask. All you do is eat and sleep."

"Hey! When did *you* start getting so responsible?"

"I'm not sure," Lily replied, with complete sincerity. "I guess I've just thought that I need to get it together a little more if I'm going to raise you up right. It's a lot of work, but it's rewarding."

Lafine's fork tumbled from her hand, clattering onto the table.

"Wh...wha...r...raise...me...?"

She slumped lifelessly back into her chair, eyes going blank. Seeing this, Veil burst out into laughter.

The three sat around the round table, eating together, in the home of the Alstea family. Mornings were often like this on the days when Veil brought special jobs from the guild and when Lily went to help the orphans in the slums with their daily tasks. Before anyone even realized it, this had become their custom.

"So, what kind of job is it today, Veil?"

"It's supposed to be guarding a merchant caravan. They're going to a little village near the capital, so we should be able to make it back by nightfall. I can't be away from the slums for too long," explained Veil, shoving a fried egg into his open mouth.

"Supposed to be?"

"The real job is to lure out and capture a bandit troop. Apparently, they've been showing up a lot around here recently. They've been going exclusively after smaller wagons, so they should be a smaller group."

"The guards gonna be inside the wagon?" asked Lafine. "Sounds easy, then. Guess I'll tag along!"

"No, there's actually going to be farming supplies that the village needs inside."

"Then I'm out. *Lame.*"

"I mean, the delivery is really the point of it. The merchants' goal is to deliver their goods, and the guild's goal is to deal with the bandits. These kinds of jobs pay pretty well. It would be a big help if you came along. It'd be useful to have more skilled people around to cover the parts of the job where Lily is...less effective."

As always, Lily's magic was explosively powerful. Allowing her to use it recklessly would absolutely result in someone's death.

Lafine shoved her own cleared plate aside and collapsed upon the table.

"No thanks. I'm going to sleep."

"Why are you only awake when you're eating?"

"Can't sleep on an empty stomach."

Lily grinned and nodded at Veil.

"See? I told you. It's hard raising this girl."

"I feel I understand this deeply." Veil gazed at Lafine as though staring at a troubled toddler.

"Ughh... I don't want to grow up! I want to stay a kid forever..."

"Aha ha, I think it's already too late for that, Lafine."

A tremor ran through Lafine's body at this innocent scolding.

Once the meal was through, Veil and Lily stood up together.

"Well then, we'll be going. Please clean up the dishes later, Lafine."

"Whaaat? Can't hear you..."

The pair both smiled wryly as Lafine, still lying down, covered her ears. She even went so far as pretending to snore.

Lily pulled her mask from her pocket and slipped it on. She then put her left hand on her right shoulder and rolled her right arm around.

"All right! Time to tear it up again today!"

"Yep. It could be dangerous, though, so don't get too excited."

"Okay."

And so, Lily Lockwood flung the door open, and stepped out once again into the unknown of the great wide world.

A Feline Friend

O NE DAY, that idiot Lily brought home a cat.

With an uncharacteristically humble expression, she set a little tortoiseshell kitten down in the middle of the living room table, of all places.

"Hey, can we keep him?"

Seriously? Why should we spend our money on pet food when we already barely have enough to eat?

I put my elbows on the table, rested my chin on my hands, and said to Lily, who was staring at me with those pure and innocent eyes, "Nooo way. Get rid of that thing. I'm no good with monsters *or* animals. They just get in the way, and they're annoying and noisy. Plus, one Lily is more than enough of a pet to take care of."

"If I put a little kitten like this out of the city gates, it would be eaten right up by monsters. Plus, this little guy doesn't have any family, just like you and me. I feel so bad for him," said Lily, looking as though she was about to cry. Did she really think that would have an effect on me? Seriously, having to pay for this thing's room and board would just put more of a burden on her, wouldn't it? How could she not mind sacrificing herself like that all the time? Dummy.

Before I realized it, the kitten had started walking across the table toward me, looking up with its nose twitching.

To be honest, it *was* kind of cute. But I couldn't be weak. Showing compassion and ending up with more burdens was something only suckers did. With one hand, I carefully pushed the kitten back to the center of the table. Its warm fur *was* rather soft...

"Please, Lafine? I'll take good care of him. Oh, but of course not just him. I'll still do my best to take care of you, too. So that you can grow into a big strong auntie one day."

What was she saying?! Why did this little brat still act like she was raising *me*?!

Veil, who had been silently watching this the entire time, muttered, "I don't think that's something a nine-year-old girl should be saying to a twenty-two-year-old woman. It's something *she* should be saying, not having said to her."

To be fair, in the Alstea household, it was in fact nine-year-old Lily who did most of the household chores. But, to make things even, I, the twenty-two-year-old, took care of most of the sleeping in and napping and eating and drinking... Well, perhaps a little too much.

"Shut up, shut up, shut *uuuup*! Why are you getting in on this, Veil?! I get it! I get it already! However, this comes with some conditions! You have to search for an owner! You said yourself that you want this kitten to have a family, don't you?"

"Yeah. We're gonna be his family! You and me, Lafine!"

"What?! Are you kidding me?! I don't care if it's a foster or just a mama cat or what, but you need to find somewhere for this guy to *go*! It can stay here just until you do that. And you're responsible for taking care of it, Lily! Got it?"

"So you're saying, if I never find anywhere, he can stay here forever?"

How optimistic! Whatever. I was tired.

"We'll see. I'm going to put in a request to the guild myself to find a foster. There's a time limit on this, so don't go getting attached to this little stray. Not that I care if you go catching feelings and have to bawl your eyes out when it comes time to give it up. Ha!" I said, standing up to return to my room—though before I did, I realized there was something I had forgotten to ask.

"Lily, what's for dinner tonight?"

"Oh, I'm gonna start making it now. Tonight we're having orc burger steaks with grated shiso."

Oh yeah! I loved the orc burger steaks she made. Thinking of food, I scarcely even noticed the kitten that was underfoot, slipping into my room alongside me. Annoyingly, this kitten seemed to enjoy sleeping on my bed, returning immediately even if I shooed it away. And so, from that day on, the kitten became my sleeping companion.

Ten days later...

I found myself in tears. The day Veil reported that an owner had been found, and Lily went to take the kitten back, I tried relentlessly to drag it back into my room.

"*Nooooo!* I'm not giving him back!!! He's my cat now!"

"But we found his real family, so we need to return him to them. Right?"

"*Nooooooo!!!*"

"Aha ha! You're twenty-two—you can't keep being so selfish."

All I could do was hurl abuse at her little back as she carried my kitten away.

"Beast! Devil! Monster! Cat snatcher!"

Turns out I was the one who caught feelings after all...

Afterword

EVERYONE WHO'S NEW to my work, pleased to meet you! And those who already know me, long time no see. I'm Kousuke Akai.

To be honest, it was over a year ago that my editor first presented me with the job of writing a spin-off story for the *Didn't I Say to Make My Abilities Average in the Next Life?!* series. At the time, I was already caught up in other work, and I wasn't confident that I should be messing around in the world that FUNA, the original author, had already so expertly crafted, so I arrogantly turned the job down.

However, as time passed, and I found myself between assignments, huddled alone in the corner of my dark room, staring up at the ceiling and counting all the stains, the opportunity was thankfully offered to me again. I was worried about what sort of horrid, stain-counting creature I was en route to becoming, so I accepted that job at lightning speed.

I then immersed myself in reading the series, reacquainting myself with the cheerfulness and charm of all the main characters. I fell in love with the intricate worldbuilding and once more truly felt all the joy this story could bring.

And so, I ran this spin-off by the editors and FUNA, taking meticulous care not to disrupt the already fully-fleshed setting and characters, and was even able to have the original illustrator, Itsuki Akata, provide some wonderful illustrations, all of which came together to produce the work you see before you, *Didn't I Say to Make My Abilities Average in the Next Life?!: Lily's Miracle*.

Thank you so much to everyone for taking the time out of their busy schedules to participate in the creation of this book.

If I talk too much about the story itself here in the afterword, it's going to get confusing for the people who read this part first, so please allow me to keep this to a short and sweet introduction.

This is a story about how no matter what challenges life throws at you, as long as you keep running straight ahead, never abandoning positive thinking, the world is sure to meet you halfway.

I hope that I can make everyone who reads this book smile, just a little bit.

—KOUSUKE AKAI

AFTERWORD (OR SOMETHING)

OUR CUTE AND SPUNKY LITTLE LILY! I HOPE
SHE GETS TO MEET UP WITH MILE AND HAVE
ALL SORTS OF ADVENTURES ONE DAY.

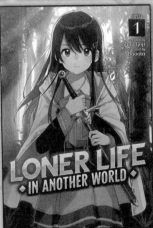